CALL ME Crazy

THE BELLAMY CREEK SERIES

Melanie Harlow

For Harlots
(You know who you are . . .)

Those fingers in my hair
That sly come-hither stare
That strips my conscience bare
It's witchcraft . . .

And I've got no defense for it
The heat is too intense for it
What good would common sense for it do?

—***Carolyn Leigh***

CALL ME Crazy

One

Enzo

There comes a day in a man's life when he enters a room with hope in his heart and a ring in his pocket, fully prepared to get down on one knee. To pledge his eternal devotion. To take his soul mate's hand in his and pop the question, promising to love, honor, and cherish her forever and ever, until death do them part, amen.

This was not that day.

However, I did have a ring in my pocket—a very nice one-point-four carat diamond solitaire on a gold band. I'd gotten a great deal on it because my cousin Paulie worked at the jewelry store, and some poor guy had just returned it. Sure, it was engraved with someone else's name, but Paulie had assured me that could be removed.

In hindsight, I probably should have done that before I proposed. But I wasn't thinking straight—I needed a wife, and I needed one *fast*.

It was all because of this ridiculous tradition in my family. In order to inherit the family construction business, Moretti & Sons, the oldest son has to be "settled down" with a wife and preferably a kid or two by the time he's thirty-five. My father, who was sixty-eight years old and ready to retire, had been threatening to leave the business to my younger brother Pietro for years now.

Fucking Pietro!

He might be thirty-two and married with his third bambino on the way, but he was *never* on time, he was *always* disorganized, and he was way too easygoing to be an effective manager. Contractors, suppliers, and clients were constantly walking all over him because he hated confrontation.

Don't get me wrong, he's my kid brother and I fucking love the guy—and my niece and nephew are awesome—but he's not the one you want running your multi-million-dollar firm.

Me? I loved confrontation. I wasn't afraid to tell someone when they were fucking up or remind them of the price they'd quoted or the deadlines they'd agreed to. I knew when to be charming and when to be a dickhead. I knew when to be a charming dickhead. And I knew how to close a deal.

At least, I thought I did.

But that was before I proposed.

I'd been seeing Reina for about three months, which I thought was a pretty decent amount of time to spend with someone, although I might not be the best judge of that since long-term commitment has never been my thing. Not that I was a jerk about it—I always made sure a woman understood exactly what I could offer her (one hell of a good time), and what I couldn't (anything resembling a relationship).

But as thirty-five closed in on me and my father's threats started to get more real, I realized it was time to man up and put a ring on someone's finger.

Reina seemed as good a candidate for Mrs. Moretti as anyone. She was a little young—she'd just turned twenty-one yesterday, in fact—a little too attached to her phone, and sometimes I had no fucking idea what she was talking about, but she checked all the other boxes for me. She was beautiful, she wasn't crazy, she got along with her family, and her mother was in her late forties and still looked good. What more could I ask for?

She checked my parents' boxes too: Catholic. Italian. My Nonna knew her Nonna.

Was I in love with her? No. But love was something that developed over time, wasn't it? I wasn't exactly sure, since I'd never been in love, but it seemed to me like something you settled into, like a couch that's a little stiff at first but grows more comfortable the more you sit on it. I figured we'd get there eventually.

The important thing right now was to secure my place at the top of Moretti & Sons, where I'd worked every damn day of my life since I was fourteen years old. I hadn't put all that blood, sweat, and tears into growing the business just to see it go to Pietro, and I sure as hell wasn't about to be the only oldest son in five generations who failed to inherit. If I had to get a wife and kid to do it, I'd get myself a wife and kid.

How hard could it be?

Turns out, a little harder than I thought.

To celebrate Reina's birthday, I'd taken her to dinner at DiFiore's, which was the nicest Italian restaurant in town and owned by my mom's cousin Big Tony. We were seated in the best booth in the place. Candles on the table. Soft music playing. As for me, I was wearing a new suit and tie. I'd gotten a haircut and trimmed my scruff. I smelled fucking fantastic, my wavy hair was doing that *thing* in the front, and I was wearing my lucky underwear.

It was on.

I waited for the server, my cousin Lara, to take away our dessert plates, and then I sat up taller and cleared my throat. My gut was clenching up a little, but I ignored it. "So how's your birthday so far?"

Reina smiled at me and tossed her long, straight dark hair. "It's great. Thanks for dinner. The ravioli was yummy."

"You're welcome." I glanced at her wine glass and noticed it was still pretty full. I'd splurged on a pricey bottle of Barolo, which I'd thought was worth every penny. "Didn't you like the wine?"

"Truth?" She shrugged. "I'm not a huge red wine person. But I didn't want to be rude."

"It's not rude to ask for what you want," I said. "Let's get you what you want."

"Can I just have a Diet Coke?"

"Of course." After signaling to Lara, I ordered Reina a Diet Coke, and once it arrived, I watched her take a sip from the straw and started over. "So. It's your birthday."

"Yes." She glanced at her phone, which was out on the table.

"Do you want your present?"

She beamed like a kid who'd just been offered a piece of candy. "You got me a present?"

"I might have." I tilted my head, giving her my best smolder.

"Enzo, you didn't have to get me anything. You took me out to dinner tonight."

"Listen, you only turn twenty-one once. I wanted to make it memorable."

"Awww. That's so sweet."

I reached inside my jacket pocket and took out the box. Opening it up, I flashed the ring toward her and cocked one eyebrow. "Well? What do you say?"

Her mouth fell open. She stared at the diamond like it was a giant spider she was afraid might attack. "What is that?"

"It's an engagement ring." I glanced inside the box, just to make sure it was actually in there.

"I—I can see that. But why are you showing me an engagement ring right now?"

"Well . . . because." Hot and sweaty all of a sudden, I loosened the knot in my tie. "I want to be engaged."

"To me?"

"Yes." I cleared my throat. "To you."

"But . . . you didn't even propose."

"Yes, I did."

"No, you didn't. You just showed me the ring."

"Oh. I guess I should propose, then." But first, I stuck two fingers in the collar of my white dress shirt and tugged. "So will you marry me?"

She stared at me for a moment and pressed her lips together. "Um, this is awkward. But no."

"What?" I blinked at her. "What do you mean, no?"

"I mean, no, I won't marry you. We've only been dating for three months, Enzo."

"I know, but time flies, and—and—soon it will be four months."

She looked confused. "Huh?"

"Look, I know this might seem a little . . . sudden," I said, tugging at my collar again. "But I really like you."

"You do?"

"Sure."

Folding her arms over her chest, Reina eyeballed me suspiciously. "Then how come you haven't tried anything?"

"What do you mean?"

"I mean, you've kissed me, but that's about it. And the few times I tried to initiate something more, you backed off."

"I was trying to respect you." I grabbed my ice water and chugged it. "I wanted you to know I was willing to wait."

She shook her head, like she didn't get it. "I know, but . . . it's weird to me. I actually thought maybe you were gay."

"Just because someone doesn't want to have sex with you doesn't mean he's gay," I said, annoyed. "And what's so weird about wanting to respect the girl you're going to marry?"

She rolled her eyes. "Enzo, for God's sake. We're not getting married."

"Why not?"

"To start, I'm only twenty-one. I've got things I want to do with my life. And when I get married—if I get married—I want my husband to be someone who respects me but also can't keep his hands off me. Someone in *love* with me."

"Love," I scoffed, frowning. "What is that, anyway?"

"It's a thing you should feel for the person you're proposing to. And . . . and what is that engraved on the band?" She plucked the ring from the velvet cushion before I could stop her. "It says 'Love Always, *Ricky*.'"

"Um . . ."

"Are you . . ." She glanced down at the ring and then up at me incredulously. "Are you proposing to me with someone *else's* ring?"

"I can explain," I said, although I realized that any explanation for that engraving was going to sound terrible.

"Don't bother." Sighing, she stuck the ring back in the slot and pushed the box toward me. "It doesn't matter, anyway."

Humiliated, I snapped the ring box shut. "Wow. I really fucked this up, didn't I?"

"Yeah. You did. But it's not the ring that's the problem." Reina leaned forward, reaching across the table to touch my forearm. "I'm not in love with you, Enzo. And you're not in love with me, are you?"

Staring at the tablecloth, I shook my head.

"And actually . . ." She took her hand back and sighed. "I don't think this is going to work. You're a little bit . . . old for me."

My head snapped up. "Huh?"

"Not that you're old in general," she said quickly. "You're just old for *me*."

I totally agreed with her, of course, but I didn't like hearing it. Reaching for my wine glass, I took a couple expensive gulps.

Reina checked her phone. "Listen, thanks for dinner, and—and everything, but I think it's best if we stop seeing each other."

"Fine," I said, guzzling more Barolo.

"My friends are across the street at The Tipsy Canoe," she said, naming a bar that had recently opened in Bellamy Creek and was popular with the younger crowd. "So I think I'm just going to walk over there."

"Let me drive you, at least." Setting my empty wine glass down, I took out my wallet and looked around for Lara so I could get the bill.

"No, really, you stay and finish the wine. I'd rather walk." She slid out of the booth and tucked her purse under her arm. "No hard feelings, right?"

I tried to smile, but it was a half-assed effort. "No hard feelings."

"Great," she said, looking down at her phone again. "See ya." She was typing something as she walked away.

Scowling, I shoved the ring box back in my jacket pocket and was pouring more wine in my glass when Lara appeared at the table.

"Hey," she said, looking surprised. "I just saw your date go out the door. She ditch you or what?"

"We mutually decided to go our separate ways," I lied.

"Tonight? Or in general?"

"In general."

"Ah." She paused. "You okay?"

"I'm fine." But I wasn't fine. My plans for the future had just been eviscerated, and it was my own fucking fault.

"You want the bill so you can get out of here?" Lara asked sympathetically.

I shrugged. "Nah. I don't have anywhere to go. Unless you need the table, I'll just sit here like an old man and drink wine by myself. This is probably what I'll be doing for the rest of my life, anyway. Might as well get used to it."

"Oh, come on. You know you won't be alone for long." Lara nudged my shoulder. "But stay as long as you like. If I need to kick you out, I'll tell you."

"Thanks. I'll leave you a good tip."

She winked at me. "I know you will."

Alone again, I drank my wine and stared at the flickering candle, wondering where the hell I'd gone wrong. Was it my fault I hadn't been in love with Reina? Should I have faked it? Should I have slept with her to "prove" it? This was a perfect example of why I'd steered clear of relationships.

Women were confusing, infuriating, moody, and temperamental. They said one thing and did another. They expected you to know exactly how to act and what to say without actually telling you. They wanted mind readers, not men. And then when you did or said the wrong thing, or *failed* to do or say the right thing, they flew into a rage and threw plates at your head or else they gave you the silent treatment for days. My parents had just celebrated their thirty-sixth anniversary, so I knew firsthand how marriage worked. My mother's mood swings and hair-trigger temper drove my father up a wall, and he could be a real stubborn, belligerent asshole sometimes. I'm talking thirty-six years of screaming fights and slamming doors and threats to leave or change the locks.

Not that they'd ever followed through. For fuck's sake, I had five younger siblings—two brothers and three sisters. And when our folks weren't fighting, all six of us agreed it was *embarrassing* how they couldn't keep their hands off each other. But it was always one extreme or the other—how the hell could anyone live like that? What was the appeal?

"Hey you. This seat taken?"

As if tonight couldn't have gotten worse, I looked up to see Bianca DeRossi—just about my *least* favorite person on Earth—standing next to the table, glass of wine in her hand.

"Doesn't look like it," I snapped.

She smiled and slid in across from me. "Thanks, I'd love to join you."

Frowning, I finished what was left in my glass and poured

myself the rest. Normally I'd never be so rude to a woman, but Bianca wasn't a regular woman. I'd known her since we were kids—our families were friends—but she'd always been a snotty little bookworm who thought she was too smart for me. Any time I tried talking to her, she clammed up and walked away. My parents forced me to take her to a dance at her all-girls Catholic high school once—didn't surprise *me* she couldn't get her own date—and she brought a fucking paperback book in her purse and kept her nose in it the entire time. So I amused myself by asking other girls to dance. How the hell was I supposed to know it would make her mad enough to tell her friends I had a small dick? She'd never gotten anywhere near it!

I only realized what she'd done a few years later when I hooked up with one of her classmates, who professed pleasant surprise at the generous size of my package. When I asked her why she'd thought I might be anything less than well-endowed, she told me what Bianca had said.

I was still mad about it.

Bianca had been living in Chicago since college, but a couple years ago she'd moved back to Bellamy Creek and had picked up aggravating me right where she'd left off. She was an interior designer and liked to buy and flip houses on the side just like I did, and somehow she managed to outbid me on every listing we competed for, all while acting sweet as pie, like we were old pals.

We weren't. I couldn't stand her. She wasn't a snotty little bookworm anymore, but she still knew exactly how to get under my skin.

Even more annoying?

She was fucking *hot*.

"What are you doing here?" I demanded.

"My family was here having dinner for my dad's birthday. But our family functions are short and sweet because Grandma Vinnie is ninety-six. She starts to fall asleep after an hour or so."

"Wow. Ninety-six." I took a break from being annoyed to appreciate a long life.

"Yes. And hitched when she was twenty-one, had five kids before she was thirty, and was married to my Grandpa Jack for seventy years before he died. Which she loves to tell me every single time I see her, right before she asks why I'm still single." Bianca took a sip of her wine.

"I've got some ideas on that."

Beneath the table, she nudged my foot with hers. "So what's with you? I thought I saw you with a date earlier. Either that or you were babysitting."

I glared at her. "Funny."

She grinned. "So who was she? Your girlfriend?"

"No. We broke up."

Her eyes widened. "Oh. Sorry to hear that."

"No, you're not."

"Enzo, this might come as a surprise to you, but I am not your enemy. I don't even dislike you—much."

"Oh yeah? Since when?"

She shrugged. "Since we're not immature and awkward kids anymore, who didn't know how to be friends with someone of the opposite sex?"

"Speak for yourself. I had plenty of friends who were girls."

Her blue eyes gleamed in the candlelight. "True. You always were a ladies' man."

I rolled my eyes. "Whatever. I'm here alone, aren't I?"

"Wait, are you expecting me to feel sorry for you? Like you couldn't walk right out of here and pick up the next girl you see? There's not a woman alive who can resist your charms, Enzo. Those dark eyes? That wavy hair? The Moretti swagger?"

"Apparently, I've lost my touch," I muttered, pouring the rest of Reina's Barolo in my glass.

She tipped her head to one side. "Eh, I doubt that. You weren't really into that girl, anyway, were you?"

I shrugged. "She was okay."

"You can do better."

"Better isn't the issue."

"What's the issue?"

"Fast."

"Why?" She laughed. "Are you going to turn into a pumpkin at midnight?"

"No, I'm going to lose Moretti & Sons to my brother Pietro if I don't get married before I'm thirty-five."

Her jaw dropped. "Seriously?"

Instead of answering, I polished off the last few sips of Barolo and set down the glass with a clunk. "I need another drink. Something stronger."

"Me too," she said, finishing the wine in her glass.

I flagged Lara down, and we ordered cocktails—a dirty vodka martini for Bianca, and bourbon on the rocks for me. Once she'd brought them, I took a sip and studied the woman across from me. Was it the wine, or was she even cuter than the last time I'd seen her?

She had skin so fair she practically glowed in the dark, bright red hair that skimmed her shoulders and glinted with gold in the candlelight, blue eyes that never missed a trick behind black-framed glasses, and a wide, lush mouth painted fire-engine red. Her nose and ears were small—actually everything about her was small, and if I remembered correctly, she hated being teased about it.

"What?" she said, growing self-conscious under my stare. She touched her hair. "Why are you looking at me like that?"

"I'm wondering what your parents fed you that stunted your growth."

Her crimson lips pursed and she sat up taller. "I am average height, thank you very much."

"Average for what, a chipmunk?"

She took a sip of her martini and clucked her tongue. "Always so obsessed with size. What *are* we to make of that, Dr. Freud? Is he worried he doesn't measure up?"

"Hey, that was *you* who started the rumor about the size of my—my *stuff*," I said angrily, puffing out my chest. "Totally unfounded, I might add."

"Okay, okay." She set her glass down and held up her palms. "It's time for me to apologize for that."

"I'm not sure I accept," I said stubbornly. "You can't insult a guy's manhood like that—without even seeing it—and just expect him to say it's no big deal. You besmirched the family jewels."

Laughing, she tucked her hair back behind one ear. "I'm truly sorry for what I said, and I shall never besmirch your jewels again."

"Why'd you do that anyway?"

She picked up her glass again and took a dainty sip. "To get back at you for asking every girl to dance but me, of course."

"What?" I snorted. "That's ridiculous. You didn't want to dance with me."

"How do you know? You never asked."

"Bianca, you brought a fucking *book* with you and read it the entire time."

She clutched at her chest. "*Twilight* isn't just a *book* to me, Enzo. It's a whole world. I still reread it every year."

"*Twilight*? Isn't that about a teenage vampire?"

"At least that vampire was a gentleman."

I rolled my eyes. "Whatever. You refused to even talk to me, and I was bored, so I asked some other girls to dance. I didn't think it was a big deal."

"Well, it hurt my feelings," she said, pointing her pert little nose at me. "I was already aware you didn't want to be there—I knew your parents made you take me. And I felt horrible about it, so I copped the bad attitude to hide my humiliation."

"Well, I didn't know any of that, because you never said anything. But I'm . . . I'm sorry I hurt your feelings."

"Your apology is accepted," she said. "Now are you going to accept mine?"

"I guess," I grumbled, taking another drink.

She lit up with a smile. "Thank you. So can we be friends now?"

"I suppose we can try," I said, "although I still don't understand why you were so stuck-up back then, always too good to talk to me."

"I wasn't stuck-up, Enzo, I was *shy*!" she exclaimed, like I should have known. "And you were always surrounded by girls batting their lashes and tossing their long blond hair and giggling like idiots at everything you said. Just because I wasn't one of them doesn't mean I thought I was too good for you. Frankly, I'm shocked you even remember me from back then. It's not like you ever noticed when I was in the room, what with your ego taking up all the space around you."

"Okay, maybe we should leave the past alone," I said, remembering why I didn't like her much. "Clearly, we are always going to disagree."

"Fine with me." She pulled the pick from her martini and ate one of the olives from it. "So how's your ego tonight? A little bruised, huh?"

"It's fine," I said, tightening the knot in my tie. "Reina obviously wasn't the right choice for a wife. I'm glad she said no."

Bianca started to choke on her olive. "Wait a minute." She fanned her face and managed to swallow. "You *proposed* to—to—what was the little girl's name?"

"Reina. And you've got no room to call someone little, *Tiny*."

As I'd hoped, the old nickname drew a brief scowl from her. "We're talking about *you* right now. Did you actually propose tonight? Like with a ring?"

I exhaled, regretting I'd mentioned it. "Yeah. I did."

Her eyes lit up. "Let me see it."

"No."

"Why not?"

"Because you just want to rub salt in my wound."

"For fuck's sake, Enzo. You're not wounded. You don't even love this girl, you just needed to put a ring on her finger so your dad would put your name on the company letterhead." She held out her hand. "Now give it here."

Something told me I was going to be sorry, but I reached into my jacket and pulled out the ring box.

She took it from me and opened it up. "It's pretty," she said with grudging admiration. Then she squinted at it, pushing her glasses up her nose. "Did you have it engraved?"

I picked up my bourbon and took a hefty swallow. "No."

"But it says . . ." She set the box down and pulled the ring from the velvet to examine it closer. Then she started laughing. "'*Love Always, Ricky*?'"

"Give me that." Leaning forward, I tried to swipe the ring from her hand, but she held it out of my reach.

"Just a second! I want to try it on."

I thumped against the back of the booth, picking up my drink again and tossing back the rest of it. Could this night get any worse?

Bianca slipped the ring on her finger—it fit—and held out her hand, studying it. "So what did you say?"

"I proposed."

"But how? Like, did you say, 'You're the love of my life and I want to be with you forever' kind of thing?"

"Uh, not exactly. I didn't want to *lie* to her. I just, you know, gave her the ring." I made a grand, sweeping gesture with one hand.

"But you must have *said* something."

"What difference does it make?" I asked irritably.

"Look, I'm only trying to help you. You obviously blew it tonight, and by your own admission, you need to find a Lucy for your Ricky sooner rather than later, right?"

I looked around for Lara. I needed another drink. And then a ride home.

"Right?" Bianca prodded me with her foot under the table again. "So let me help you."

"The only way you could help me is to marry me," I grumbled, waving Lara over. "And since that's out of the question, this discussion is over."

"Well, wait a minute. Who said it's out of the question?"

I stared at her like she'd sprouted horns. "Huh?"

Bianca continued to study the ring on her finger. "I'm just thinking out loud here. But it seems to me we each have a goal, and they could both be accomplished with one simple—fake—relationship."

I shook my head, as if to clear it, but the fog remained. "I know I'm drunk, but what the hell are you talking about?"

She sighed and picked up her martini for a sip. "I'm talking about the fact that *you* need a wife to get what *you* want. I'm willing to *be* that wife—temporarily, and under the strictest of conditions—if you'll agree to give me what *I* want."

I shook my head. "Oh, no. No fucking way. I see what you're doing here. I'm not paying you to fake being my wife."

Bianca rolled her eyes. "Give me a break, Enzo. I don't want your money. Nor do I need it."

"Then I don't understand," I said, feeling—once again—completely baffled by a woman. "What could you possibly want that I could give you?"

The smile that crept over those hellfire lips should have been a warning. "A baby."

Two

Bianca

THE LOOK ON ENZO'S FACE WAS PRICELESS. "A WHAT?"

"A baby."

His dark eyes clouded over with confusion. "Whose baby?"

"Mine. And . . ." I ate the second olive off the pick. "Yours."

"I don't have a baby."

I sighed. "Enzo, I know you're somewhat inebriated, but try to keep up. You need a wife. I would like a baby. One and one can make three."

Enzo continued staring at me as if he didn't know who I was. "This makes no sense."

"It makes perfect sense, actually."

His brow furrowed. "I don't want to marry you."

"You don't want to marry anyone," I pointed out.

"True."

"At least if you marry me, there's an agreed-upon expiration date. We only have to stay married long enough to get you what you want." I ate the third olive. "And what I want, of course."

"That's the other thing. What is this about a *baby*?" Even

with consternation creasing his forehead and tightening his jaw, he was stupidly handsome. He always had been.

I cleared my throat. "Well, the baby is something I've been thinking about for a while. I've always wanted children, but I haven't met *the one* yet, and unfortunately for a woman, the biological clock is an actual thing. And mine is ticking."

"How old are you?"

"I'll be thirty-three next month."

"That's not that old. My mother had my brother Matteo when she was like thirty-eight or something."

"I've got some additional reproductive health concerns, okay?" Uncomfortable discussing them with him, I took a sip of my martini. "Without going into detail, I'll just say that it would be better for me to try to get pregnant sooner rather than later. It's likely I'll struggle to conceive, so putting it off will only be worse for me."

He looked like he might ask more about it but closed his mouth and took a drink. "So how would that even work? Would we have to actually—"

"No!" I set my drink down so fast, some of it splashed onto the tablecloth. "It would all be done in a fertility clinic. You'd donate your . . . you know." I found myself struggling to say the word *sperm*. "Genetic material."

One of his dark eyebrows peaked. "My genetic material?"

"Yes." My face warmed, and I knew a hot pink blush was creeping into my cheeks. "The procedure is called an intrauterine insemination. You provide the, um, DNA, it gets washed and concentrated, and then a nurse performs the . . . placement into my uterus."

"Oh, like the thing with the turkey baster? I've heard about that."

I sighed and sat up straight, feeling like a principal dealing with a troublesome schoolboy. "Yes, sort of."

"That doesn't sound very sexy," he said, lifting his glass again—but not before I caught the grin creeping onto his lips.

"It's not supposed to be sexy," I said stiffly. "It's science."

"Okay, so what then, you get pregnant with our science baby and then I'm supposed to divorce you while you're pregnant? No fucking way. I'll look like a monster."

"We can wait until after it's born if you want," I said quickly. "I'm just not sure how long it will take for me to get pregnant. I suppose we could write it into our contract that if I don't get pregnant within a certain amount of time, the whole thing is null and void."

Enzo thought for a moment and shook his head. "But if you *do* get pregnant, I'm an asshole for leaving."

I held up both hands. "I'll take all the blame. I'll leave you."

"But I must have done something to make you leave. I'm the asshole in all your ideas," he complained. "No. If we do this, it would have to be an amicable parting. No one gets the blame."

"Okay, fine. We'd split up as friends."

"We're not even friends right now."

I tossed a hand up. "So we'll split up as non-friends! However you want to end things, Enzo, I'll agree to it. As long as I leave with the baby."

Enzo sat up taller. "That's the other thing. I'm supposed to just father this baby and never see it again?"

"I never said that. You can see him or her whenever you'd like. I won't move away or anything. I want to live near my family—that's why I moved back to Bellamy Creek in the first place."

"So I'd be like . . . Weekend Dad or something?" He squinted and gazed off into the distance, like he was trying to picture it.

"If you want."

After a solid thirty seconds of staring into the future, he shook his head. "I don't know. It doesn't seem right to do to a kid."

"Enzo." I reached across the table and put a hand on his, causing him to look down in surprise. "I've been thinking about having a baby on my own for a couple years now. I've researched fertility clinics, looked over donor profiles, talked with my family and my therapist."

"What did they say?"

"My therapist understands. My family does not." I pressed my lips together. "They're totally against it. They cannot imagine why I'd want to get pregnant with a stranger's baby or raise a child on my own. But they're Catholic and old-fashioned, and they want for me what they had for themselves, and it's just not going to happen—not in time for me to have a baby, anyway. I know I could always adopt, and I absolutely would, although I think it's more difficult for an unmarried woman to adopt than for a couple. I admit, I haven't done all the research. Because I really would like to experience being pregnant and giving birth if I can. I know I'll be a good mom."

Enzo's eyes were on our hands. He swallowed.

"You cannot imagine the things people say to me," I told him, a lump trying to form in my throat.

He looked up. "Like what?"

"Like, 'At your age, you should lower your standards and just find a man willing to commit.' Or 'You may have to settle down with a man who already has kids, if you really want them.' Or 'You're a beautiful woman. It can't be *that* hard to get knocked up.'"

"Someone said that to you?" Enzo appeared appropriately horrified.

"Yes. People say that shit to women all the time."

"Fuck." He shook his head, like he had no idea what jerks people could be.

But this was no time for a lesson on how society treats women and their bodies.

"You're probably wondering, 'Why me?'" I went on.

His expression morphed into something more familiar—three parts cocky, one part amused. "Not really."

Laughing, I took my hand back. "Well, I'll tell you anyway."

"Please do." He sipped his bourbon, knowing he'd enjoy this.

"I know we've had our differences in the past, but we go back a long way, and that means something to me. Our families go back a long way. There's trust and loyalty and respect. There's a history of . . . of showing up for each other. And I was just thinking, even with our somewhat rocky past, that *we'd* show up for each other. Wouldn't we?"

He took a drink and swirled what was left in the glass. "Nothing means more to me than family. That's true."

"I think beneath it all, we share the same traditional family values—albeit with some modern adjustments," I said. "I don't think a woman should have to be married to have a baby, and you don't think a man should have to be married to inherit the family business."

Enzo thought for a moment. "But I believe in honesty too, and this plan of yours involves lying to our families and friends. And my closest friends *are* family to me."

"I know, and I don't love that part of it. But I do like that about *you,*" I added quickly, "the fact that you'd hesitate before deceiving the people you love. It's part of what makes me want you to be the father of my baby, despite your enormously inflated ego. Deep down, like way deep, buried beneath layer upon layer of vanity, pride, and self-absorption—"

"Okay, okay." He stopped me with a hand. "Enough."

I smiled and went on. "Deep down, I do believe you are a decent man. Honorable. Trustworthy. Protective of those you care about."

"Don't forget about my face," he said, giving off that Enzo Moretti heat that had probably melted more panties than I'd ever owned.

"Your face?" I squinted, like I hadn't really considered the fact that he was the best-looking guy I'd ever known. "I suppose it's passably attractive. I've never really looked that close."

He laughed, shaking his head. "Fine, be that way. I will donate my passable looks to your turkey-baster baby."

"You will?" My heart started to race.

"Why not?" He shrugged, as if he was agreeing to go out for pizza with me. "I'm not sure we're going to fool anybody, but what the hell? I've got nothing to lose. I do want to be a dad, and I'm not getting any younger. And fake-marrying you sounds better than real-marrying anyone else—as long as it's temporary."

"I suppose that's the best proposal I'm going to get, huh?" I looked at the ring on my finger. "Well, Ricky, I guess you've got yourself a Lucy."

"You did *what*?" My younger sister Ellie nearly went off the back of the treadmill next to me at the gym. She had to grab the rails to keep on the belt.

"I asked Enzo Moretti to be the father of my baby, and in return, I offered to marry him."

"Bianca, what the hell?" Ellie's feet scrambled beneath her to regain her balance. "Why would you do that? It sounds psychotic."

"It's not psychotic. It's very logical, in fact." I bumped up my speed from a power walk to a light jog. "It's going to get both of us exactly what we want with the added bonus of being a temporary situation."

"Temporary? Uh, last I checked, a baby is forever."

I laughed. "I know the *baby* is forever, but the marriage won't be. It's just a marriage of convenience. Happens all the time in books."

"Yeah, but this isn't a book, Tiny—it's real life. What you're talking about sounds insane! A fake wedding?"

"Shhhh!" I scolded, looking around to make sure no one had heard. It was nine a.m. on Sunday, so the gym wasn't too crowded since most people were still at church. I'd gone to Mass the previous afternoon with my family before dinner. I couldn't afford to play hooky since I was asking God for a pretty big favor in the next few months—possibly a near-miracle, if my fertility specialist was right. "The wedding won't be fake. Just our feelings."

"So why even bother with a real marriage?"

"Well, we talked about that, and we agreed that we really do have to get married in order for this to work. His dad has to be convinced it's legit. Also, I'd like it to be legal for the baby's sake."

She shook her head. "This is nuts."

"But it's happening."

Ellie let that sink in as she increased the incline on her treadmill. She was three years younger than me, and we shared our mother's auburn hair and light eyes, although she kept her hair more strawberry blond and was a good three inches taller than my five-foot-one. In contrast, our younger brother JJ was tall like our dad, and he'd inherited our father's dark hair and olive skin too. Ellie and I used to complain every summer that he was able to get a beautiful golden tan while she and I burned horribly if we didn't wear long sleeves and bucket hats at the beach.

"So what are you going to tell Mom and Dad?" she asked. "It's not like you can pretend you've been dating him all this time."

"No," I agreed. "That's why I'm not wearing the ring yet."

Ellie had to grab the rails again. "He already gave you a *ring*?"

"Yes." I had to chuckle. "Things progressed quickly last night. And that's what I'm going to tell the family. We ran into each other at DiFiore's after Dad's birthday dinner. We talked for hours. We fell madly in love."

Ellie shook her head. "No one will believe it."

"Listen, I need your support on this," I pleaded. "You have to back me up, Ellie—or I agree, it won't work."

"But—"

"I was there for you when you came out to Mom and Dad and told them about Sierra," I reminded her.

"That's different," she argued. "I am *actually* a lesbian. Sierra and I are genuinely in love. You're asking me to back you up in a lie."

"Right. Sorry," I said, feeling shitty. "I just really want you on my side."

"I am on your side." She exhaled loudly. "I'm not sure it's the best way to go about having a baby, but if you're determined to do it, I'll support you. What do I have to do?"

I flashed her a grateful smile. "Just be publicly happy for me. Shut down any doubts anyone raises that this isn't the real thing. Be amazed that it happened and yet totally convinced this is fate."

"That's a tall order. You couldn't stand Enzo Moretti when you were young."

"Honestly, there are some things about him that still drive me nuts," I confessed. "But I don't need to love him for this. In fact, it works better if I don't."

"What do you mean?"

"Because when it's time to end it all, I won't be in pieces about it. I'll be just fine walking away. And besides, I didn't really *hate* him back then," I said. "I just hated the fact that girls were always tripping over themselves to be with him, and he lapped up all the attention like a Golden Retriever. I thought he was obnoxious and conceited."

"Fair enough."

"And maybe I was a little jealous," I admitted.

"Jealous?" She glanced over at me in surprise. "Of him?"

"Kind of. Or maybe I was jealous of those flirty girls." I tried to puzzle it out. "I was just so shy. I *wanted* him to pay attention to me, but I didn't know how to show it. He was just so good-looking and confident. I was tongue-tied around him. So I pretended to hate him. It was easier than admitting I liked him. Know what I mean?"

"I guess."

"But that's all ancient history. We made our peace with each other last night and agreed to leave the past in the past. What matters is the future."

"So when are you getting married?"

"Not sure yet. We're actually having dinner tonight to hammer out the details of the contract. We both have some stipulations we want in writing."

"This is so weird. It sounds like a business deal, not an engagement."

"That's exactly what it is. We're clear on the mission, but we're going to clarify our vision, define our purpose, discuss the timeline."

"Oh my God." Ellie's expression was agonized as she placed her hands over her heart. "Romance is really dead, isn't it?"

"I don't *want* romance, Ellie," I said, growing frustrated. "Look, I tried for romance. I was with Tate for five solid years before I realized he was never going to marry me—I wasted *five years* of my life believing his lies and letting him push aside all the serious conversations I tried to have about the future. And now there isn't anything I wouldn't do to get just one of those years back. What if it's too late for me?"

"I'm sorry, B," Ellie said, a little softer. "I know how hurt you were after Tate. If you're determined to do this thing, I support you."

"I'm more than determined, Ellie. I want to have a baby, and I'm done waiting for it. Why shouldn't I get to experience being a mom just because I haven't found real love? I was willing to use an anonymous donor, but thankfully, I don't have to. My child can actually know its father."

"And Enzo is up for that?" she asked. "Raising a child with you?"

"He said he was." I hesitated, then admitted what I was afraid of. "But he was also drunk. Tonight, I want to have a completely sober conversation about this."

"Good idea." She peeked at me sideways. "What will you do if he says no?"

I took a deep breath, let it out, and increased my speed to a run. "I'll move on. That's the beauty of this, Ellie. I'm not giving Enzo Moretti my heart to break."

She thought for a moment. "So are you actually going to *do it* with him?"

"No! I'll still have an artificial insemination. He'll just provide the sperm."

She giggled. "Too bad. Seems like if you're going to marry a guy as hot as Enzo Moretti, you should at least get a couple perks out of it, like seeing him naked."

"I don't *want* to see him naked," I said. But then I had to turn the speed of my treadmill down.

I was having trouble breathing, and my heart was racing a little too fast.

Enzo knocked on my door that night just after six.

I lived in a ground-floor condo right on the harbor, which I loved, although it was small—just 900 square feet—and I never did get around to buying a boat to put in the slip that came along with the lease. But it was the perfect size for one person, with an open-concept kitchen and living room, two bedrooms, a bath and a half. And since I hadn't planned on having a roommate when I moved back to Bellamy Creek—let alone a spouse—it had seemed like a good buy at the time.

I wondered where Enzo lived. Would I have to give up my condo and move in with him? Where would I go when I left? As I went to answer his knock, I realized there were a lot of pieces to this puzzle we'd have to make fit.

Pulling open the door, I ignored the little *ka-whump* I always experienced in my chest at the sight of him. Probably every woman who laid eyes on him felt that *ka-whump*. "Hey," I said. "Come on in."

He stepped into the entryway, and I shut the door against the late February chill. "This is for you," he said, handing me a bottle of Nebbiolo. "It's one of my favorites, but don't let me have any. My head still hurts from last night."

"Thank you." I went over and placed it on the kitchen island, which also functioned as my dining table and was already set for two. "Can I take your coat?"

He shrugged out of a black wool double-breasted coat. Beneath it he had on dark jeans and a black cashmere sweater over a white-collared shirt. His clothes fit him as if they'd been custom tailored, but then, he had a body that just looked good in fitted clothing—lean and muscular but not bulky, with just the right amount of brawn to his chest. His hands, I'd noticed at the table last night, were surprisingly elegant for someone who worked with them, with long, graceful fingers, a neat manicure, and thick, masculine wrists. The kind of hands you could imagine aggressively pounding a hammer or ripping out drywall but also gliding smoothly over your bare skin.

Turning away from him, I clamped down on the troublesome thought and headed for the closet, where I hung his coat next to mine.

"Smells great in here," he said, looking at the stove, where a couple pots were on the burners. "What are we having?"

"Pappardelle with sausage, kale, and spicy tomato sauce." I went over and lifted the lid on my sauce, taking a quick taste. "Can I get you something to drink?"

"Water's fine."

I grabbed a bottle of water from the fridge and handed it to him. "Rehydrating?"

He grimaced, leaning back against the counter. "Yeah. Next

time I think it's a good idea to drink an entire bottle of Barolo with bourbon for dessert, remind me of the headache I have today. And how I couldn't drive myself home. And how I had to go get my car before church."

"You got up for church this morning? I'm impressed." I had to elbow him aside to grab a large serving bowl from a low cupboard.

"Of course I did." He sounded shocked I'd question his devotion to Jesus as he uncapped his water bottle. "Father Mike and I are tight these days."

"Oh yeah? And why's that?"

"Because I needed a miracle to avoid getting married, and I figured Father Mike might have an in. Also I wanted God to see me helping my Nonna into the pew, getting on my knees to pray, putting money in the collection basket, admitting I'm a sinner, et cetera, et cetera, et cetera." He tipped up the water bottle.

Shaking my head, I opened the oven and took out the loaf of bread warming inside. "I'm not sure God's going to look favorably enough on your *et cetera* brand of piety to provide a miracle. What would that even look like?"

"My dad would change his mind about this stupid settling down bullshit. I could just live my life the way I want to live it."

"I thought you said you *wanted* a family," I said, grabbing a bread knife and slicing the loaf.

"I do. But why does he have to put this arbitrary number on it? Why can't I just do it when I'm ready?"

"It does seem unfair," I told him. "But then again, so does the whole biological clock thing. Men can reliably and safely father children *long* past the age women can easily conceive them."

"Yeah, that seems like bullshit too," he agreed. "Do you want me to do something to help you?"

I glanced at him over one shoulder, quirking one brow. "You cook?"

"Yes, I *cook*." He rolled his eyes. "I moved out of my parents' house when I was eighteen. I would have starved if I couldn't cook."

"In that case, can you check the pasta? I think it's probably done." I glanced at him over my shoulder. "Grab a fork from that drawer to your right."

He set his water bottle down, washed his hands at the sink, and took a fork from the drawer. Bumping it closed with his hip, he lifted a long, flat pappardelle noodle from the simmering pot on the stove. After letting it cool for a second, he plucked it off the fork with his fingers and sank his teeth into one end. Then he nodded. "Done."

"Okay, switch the gas off on that burner, please. And the one under the sauce."

He did as I asked while I opened an upper cupboard door and tried to reach the pasta bowls on the third shelf. But I was wearing ballet flats, and I couldn't quite get my fingertips on the edges. My kitchen was tiny, but the design made good use of vertical space, meaning the cupboards went all the way to the ceiling. Normally, I'd just climb onto the stone counter, but I didn't want to do that with Enzo here.

"Need help?"

I gritted my teeth. "Yes."

He came up behind me—so close I could smell his cologne, which made my lady parts awaken from a deep slumber—and easily brought two wide, shallow bowls down, setting them in front of me. "There you go. You should have asked them to put a rolling ladder in here for you. Like at a library."

"Very funny. If you want to be useful, grab that colander and drain the pasta. Reserve about a cup of the water." Breathing easier when he moved away from me, I placed the sliced bread in a basket lined with a linen napkin and set it on the table. The salad and salad plates were already out, as were bread plates, wine and water glasses, and silverware.

Back in the kitchen, I carefully stepped around him to

retrieve some serving utensils from a drawer. I wasn't sure what my problem was tonight, but it was important to remember that he was only here for business negotiations. This wasn't a date. We were barely even friends. And just because it had been a *really* long time since I'd been intimate with a man did not mean I should be thinking about what he looked like naked.

"You want this in the sauce?" he asked me, holding the colander full of steaming pappardelle.

"Yes. Thanks." I watched him carefully tip the pasta into the sauce. "I'll take it from here. You can sit down if you want."

"Okay." He set the colander in the sink. "Can I pour you a glass of wine?"

"Uh, sure." I wanted to keep my wits sharp tonight, but figured one glass wouldn't hurt. It might even help take the edge off whatever physical attraction I felt for him.

"Opener?"

I pulled it from a drawer and handed it to him, careful not to let our fingers touch.

While he opened the wine, I faced away from him and took a breath before finishing the pasta, transferring it to the serving bowl and grating a little more parmesan onto the dish. From the fridge I pulled out some fresh basil and quickly chopped a small handful, sprinkling it over the top.

When I turned around, Enzo took the large, heavy bowl from me and placed it on the island. "This looks incredible."

"You don't have to sound so surprised." Lowering myself onto one of the counter stools, I took a sip from the glass of wine he'd poured me.

"That was a compliment," he said, scowling. "See, this is the problem with women. You try to say something nice, and they don't know how to just say thank you."

"I'll try to remember that," I muttered, grateful he'd said something to remind me why I would *never* be romantically interested in him.

Never, I repeated, watching those hands as he served us both salad and pasta.

Never.

Never.

Never.

Three

Enzo

"So," she said as we began to eat, "should we wait until after dinner to talk business?"

"No need," I said, drizzling olive oil and then vinegar over my salad. "We can talk now if you'd like. And if there's anything we need to get in writing, we can do it when we're finished."

She took a sip of wine. "So you're still up for this?"

"*I* am. Are you?" My tone came out more challenging than I'd intended.

"Yes. I just felt like maybe I should double-check with you, since your decision-making abilities were impaired last night." She didn't even bother to hide her smile.

"Well, today I'm stone cold sober, and I'm still in."

"Excellent. So am I." She stuck a forkful of salad in her mouth.

"So the way I see it, there are three phases to this project," I said, feeling like I was pitching a new construction deal. "The engagement, the marriage—which includes the baby—and the breakup."

"Sounds about right."

"I don't think we should wait on the engagement. It might seem like it's coming out of left field, but we should probably fake the whole falling in love thing quickly, and just make the announcement we're married." I took a bite of pasta—it was fucking delicious. Her cooking would definitely be a perk. "I figure we can do like a City Hall thing and tell them after the fact."

She took another sip of wine and set the glass down slowly. "So there won't be an actual wedding? With guests?"

"I wasn't planning on it. Why? You want one?"

"Not a big one. But what if this is the only chance I ever have to wear a white dress and have my father walk me down the aisle?"

I thought about that as I chewed. "Can it be the aisle at City Hall?"

She considered it. "I suppose I could deal with that. It might even be better because then we won't have to lie to a priest. I was nervous about that."

"Same," I said, glad we agreed on something. "I think it's best if we keep God out of this. Otherwise, one of us might be struck by lightning or something."

She nodded. "So the story will go that we ran into each other after dinner last night and realized, lo and behold, that we've been wrong about each other all these years, and suddenly we're head over heels."

I shrugged and stuck more pasta in my mouth. "Whatever."

"Probably we need to *date* for at least a month before you propose, don't you think?" She put little air quotes around the word. "Lest our families think we've completely lost our minds?"

After giving it some thought, I said, "Yeah, you might be right. I don't want my dad to pull some bullshit where he says we have to be together for a certain amount of time before he'll give me the business. He has to believe we're in love and this is real." I eyeballed her critically. "You sure you're going to be able to pull this off?"

She stared right back. "Are *you*?"

My spine straightened. "Yes. I'll have you know, I'm a great actor. I played Romeo when I was a senior in high school."

Her expression said, *Fuck off, you did not*. "What?"

"I'm serious. Some girl I liked at the time was all into theater and shit, and she convinced me to try out. I didn't really think I'd get the role, but I did. And she was so psyched about it, she gave me a blowjob that very day after school." I shrugged. "So I figured I should actually do the play."

Bianca was shaking her head. "Of *course* that's why you did the play."

"I was good too." I clutched at my chest and spoke in a dramatic, raspy voice. "*Thus with a kiss, I die.*"

She burst out laughing. "Just when I think you can't be any more ridiculous."

"Whatever." I started eating again. "My point is that I know I can be convincing. I hope you're up for the challenge."

"I will admit that acting wildly in love with you is going to be a challenge, but I will do my best," she said, twirling pasta on her fork. "Don't expect any blowjobs though."

I snorted. Bianca had probably never given a blowjob in her life. "I wouldn't dare. So what *will* be allowed? We have to give them something. Hand holding?"

"Sure."

"Can I kiss your cheek?"

"I suppose," she said with a sigh, like it would truly be a hardship for her. "Just for show. But no kissing on the lips."

"Agreed. But if I put my arm around you, are you going to slap me?"

"Just keep your hands where they belong, Enzo, and we'll be fine."

"Works for me," I said, although I found my eyes wandering over the small curves of her breasts in the tight black sweater she wore. For a moment, I imagined sliding between the sheets with her, but even when I looked at her in my fantasy, she was wearing her glasses and had her nose stuck in a book about teenage vampires.

"What's so funny?" she demanded.

"Nothing." I hadn't even realized I'd started to chuckle.

Her eyes narrowed, and I got the feeling she'd read my mind somehow and knew I was laughing at her.

"So the marriage," she said tartly. "I've got some rules."

"Hit me."

"It's purely for show. There is no *marriage bed*. There will be no consummation. Not on the wedding night or any night after."

"Party pooper."

"And we'll do the insemination right away."

"No problem. I cannot wait to inseminate you from one room away."

"And if it doesn't work the first time, I'd like two more tries. If it doesn't work after three tries, we can move to the divorce phase." She looked upset as she poked at her pasta.

"You don't think it's going to work?"

Her shoulders rose. "Hard to say. Women who have PCOS like I do have reduced odds of conceiving."

"Well, that's because they've never tried it with a Moretti." I thumped my chest. "The men in my family have very strong genes."

"Oh, good Lord." She rolled her eyes. "It doesn't have anything to do with your genes, Enzo. It has to do with *my* eggs. But I don't really want to talk about that now."

"Suit yourself."

She took a breath and met my eyes. "I'd like to give it three tries. If you're okay with it."

I shrugged. "I'm fine with it. I can jerk off three times."

"Can you not say it like that?" She wrinkled her nose.

"That's what it is, right? Why not call a spade a spade?"

"I prefer *providing a sample.* You will *provide a sample* three times."

"If it makes you feel better," I said. "But it's exactly the same—"

"If it *does* work," she went on, interrupting me, "we should probably at least stay married until it's born. That means we're potentially committing to being married for up to a year or more. Maybe fifteen months."

"I was assuming that would be the case," I said. "I think anything less is suspicious anyway."

She took another drink of her wine. "Should we discuss phase three? The breakup and divorce?"

"Already trying to get rid of me?"

"The way I see it, there are two possible scenarios."

"Go ahead. What are they?"

"First, if I don't get pregnant, we can just blame that."

I shook my head. "No way. Makes me an asshole, remember?"

She touched her chest. "I'll take the blame. Look, I can't explain this fully, but infertility is really hard on women. It affects them in ways people who've never been there can't understand. But trust me when I say that it could have a detrimental effect on a marriage, especially one that was too rash and ill-advised in the first place."

What choice did I have but to believe her? "Okay."

"The second scenario is more complicated. If there *is* a baby."

I set down my fork and took a big drink of water. "Yeah, I agree. If I hadn't passed out last night, the thought of it would have kept me up."

"This is the most serious part of this, because it's the part that's *real,* and the part that's actually *forever.*"

"Right." My throat was doing something weird, and the water wasn't going down smoothly. I coughed into my elbow.

Bianca put her fork down, adjusted her glasses, and placed her hands in her lap. Her expression was concerned. "I want you to take some time to think about this, Enzo. This isn't like a sperm donor situation. Because of our '*marriage*'"—she made quote marks in the air again—"people will know you're the baby's father. Like I said before, I won't ask anything of you, but if you want to co-parent with me, you can. We could work out custody and visitation arrangements. On the flip side, if you want to walk away completely, you can."

Anger boiled up inside me, and I glared at her. "Fuck that. I'm not an asshole, Bianca. If I father a child, I'll *be* its father. I'm not a man who walks away from my responsibilities."

"Okay."

"And I told you. I've always wanted kids," I went on heatedly, as if she'd insinuated otherwise.

"I get that, but I just want you to take some time to think about whether or not you're ready for one at *this* point in your life, and with *these* circumstances. You *will be* a single dad."

I looked her right in the eye. "I know. I said I was up for this, and I meant it." It was the truth. Not that I wasn't nervous, but I *did* want kids. And I didn't want to be an old man before I became a father. A kid deserved a dad who could run the bases with him, wrestle and play catch, teach him to swim and fish and ride a bike, coach his teams. So wasn't this the best possible way to go?

"Okay. So this is the last thing I'm going to say on this topic." Bianca took a breath. "I know you want to run your own company. But are you sure this is the only way to get it?"

"Of course I'm sure. That's what I've been saying."

"What about starting your own company? Not taking over your father's."

My eyes widened. "Starting over from scratch? Fuck that.

This is my birthright, Bianca. I'm the oldest Moretti son, and I deserve this, just like the previous five generations of oldest sons. I'm just as worthy as the rest of them. I can prove it."

"I believe you," she said quietly, and somehow I felt like she did.

"Good. Then it's settled." Without saying anything further, I ate the rest of my pasta, served myself some more, and finished that too. Then I grabbed a piece of bread and mopped up the sauce left in the bottom of the bowl.

When I finally looked up, I saw Bianca sopping up sauce with bread just like I had, then licking her fingers. Her appetite was sexy.

While she didn't know I was watching, I covertly studied her profile and wondered what a child of ours would look like. Would they get her straight red hair or my thick brown waves? My dark eyes or her baby blues? Her alabaster skin or my olive complexion? Her petite stature or my height? Would it be a boy or a girl? Chubby or small? Sweet-natured or temperamental?

She looked over and caught me staring, and her expression turned angry. "Quit it," she said, sucking sauce from her thumb. "You're creeping me out."

"Sorry." *Definitely temperamental,* I decided. I pictured myself pacing the floor at night, holding a fat, screaming baby with wild red hair and briefly had second thoughts.

"Want some coffee?" she asked, sliding off her stool.

"Sure." I rose to my feet to help her clean up.

"I'm impressed," she said, watching me set my dishes in the sink and rinse them.

"Thank you."

"I meant with your mother. You have nice manners."

I poked her in the side and she giggled, scooting away from me. "Yeah, well, when she wasn't busy screaming at my father, she managed to raise polite kids."

We cleared off the island, and while I loaded the dishwasher, she put the food away. "You want to take some pasta home?" she asked.

"Are you kidding? Yes, please."

She grabbed a plastic container from a cupboard, filled it with pappardelle, and snapped the lid on. "Don't forget to take it. It'll be in the fridge."

"Okay. Thanks. Hey, can I use your bathroom?"

"Sure. Around the corner on your right."

When I came out of the bathroom, instead of going left to head back to the kitchen, I peeked into the small room across the hall. It was a bedroom set up like an office, but it also had a couch, which looked like it might be a pull-out. Spying a bunch of framed photos on the bookshelves behind her desk, I switched the light on and moved deeper into the room to check them out.

They were mostly family pictures—some recent, some from her childhood, some vintage shots in black and white—but she also had a couple travel photos too. I could tell she'd been to Italy at least once, and it looked like she'd been to Paris and London as well.

Taking a snapshot of Bianca and her immediate family at what might have been her high school graduation off the shelf, I studied it. She looked much the same at eighteen as she did fifteen years later—same black-framed glasses, same wide-mouthed grin, same smooth, bright complexion and fiery hair. She definitely looked like her mom. Bianca DeRossi was an Italian name, but the actual Bianca looked about as Irish as a person could be. I made a mental note to crack a few leprechaun jokes at some point.

"You get lost?"

I turned to see Bianca in the doorway. "Just snooping in your office. Making sure you're not a secret psychopath."

"I don't keep the bodies in my office, Enzo. Give me a little credit."

Smiling, I set the frame back on the shelf. "You like traveling, huh?"

"Love it. It's where I get all my design inspiration."

"What's your favorite place? I should probably know this stuff about you."

"Good point." She came around the desk and stood next to me. She smelled like garlic and tomato sauce, which was actually kind of sexy. "I'd say Florence. No, the Amalfi Coast. No, maybe Capri."

I nodded. "I like a woman who gives a straight answer."

She poked my shoulder. "At least they're all in one country. What about you?"

"I like Italy too. I'd say Rome or Florence, for the architecture."

"What do you know, we agree on something. If we were going on a real honeymoon, we could have gone to Italy."

"Who's that?" I pointed at one of the black and white photographs—a wedding picture, from the looks of it.

"Oh, those are Grandma Vinnie's parents—my great-grandparents. Their last name was Lupo. They were married in 1923."

I studied the couple. "So that's your great-grandmother? You look like her."

"You're just saying that because she's short. Everyone called *her* Tiny too. That's where my nickname comes from."

I laughed. "It's not just because she's short. It's her face too. The heart shape of it." Bianca had a more lush mouth, but I didn't feel like that was something I could say.

"She had red hair too," Bianca said. "I mean, she died when I was only three, so I don't remember her, and her hair was white by then anyway, but I've heard stories about her. Apparently, she was a real pistol."

"Oh yeah?" I gave her a sideways grin, nudging her with my elbow. "Your namesake was a pistol? *There's* a surprise."

She stuck her tongue out at me. "Do *you* know any family history?"

"Very little," I admitted. "I should ask my parents about it. Apparently my great-grandfather, the one I'm named for, was into some sinister business. Mobster stuff."

"That's funny, because mine was too. They both were," Bianca said, gesturing at the old wedding photo. "They ran whisky into Detroit from Canada during Prohibition."

"Seriously?" I looked at the petite woman and her short, barrel-chested husband. There *was* something sly about the smiles on their faces. "That's pretty cool. My great-grandfather lived in Detroit too. Maybe they knew each other."

Bianca laughed. "Wouldn't that be something? Come on, let's have coffee and dessert. I've got a sweet tooth."

"Good to know," I said, following her from the room and trying not to look at her cute round butt in her tight jeans.

Sinister business indeed.

"What's that?" I said, eyeing the pad of paper and pen she'd placed on the island along with two cups of coffee and a plate of pizzelle sprinkled with powdered sugar.

"That's for us to draw up the most important rules of our deal. I figure we don't need everything in writing, maybe just the top five things." She sipped her coffee, then she picked up the pen. "I'll go first. *No sex,*" she said, writing it down in all caps, as if I'd been pawing her all night.

I rolled my eyes. "Fine."

"With *anyone,*" she went on, pushing her glasses up her nose. "Not as long as we're married. I don't want it going around that you're cheating on me."

"Well, *I* don't want it going around that I'm a cheater."

"Good, then we agree," she said breezily, picking up a cookie and taking a bite.

Aggravated at the thought of a yearlong dry spell, I grabbed a cookie too. I wasn't much of a sweets eater, but I did like pizzelle. "Did you make these?"

"Yes."

"They're good."

"Thank you. Okay, what's *your* top rule?"

I thought for a minute, taking another bite. "Don't nag me."

"What?"

"My mother is always on my dad about every little thing—he got the floor dirty, he left the seat up, he forgot their anniversary, he didn't make the dinner reservation, the volume on the TV is too loud . . ." I shook my head. "It's like a constant stream of criticism."

"Fair enough. No nagging," she wrote down.

"Add something else to that," I said, finishing my first cookie and taking another one. "Add that if something is really bothering you, you're going to tell me what it is and not expect me to guess at it like a mind reader. Like, you won't go into a room and slam the door and make me wonder what I did wrong or what you're upset about."

She gave me a look but did what I asked. "Item two *A*, no mind-reading expectations."

"Okay, what's next?" I asked, brushing the powdered sugar off my hands on my pants.

Bianca thought for a moment. "We have to be able to trust each other. So no lying."

"Agreed. And no giving away the secret to anyone," I said seriously. "No one else can know about this."

She looked guilty. "I told my sister."

"You what!"

"I told my sister, Ellie. But we can trust her," she went on. "Look, we're going to need support from people close to us. And I felt like Ellie was going to see through it anyway. Pick one friend or one of your siblings to tell."

Frowning, I thought it over as I took a sip of coffee. My siblings were out—they were shit at keeping secrets. And choosing one of my three best guy friends would be tough. I'd been close to Griffin Dempsey, Cole Mitchell, and Beckett Weaver since middle school. They were like brothers to me. All of them would be supportive of me, no matter what—although they'd all think this was fucking nuts. "I can't choose between my friends," I said.

"How many are we talking?"

"Three."

She frowned. "That's too many. Put their names in a hat."

"Seriously?"

"Yes." She flipped to a new sheet of paper. "Who are they?"

I recited their names, and she wrote them down on three separate scraps of paper, folded them up, and put them in front of me.

"Close your eyes and pick one," she instructed.

I did, and when I unfolded it, the name on the paper was Cole Mitchell. On one hand, he was the best choice because he knew Bianca the best—she'd helped him decorate his new house. On the other, Cole was the worst liar on the planet. I wasn't sure he could fake the amount of enthusiasm required.

"Well? What does it say?" she prodded.

"Cole."

She smiled. "That's a great choice."

"I'm not sure. Cole sucks at lying."

"We're not exactly asking him to lie. We're just trusting him with a secret."

"I guess."

Turning her attention to the list again, she recited as she wrote. "Number three: No lying to each other. Number four: No telling anyone except Ellie DeRossi and Cole Mitchell."

"Fine."

"Wait—what about their significant others? Are we going to expect them not to tell Cheyenne or Sierra?"

I frowned. "I guess not. But that's it. The more people who know, the more likely it is the secret gets out."

“Agreed.” Bianca made the amendment and studied the list. “We need one more. We have no sex, no nagging or mind reading, no lying, no telling anyone outside the circle of trust. What can we add?”

I pondered the question and the situation and came up with something. “No falling in love with me,” I said, crossing my arms over my chest.

Her jaw dropped. “What?”

“You heard me.” Our eyes met like swords crossing.

A slow smile tugged at her lips. “Wait a minute. That’s a joke, right?”

“I’m totally serious, Bianca. The one thing that could ruin this entire operation is if you get all hormonal and emotional, and you develop *feelings* for me.”

“Ha!” she squawked, kicking her feet. “Fat chance!”

“Then write it down,” I insisted, stabbing her list with my index finger.

“Oh, yes, of course. Let me get this down quickly, before I forget.” She dictated as she scrawled, “Special rule for Bianca: No falling in love with Enzo Moretti, and if you forget for one moment what a cocky, arrogant, egotistical, presumptuous, swaggering *ass* he is, just come back and look at this list.”

“Erase that last part,” I demanded.

“No way,” she said, adding several exclamation points.

“Look, the only reason I want that in there is because I’ve been in this situation before, okay? Where I think a woman and I are on the exact same page, just hanging out and having fun, and then she suddenly gets feelings for me, and the fun is over. She starts expecting me to be someone else, and then I’m an asshole when I don’t change.”

“Enzo,” Bianca said quietly, a ghost of a smile still on her lips. “I promise, I know exactly who you are. And I will never expect you to be anybody else.”

I think she meant it as a compliment.

But I wasn’t sure.

At the Bulldog Pub the following Friday night, Cole paused with his beer bottle halfway to his mouth. "Wait a minute. What did you say?"

"I'm going to marry Bianca DeRossi." We were waiting for Griffin and Beckett to meet us for a few beers and some wings. I'd asked Cole to come a little early.

"When?"

"Maybe a month or so. We don't want to rush it."

He set the bottle down on the table with a thunk and looked at me as if I'd lost my mind. "*Why*?"

"So that my dad will give me Moretti & Sons. You know the condition—married and settled by age thirty-five or else."

"I know, but . . ." Cole shook his head. "Marrying Bianca? That's fucking nuts. You can't stand her."

"It's only temporary. And besides, she's growing on me—slightly," I clarified, taking a sip from my beer.

Cole washed down his shock with a few swallows of craft ale and set the bottle down again. "Temporary? Like how long?"

"Not that long. Maybe a year or so. Just long enough for the baby to be born."

Cole's eyes nearly popped out onto the table. "Baby!"

I shrugged. "Yeah. Bianca wants a baby. I need a wife. The pieces just sort of fit together."

He continued to gape at me. "I feel like I'm in the Twilight Zone."

"Look, we've worked it all out. It's more of a business deal than anything else. We have a mission, a purpose, a plan."

"Um, that plan includes the creation of another human being. Do you know what you're getting into? And if you guys split, you'll still be a father."

"I know."

"A *single father*. It's not easy." Cole had a daughter from his first marriage to his high school sweetheart, who'd died from a blood clot giving birth. He'd raised Mariah on his own for like ten years, although he'd lived with his widowed mother until just a couple months ago. That was when he'd fallen in love with Griffin's younger sister, Cheyenne, and now the two of them were engaged and living together in the house he'd bought right around Christmas.

"I know," I said. "We've talked about all this. And I've thought about it. I think being a single dad sounds awesome. You get all of the perks of being a father without having to deal with a wife driving you nuts. You can do everything *your way* without any interference or arguing."

"Or any help," Cole pointed out.

I shrugged. "I've got a mother and sisters if I need help. And there might not be a baby anyway. Bianca isn't sure she can even get pregnant."

"Why not?"

"She's got some kind of problem with her eggs," I said, feeling kind of shitty that I hadn't paid closer attention when she was explaining it. "And it's only getting worse, so she wants to try getting pregnant sooner rather than later. She was going to use a sperm donor, but she said her family was totally against the idea and she didn't love the thought of a total stranger being her baby's father."

"But she loves the thought of *you*?" Again, Cole shook his head. "This is just so weird. You guys do nothing but bicker and poke at each other when you're in the same room."

"We're working on that," I said, although it wasn't really true. "And she apologized for the thing she said about my dick being small."

"Well, I guess that's all that matters," Cole said, laughing.

"Listen, I know it sounds a little extreme, but she and I are in agreement on this. We each have a goal, and we're helping each other reach those goals. And when it's done, we'll part as friends and work out the arrangements for co-parenting the baby."

Cole did not look convinced.

"What we need from our friends is unconditional support," I went on, a little aggravated that I wasn't getting it. "We understand that this isn't the way most people would go about getting what they want, but maybe most people aren't as"—I struggled for a word—"as brave as we are. As determined. As willing to do whatever it takes to get where we want to be. We're not getting any younger, you know."

"I know," he said.

"And good for you and for Griffin that you found the real thing with someone, but Bianca and I haven't."

Cole cocked a brow. "Have you even tried?"

"That's not the point," I said, running a hand over my hair. "The point is that this is what we're doing, and we need our friends and family to support us."

"You're going to tell your *family* the truth?" He looked shocked and confused.

"Hell no! The only people who will know the truth are Bianca's sister Ellie and you. That's in the contract."

Cole groaned. "Fuck, Moretti. You know I'm shit at lying. My lip does that weird thing, and I get all sweaty."

"You won't have to lie," I said, trying to sound reassuring. "You just have to keep a secret. And be excited for me."

"I can manage that. Actually," he went on, a grin tugging at his mouth. "I might enjoy this."

"Why?"

"Because," he said, laughing now. "I know you. And her. She's going to drive you crazy."

Grimacing, I lifted my beer to my lips for a long drink.

I had a feeling he was right.

Four

Bianca

ONE MONTH LATER

"YOU READY?"

"I think so." Enzo's voice cracked.

"Don't be nervous. We're totally prepared for this."

"Are we?"

We were sitting in his car outside DiFiore's working up our nerve to go in and announce our engagement to our families. We had a seven o'clock reservation, and it was already six fifty-five, so everyone was probably already waiting inside: Mr. and Mrs. Moretti, my parents and Grandma Vinnie, Ellie and Sierra, my twenty-six-year-old brother JJ, who worked construction for Moretti & Sons, Enzo's brother Pietro and his wife Lynne, his brother Carlo, and his sisters Eve, Talia, and Cat. My thirty-third birthday had been Tuesday, so the guise was that this was a birthday celebration Enzo had planned for me.

"We are, Enzo. As far as our families know, we've been dating for over a month. We spend all our time together. We can't get enough."

In reality, all the evenings we'd been spending together had been dedicated to learning as much as possible about each other so we could be more convincing. We'd watched each other's favorite movies and TV series—I'd probably enjoyed the Bond flicks and *The Sopranos* more than he'd liked *The Notebook* and *Fleabag*, but we were glad to discover a shared affinity for *Schitt's Creek*, Judd Apatow movies, and (what else?), *I Love Lucy*.

But our efforts hardly mattered—our families were overjoyed at our sudden love affair and barely questioned it.

"Right," he said. "Can't get enough."

"What's my middle name?" I asked.

"Jane. What's mine?"

"Thomas. Where did I go to college?"

"Columbia. How long have I worked for my dad?"

"Since you were fourteen. What instrument did I play in high school?"

"Violin. What position do I play on the Bellamy Creek Bulldogs?"

I smiled. "Oh, yes. Can't forget old man baseball. You're the second baseman."

"And the fastest runner," he added. "I stole home in the championship game against the Mason City Mavericks last year, which gave us the lead. We won by one run." He held up one finger, making sure I knew exactly how important his stolen base had been.

"You are very fast," I said, patting his leg.

"Okay, what else?"

I took a deep breath. "Your favorite food is a meatball sandwich, your favorite city is Rome, your favorite color is blue. You're good at math, you like books about architecture, you have an excellent memory. You speak some Italian, which I love. You like to bring me flowers, and I like cooking for you. You snore, but I don't mind."

"I don't snore!" Enzo shrank back, offended. "And how would you know, anyway? We've never spent the night together."

"Because we've also discovered our shared old-fashioned values," I reminded him. "We don't believe in sex before marriage."

He made a face. "We're not going to say that out loud, are we?"

"No. It will just be implied." I smiled sweetly. "Now you go. What do you know about me?"

He inhaled and exhaled, running a hand over his chiseled jaw. "You have a sweet tooth and you sometimes eat cookies for breakfast—not that I've seen you do it, of course. You're near-sighted, and without your glasses, you're blind as a bat. Your favorite flowers are white roses. Your great-grandparents were bootleggers. You love traveling, especially to Italy. You moved home from Chicago to be closer to your family."

"That's good," I interrupted. "Work that in for sure. The importance of family is another belief we have in common. Also wanting to raise a family in Bellamy Creek."

"Right."

"Now what's something you love about me?"

He scratched his chin. "Umm . . ."

"Enzo!" I swatted his arm.

"I'm *thinking*!"

"Well, you need to think faster. We have to get in there."

"Okay." He pursed his lips. "Your cooking."

"And?"

"You're good at your job. You work hard. I like that you started your own little design company."

"Don't say it like that—it's patronizing."

"Fine," he said through gritted teeth. "But I don't get what the big deal is. It's a design company. It's little. You only have one employee—yourself."

"Never mind. Okay, what else? There has to be a more personal thing."

He frowned at me. "No nagging, remember? It's in the contract."

"We're not married yet, and we won't be if you can't get this right. I get to nag for a moment."

"Okay. More personal." He appeared to think hard. "I like the way your butt looks in those jeans with the rip in the knee."

I sighed heavily, even though his comment pleased me. "Less pervy, please."

"It makes me laugh when you're too short to reach your high kitchen cabinets?"

"Oh, forget it." I unbuckled my seatbelt.

"No, wait! I can think of one." He snapped his fingers. "You've got what my dad calls moxie."

"Moxie?"

"Yeah. It means courage. Determination. You can handle what comes at you and land on your feet."

That was actually a nice compliment. "Thank you, I'll take it. Let's go in."

"I'll get the door for you. Stay there." He jumped out the driver's side then stuck his head back in. "Sweet pea."

I made a face. "Sweet pea? I don't know about that."

He came around and helped me down from his SUV. "Sugar pie?" he asked as he took my arm and escorted me toward the entrance.

"Ew. No."

"Dollface?"

"What is this, nineteen-twenty?"

"Come on, I need to call you something cute." He pulled open the restaurant door and grinned. "I've got it."

"What?"

"I'll call you *mia polpetta*."

My heart fluttered. "Italian! That's good, I like it. What does it mean?" I asked as I led the way toward the room at the back we'd booked to accommodate our large group.

Behind me, Enzo put his hand on the small of my back and began to laugh. "My little meatball. Now smile, *polpetta,* we're on."

I managed to give him an icy glare over my shoulder before turning my gaze forward again and plastering on my best I'm-the-luckiest-girl-in-the-world expression.

I'd murder him later.

The plan was simple.

After we walked in and said hello to everyone, with all the requisite hugs and cheek kisses an Italian greeting required, Ellie would "notice" my ring. Then Enzo and I would look at each other, I'd blush becomingly, and he'd announce that he'd popped the question on my actual birthday. We'd been bursting to tell them for four days. And we were even more excited to actually tie the knot, so we were just going to have a simple ceremony at City Hall within the next couple weeks. We'd already applied for our marriage license, and we were just waiting to hear back from the judge. The ceremony would be very small, but we were planning a party afterward, at which all would be welcome.

Easy peasy.

We hoped.

"Oh my God—Bianca, what is that on your finger?" Ellie said loudly, once we were all seated and sipping our drinks. I'd ordered a Prosecco and even though I'm right-handed, made sure to pick up the glass with my left, putting the ring on full display.

Enzo and I exchanged an "adoring" look we'd rehearsed. (After a lot of laughter and failed attempts—"You look like you have a trapped fart, can you try a little harder please?"—we thought we had it down.)

"*That*," I said, setting my glass on the table and folding my wrist down to show off my diamond, "is my engagement ring."

A chorus of gasps, shouts, and a couple *Grazie Dio*'s went up. Mrs. Moretti crossed herself. My mother grabbed my father's arm. Enzo's sisters squealed. Inside, I said a quick prayer no one would ask me to take it off so they could look closer—the damn thing still said *Love Always, Ricky* inside.

"Seriously?" my brother said, as if he couldn't imagine why anyone would want to marry me.

"Congratulations," offered Sierra.

"Wait. *You're* getting married?" Pietro asked.

"Yes," Enzo said, putting his arm around me, which was approved choreography.

"When?" Ellie asked, right on cue.

"Soon, actually." I patted Enzo's hand, which felt big and heavy on my shoulder. We'd practiced the move last night too—"What do you think? Chair or actual shoulder?"—and decided we'd better go with the more intimate gesture. In fact, his fingers were nearly grazing the top of my breast. Had he done that on purpose? Either way, it sent a little electrical pulse zipping up my spine. "We already applied for a license. So hopefully within a week or two."

"What?" My mother exchanged a frantic glance with Mrs. Moretti. "You can't get married in a week or two. That's not enough time to send out all the invitations."

"We want a small wedding, Mom," I said. "Just us and two witnesses at City Hall."

From the looks on everyone's faces, you'd have thought I said we were getting married in the alley behind the Bulldog Pub.

"City Hall!" Mrs. Moretti clutched her chest like she might be having a heart attack. "But you're both Catholic!"

"We know, Ma, but we'd just prefer to keep it simple," said Enzo.

"Intimate," I clarified.

"You mean we can't even come?" Mrs. Moretti's face was rapidly turning white.

"You can come if you want," replied Enzo. "But we're keeping the ceremony very small. We'll have a party afterward that everyone can come to."

"Is this for real?" Enzo's sister Talia asked. "Haven't you guys only been dating for like a month?"

I opened my mouth with a rehearsed reply, but it wasn't even necessary. Mrs. Moretti reached over her husband to flick Talia's ear.

"Ow!" she said. "*Ma*!"

"Hush up, Talia!" her mother scolded. "When you *know*, you *know*. It's about time Enzo settled down." Her expression turned smug. "And I always had a feeling about them, from the time they were younger."

"I did too, Marisol," my mother added.

"Can I have your condo?" my brother asked.

My father cleared his throat and rose to his feet. "A toast," he said, lifting his wine glass. "To the happy future of Bianca and Enzo, and the union of our families!"

Mr. Moretti, who had been observing the scene without commenting, also stood. He was tall, like Enzo, but doughy through the middle where Enzo was lean and muscular. It was easy to see where Enzo had gotten his looks, because his father was still a handsome man, even if his hands were less elegant and his hair not quite as thick. As he raised his glass of red wine, I felt Enzo's arm go a little stiff—would his father see through our ruse?

"To Bianca and Enzo," he said in his deep, gruff voice. "*Per cent'anni*."

I smiled and raised my glass of Prosecco, although the thought of a hundred years with Enzo made me want to bolt for the door. Beside me, Enzo squirmed, and I knew he was thinking the same thing, but he lifted his glass as well.

Once everyone was seated again and the congratulations had quieted, Mrs. Moretti pulled out her phone. For a moment, I thought she was going to ask us if she could take our picture, but she appeared to be texting someone.

"Mom, what happened to no phones at the table?" asked Cat, Enzo's youngest sister.

"I'll put it away in a minute," her mother said impatiently. "I just need to message the priest."

Enzo nearly choked. "What?"

"I'm texting Father Mike. Just because you're getting married at City Hall doesn't mean he can't bless your marriage."

Enzo and I exchanged a frantic glance.

"That's a wonderful idea, Marisol," my mother agreed.

Under the table, Enzo nudged my foot.

"We don't really want anything too, um, *involved*," I said, glancing at him. "Do we, babe?"

He shook his head. "Definitely not."

"You really don't want a big wedding?" Pietro's wife Lynne looked at me with surprise. "We had like three hundred people at ours. It was super fun."

"We really don't." I smiled at her and tipped my head onto Enzo's shoulder. "We just want to be married."

"Isn't that sweet?" My mother's eyes misted over. "They're so in love, they just want to be husband and wife as soon as possible."

"Why the rush?" asked my brother JJ. "You knocked up or something?"

"John Patrick DeRossi, what is the matter with you?" My mother was outraged.

"I'm not pregnant," I assured everyone at the table.

"But you want children, right?" Mrs. Moretti nodded at me, as if to encourage an affirmative answer.

"Yes. We do."

Both our mothers looked so elated I thought they might rocket right out of their chairs.

"I think I'm going to cry. It's like all my prayers are being answered in the space of ten minutes." Mrs. Moretti fanned her face and turned her eyes to the ceiling. "Thank you," she whispered.

"Anyway, Ma, we really don't want a priest. I'm already in touch with Judge Reinhart—we did a kitchen reno for him and his wife last year—and I'm just waiting for him to get back to me with a date."

"James Reinhart?" Mr. Moretti nodded. "I'll call him tomorrow. We gave him a great deal on that home renovation, and he said if I ever needed anything to give him a call."

Enzo spoke up. "Pop, we've got this. You don't need to—"

"Consider it done," Mr. Moretti spoke with finality. "I'll get that wedding date for you by the end of the week."

Enzo and I looked at each other—a completely unrehearsed look of *oh shit, this just got real.*

I recovered first, flashing Enzo's father a grin. "Thanks, Mr. Moretti. We'd appreciate that."

"So Enzo, how did you propose?" asked his sister Eve.

We were prepared for this question, and I had the first line.

"It was very romantic," I said, trying not to laugh as I recalled his drunk ass showing me the ring engraved for someone else. "He even got down on one knee."

"Where were you?" asked Cat.

"At my condo," I answered.

"Were you surprised?" Lynne asked.

"She was shocked." Enzo sounded pleased with himself as he put his arm around me again. "Shocked and delighted. She couldn't say yes fast enough. And she cried tears of joy."

That was *not* in the script.

Before I could help myself, I gave him an annoyed look, which he responded to by stepping on my foot. I quickly tried to shift my face into an expression of adoration. "It was quite the surprise," I said through my teeth.

"I'm sure it was," Talia said, amused. "Whoever thought Enzo would be the type to get down on one knee?"

"Both knees, actually," I said, adding my own bit of improvised dialogue. "Almost like he was *begging* me to spend the rest of our lives together. He just kept saying over and over again how much he loved me. How he can't wait for me to be his wife."

Enzo dug his fingertips into my shoulder. "You're just so lovable, *mia polpetta*," he said, his jaw tight, staring murderously into my eyes. "Once I got past your prickly surface, I discovered a truly big heart."

"And once *I* realized there was more to you than your big fat ego, I couldn't help falling in love." I bit back a laugh. "In fact, I find your insufferable arrogance sort of charming now."

"And I find your know-it-all attitude and general air of imperious self-importance downright *entrancing*," he said angrily. He was gripping my shoulder hard enough to leave a bruise. "I am so be*witched* by you, sweetheart, I can hardly see straight."

To my left, Ellie cleared her throat. "Wow. Clearly you were meant to be."

"Clearly," I said, and then I couldn't resist planting a kiss smack on Enzo's lips. His mouth was warm and firm and felt nice against mine, so nice I dragged out the kiss for a few seconds longer than planned. A warmth blossomed deep in my belly and spread through my limbs. When I pulled away, Enzo's expression told me how stunned he was. Frankly, I was kind of stunned too—my body had reacted as if the kiss was real.

It wasn't, though. Was it? I was just playing a role.

So why were my toes still tingling?

"Aww, now isn't that sweet?" My mother sighed and picked up her wine glass. "You two are going to be together forever. I just know it."

While we were waiting for dessert and coffee to be served, my sister grabbed my arm. "Ladies' room, please," she murmured.

I turned to Enzo. "I'll be right back, honey," I said, patting his arm as if he might miss me.

He nodded and picked up his wine glass. He'd been a little quiet throughout the meal, but I figured it was just the stress of putting our "relationship" to the test for the first time on such a big stage.

I followed Ellie to the bathroom, and the minute we were alone behind the closed door, she whirled on me and clutched her head. "Oh my God! I can't believe you guys are going through with this. Look at me. I'm sweating." She pulled the armpits of her blouse away from her body.

I laughed. "Relax. It's going great. Mom and Dad are so happy, they're not even questioning the fact that we're obviously rushing into something that will be a big fat mistake." We entered the side-by-side stalls and continued talking.

"Neither are the Morettis," Ellie commented. "Except maybe Pietro."

"Well, he's about to lose the opportunity to be head of the family firm. Understandable why he might be reluctant to offer his heartiest congrats."

"Mr. Moretti seems a bit quiet too. Think he's got doubts?"

I'd noticed his silence—which had mirrored Enzo's—and his curious eyes on us all night. "Hard to say for sure, but he certainly volunteered to reach out to the judge quickly enough."

"Maybe he expected you guys to argue against it."

"Hopefully, he noticed that we didn't." We came out of the stalls and washed our hands beside one another at the sinks. "We don't see any reason to push it back."

She rinsed her hands, shaking her head. "I still can't believe you guys are going through with it. At least you're marrying someone hot. Sometimes it's hard to look away from his face. And I'm not even attracted to men."

I laughed, reaching for the stack of towels on the counter. "He's handsome. I agree."

"Do you guys get along at *all*?"

"Nope." Grinning, I dug into my purse for my lipstick. "I mean, we're learning better how to fake it, and occasionally I get this glimmer of appreciation or maybe even gratitude for him, but then he says something truly loathsome and I remember why he's the worst."

She laughed, fussing with her hair in the mirror. "I don't know, you have pretty good chemistry. Sparks were definitely flying between you at the table."

"For all the wrong reasons," I said pointedly. "Our chemistry is not the good kind."

She shrugged. "Sparks are sparks. And it would not surprise me at all if eventually something catches fire."

I rolled my eyes and reapplied lipstick. "Not happening."

Facing me, her expression was wry. "You're telling me you're not attracted to him whatsoever?"

"Nope." But I could feel the heat in my cheeks, and a moment later they bloomed like red roses. "Plus we've agreed there will be no messing around. It's in the contract."

She burst out laughing. "You guys actually made a contract?"

"Yes. We had to lay the ground rules," I insisted, recapping my lipstick and tucking it back into my bag.

"So what was that kiss out there?"

The roses in my cheeks deepened their hue, but I turned to face her, meeting her eyes. *That kiss. That kiss. That kiss.* "That was for show."

"Looked real to me."

"That's because I'm a good actress. Let's get back to the table." Shouldering past her, I pushed open the door, and she followed close on my heels.

"You know, you're really not that good an actress," she said, her tone amused. "Just saying."

I was about to argue with her when Enzo looked up from the table, and our eyes locked. My stomach went weightless, and I nearly tripped over my feet. Damn, that asshole was gorgeous. I had to admit, it really wasn't hard to fake an attraction to him.

But it *was* fake.

Wasn't it?

"What the hell was that?" Enzo exploded as soon as we were alone in his car.

"That was our engagement dinner. I thought it went well, by the way," I said, buckling my seatbelt.

"I meant that kiss. What the fuck was up with that?" He started the engine, glaring at me in the dark.

I shrugged, while inside all I could think was, *That kiss. That kiss. That kiss.* "Kissing is something a real couple would do at their engagement dinner, don't you think? I was trying to be authentic."

He backed out of the parking spot and swerved out of the lot. His right hand was gripping the steering wheel tightly. His left hand was clenched into a fist in his lap. "You were the one who said no kissing allowed, and I agreed."

"Sorry," I said with a shrug. "I didn't realize it would bother you so much."

"It's not that it *bothered* me. I was just . . . unprepared. I think we need to agree on that stuff ahead of time."

Amused by how rattled he was—at least I wasn't alone—I looked over at him. "Enzo, if we're going to fake being in love, we're going to have to do things couples in love do when we're in front of other people. It's part of the act. I mean, we're going to have to kiss at the ceremony, right?"

"That's different," he argued. "That's expected. This was *unexpected*. And it threw me."

"Okay, okay. Sheesh." I reached over and poked his leg. "I'll give you a warning next time, how's that?"

"I don't need a *warning,* Bianca. Now that I know that kissing is approved, I'll be fine." He glanced at me sideways. "I didn't realize you'd have such a hard time controlling yourself around me."

My jaw dropped. "I don't have a hard time controlling myself around you, Enzo. I *told* you, I was playing the game."

"Right," he said knowingly. "The game."

I felt my hackles go up like a kite. "Speaking of unapproved moves, what was all that BS about me crying tears of joy when you proposed?"

He shrugged. "That's what girls are supposed to do when they're happy, isn't it? I was just trying to be authentic," he said, tossing my words back at me.

"You weren't being authentic, you were being obnoxious. My *prickly surface*?"

"Listen, you weren't any better, telling them I *begged* you to be my wife." He made a noise from the back of his throat. "Please. I've never begged a woman to do anything in my life."

"That was before. Now that you're in love with *me,* everything is different. You *definitely* begged."

He muttered something I didn't quite catch, but I'm pretty sure it involved me, where I could go, and what I could do with myself when I got there.

"Listen, let's not fight," I said. "We've got issues to deal with. Do you think your dad can really get the judge to give us a wedding date by the end of the week?"

"Probably. My dad can be very persuasive." He glanced over at me. "So we should be prepared to move fast."

"Okay."

He must have heard the slight quiver in my voice. "If you're going to back out, Bianca, do it now. Last chance."

Shaking my head, I sat up taller in his front seat. "If you're still in, I'm still in."

"I'm still in. We should talk about where we're going to live," Enzo said. "My place or yours."

"Oh yeah. I guess one of us has to move, huh?"

Enzo laughed. "Uh, yes. I don't think it would be too convincing if we lived separately."

I thought for a moment about my nine-hundred-square foot condo and his three-bedroom house, which wasn't huge, but definitely offered more space than my place. "Your place is bigger. I suppose it makes more sense. But I hate to give up my condo . . . eventually I'm going to need it back."

"So keep it," he said. "Let JJ live there."

I winced at the thought. "I guess. But I'll have to kick him out when I need to move back in. I don't want to live with him or be stuck with nowhere to go."

"You won't have *nowhere to go*, Bianca." Enzo sounded irritated with me. "Do you think I'd put you out on the street with our baby? If it comes to it, I can always go stay at Beckett's."

I looked over at him. "Really? You'd move out of your own house for me?"

He shrugged. "Sure."

"Thanks," I said, feeling an odd catch in my chest.

A few minutes later, he pulled up in front of my building, and I unbuckled my seatbelt. "Thanks for the ride. And for dinner." Enzo had paid the entire bill, which had been sizable.

"You're welcome."

I glanced at the digital clock on the dash. It was only nine. "Do you want to come in for a drink or something?"

"I guess I could."

"No pressure," I said quickly. "If you've got other plans, it's fine."

"No other plans," he said, swinging around so he could park in one of the spots marked *Guest*. "I'm just surprised you'd want to spend any more time with me than necessary."

"I'm trying to get used to you," I joked. "It's like exposure therapy. And pretty soon, all our Saturday nights are going to be spent together."

"Can't wait," he said, his voice dripping sarcasm. Then he turned off the engine, and stared out the windshield at the harbor, ghostly in the dark. "You got any whiskey?"

"I do, in fact. And I make a mean Manhattan if you're interested."

He gave me the side-eye. "I'm interested."

My heartbeat quickened whenever he looked at me that way, with that *I'm game if you're game* expression. I made sure to keep my tone neutral. "Then come on in."

Five

Enzo

"WHAT SHOULD WE DRINK TO?" BIANCA ASKED, taking a seat at the opposite end of the couch and raising her Manhattan toward mine.

"To a long and happy life—apart," I suggested, leaning over and tapping my glass against hers.

She took a sip and tucked her feet beneath her. All the drapes were closed, only one floor lamp was on, and she'd turned on the gas fireplace, so the room was warm and intimate. In another life, with another woman, I'd have been moving a little closer to her on the couch, sliding a palm up her thigh, working my mouth from her throat to her lips. She had such perfect lips, and when she'd kissed me at the table, I'd nearly lost my mind. My dick had responded as if she'd put her hand in my pants.

The entire rest of the meal I'd been annoyed with her—and with my body's reaction to her. But how was I supposed to control that?

She wasn't supposed to fucking kiss me! That had been *her rule,* and she'd broken it. And now kissing was fair play in the game—what the hell was I going to do about that? How was I supposed to not get hard when she leaned into me, put those lips on mine, and looked at me like she wanted me? Was it *all* for show?

It had to be, because the minute we were alone, she was always angry about something. But God, it turned me on how mad she got. Pissing her off was like my new favorite sport.

What the hell was wrong with me?

"Flip any houses lately?" she asked.

"Not really. You?"

"Not in a while. I was working with a friend in Chicago who was sort of the money behind the deals—I did all the legwork, supervised the renovations, and then I turned it over to a real estate agent friend to make the sale—but the friend in Chicago lost big on a few risky stock investments and pulled back." She shrugged. "And I knew I needed to save up for fertility treatments. They're not cheap."

"Got it." I took another sip of my drink. "Did you like living in Chicago?"

"I did, believe it or not. I never really thought of myself as a city girl, and I hated the traffic, but I did like the convenience of having lots of shopping and dining options right there in my neighborhood."

"Where in Chicago did you live?"

She leaned back against one end of the couch, stretching her legs out, her feet nearly touching my thigh. She wore black socks with gray polka dots on them, and when she wiggled her toes, they cracked. "When I first moved down there, I lived on campus. Then I had an apartment with a girlfriend in Bucktown." Her eyes dropped to her drink. "But for the last four years, I lived with my boyfriend downtown. He had a condo on Lake Shore Drive."

"Fancy," I remarked, wondering why I hated this boyfriend without even knowing his name.

She nodded without smiling. "It was."

"Four years, huh? That's a long time."

"We were actually together for five."

I drank again. "What was his name?"

"Tate DuCharme."

Figured he'd even have an asshole name. "So what happened?"

She exhaled and stared into her glass, and for a second I thought she was going to tell me it was none of my business and then I'd have to argue that her relationship history would be something I'd know about if we were really in love, disguising the fact that I was just really fucking curious. But she surprised me again.

"What happened was that I was an idiot," she said, her tone bitter. "I believed his lies, I let him convince me he just needed more time, and I turned a blind eye to all the signs he would never be ready for a lifetime commitment."

"Why'd you do all that?"

"Because I loved him." Her eyes met mine, and they were bright with tears. She'd worn contacts tonight instead of her glasses. It made her look different. "And I wanted him to love me back the same way. But no amount of wanting could make that true."

"But he must have loved you," I argued. "Why else would he date you for five years?"

She shrugged, taking another sip of her Manhattan. "Maybe he loved me. But not enough. And what's the use of that?"

I didn't have an answer.

"He always had some condition that had to be met, or some goal he had to reach, before he could think about the next phase of his life—getting married and having a family, which is what he *said* he ultimately wanted. For a while, it was turning thirty, then it was making partner at his firm, then it was landing this certain big client, then it was closing the case." She shook her head. "But there was always another big client and the next big case. I realized I was never going to come first. And then I realized that it was all lies anyway—he was sleeping with a woman at his firm."

"Seriously? What a prick." I felt like kicking his ass. If you want your sexual independence, fine—but don't lie about it. I tossed back the rest of my drink in an angry gesture.

"And she probably wasn't the first."

"I'm sorry, Bianca," I said, wondering if I'd ever uttered those words before and meant them.

"The worst thing was, even after that came to light, I went to him and said, 'Last chance. If you want a life with me, it starts now.' And he said he wasn't willing to give up the life he had for the future we'd planned."

"Fuck." Now I really wanted to beat the shit out of him. "What did you do?"

She tipped up the last of her cocktail. "I left him that night and went to stay with a friend. Quit my job the next day. Two weeks later, I moved back here."

"You did the right thing. That asshole didn't deserve you."

"Thanks. So what about you?" she asked, swirling the cherry around the bottom of her glass. Not one of those fake maraschino ones, either—she had little jars of Michigan cherries she'd brandied herself. I dug that.

"What *about* me?" Setting my empty glass on the table, I propped my head in my hand along the back of the couch, pulling one knee up on the cushion between us. The bottoms of her feet were now resting against my shin.

"What's been your longest relationship?" She plucked the cherry from her glass and ate it.

"Define relationship."

She grinned. "It's a thing where you date one person exclusively for a somewhat lengthy period of time."

"Hmm." I pretended to think. "I believe there was a girl in high school that I drove home from school every day for like four months."

She poked me with her toes. "That's not a relationship, that's a carpool."

"If her parents weren't home, sometimes she'd invite me in and give me a hand job in her bedroom. Does that help?"

Her nose wrinkled. "No. You're a pig."

"Oh relax, I actually liked that girl." I grabbed her toes and tugged. "And I returned the favor."

"Did you?" Her eyebrows arched. Her toes pointed.

"Of course I did. I'm a gentleman and a feminist. I always return a favor."

She set her glass down on the table and folded her arms over her chest, eyeballing me shrewdly. "What about Juliet?"

"Who?"

"Juliet. The one who blew you in the parking lot after the Romeo audition."

"What about her?"

"Did you return *that* favor?"

"Not in the parking lot. But yes, I did."

"Interesting."

"Why's that interesting?"

She shrugged. "I don't know. Some guys don't like returning that favor."

"Some guys are idiots."

She glanced over at the fireplace, the flames dancing in her eyes. "Are you good at it?"

My jaw nearly hit my chest. "Huh?"

"Are you *good* at it?" Her expression turned sly. "I mean, what if I want to brag about your sexual prowess or something?"

"To *who*?"

"I don't know." Her shoulders rose. "Girls talk sometimes."

Recovering—sort of—I sat up a little taller. "Well, you can safely brag about my talent in that capacity. I know my way around a woman's orgasm."

"Do you?" She looked intrigued. It was hot as fuck, and I couldn't resist giving her more than she asked for.

"Yes. I'm patient, intuitive, and *very, very* good with my tongue."

Her face turned the color of brandied cherries, but she held my gaze.

"And with my lips, my hands, and my—"

"Okay, that's enough," she said, suddenly swinging her feet onto the floor. "It's getting late, and I have to get up for church tomorrow."

"Same." I couldn't resist smiling as I rose to my feet. It was hard not to feel like I'd won that round. "And a gentleman knows when to make his exit."

She walked me to the door, took my coat from the closet, and handed it to me.

"Thanks for the drink," I said, pulling it on. I enjoyed the way she watched my fingers work their way up the buttons.

"You're welcome." She pulled open the door, and a cold March wind blew in, causing her to shiver.

"You know, I could stay over," I offered facetiously. "Keep you nice and warm all night long."

"Nope," she said, shoving me out onto her welcome mat. "Goodnight, Enzo."

I turned around, bracing my hands on the top of the doorframe. "No kiss?"

She looked at my lips, and for a fraction of a second, I thought she might do it.

But then she stepped back and shut the door in my face.

Laughing, I turned around and walked to my car. It was tough to say what I liked more—when she dropped the gloves to be sweet and vulnerable with me, like when she'd told me about Tate, or when she put up her dukes and went for the uppercut. Both versions of her had their appeal.

But later that night, it was the feisty, pugnacious Bianca who appeared in my dreams, wearing nothing but a checkered apron, shrieking as I chased her around my house. When I caught her, she put up a pretty good fight, landing a right hook to my face, a solid jab to my gut, and a shockingly powerful cross to my chest that knocked the wind out of me. In fact, that one knocked me over backward, and she landed on top of me.

In one smooth motion, I flipped her onto her back, pinned those arms above her head, and looked into her electric blue eyes. Both of us were breathing hard as I—

Buzz. Buzz. Buzz. Buzz.

I opened my eyes, confused, disoriented, hard as steel and mad as hell. My first instinct was to stop the noise, and I reached over, grabbed my phone, shut off my alarm, then angrily slammed the damn thing down on the mattress.

My next instinct was to jerk off, and I reached into my boxer briefs, sheathing my iron cock with my fist and yanking furiously. Exactly who or what I was angry with, I wasn't sure. Was it Bianca for tempting me? Was it myself for being attracted to her? Was it the universe, for trapping me in this situation where I had to fake a marriage with a woman I was beginning to have real feelings for?

No, I insisted over and over again as I thrust into my palm, my stomach muscles clenching. *No, no, no.* No feelings. This thing with Bianca was all for show. I couldn't fall for her. I didn't even like her. She drove me crazy. Insane. Out of my mind. It was my dream getting to me, that was all. That dream, where I'd chased her around, her round little ass taunting me beneath the bow of her apron, her bare feet pounding as she ran up the stairs to get away from me, her laughter bouncing off the walls.

I loved that she fought me. God, she knew exactly how to get my adrenaline pumping. I wished I could spank her for it. And if I fucked her, it wouldn't be sweet. It wouldn't be gentle. I would pound into her with all the passion and fury and turmoil she made me feel. I would make *her* beg—for more, and then for mercy. And when I felt her body seize, when her nails dug into my back, when she arched and bucked and thrashed beneath me, I'd bury my cock deep inside her and come so hard she felt it like a punishment.

Next thing I knew, I was groaning and grunting aloud, my cock throbbing, my stomach and hand a hot dripping mess. Breathing hard, I lay there for a moment on my back, eyes closed, the image of Bianca in my head.

"Get out," I told her, aggrieved that the best orgasm I'd had in months had been while fantasizing about her. "Get out and stay out, you redheaded siren."

In the shower, I gave myself a rule—no more picturing her while I got myself off. The fact that I was attracted to her, even starting to like her, was messing with me. I couldn't let it foil my plans.

Eye on the prize, Moretti, I told myself.

And the prize was Moretti & Sons.

I had to remember that.

On Tuesday morning before I left for work, my father texted me.

Pop: Judge Reinhart got back to me. He'll marry you and Bianca on Friday afternoon at 4:45 pm.

Immediately, I messaged Bianca. **It's on. Friday 4:45.**

Bianca: Wow. Okay.

Me: Are we still doing this?

Bianca: Stop asking me that. Your insecurity is tiresome.

Me: So is your smart ass mouth.

Bianca: Come for dinner.

Me: Tonight?

Bianca: Yes. We're getting married in three days. I feel like a plan might be a good thing.

Me: Right. In the meantime, let your family know.

Bianca: Will do. Come at seven.

Me: You're so fucking bossy.

Bianca: Well, maybe there will be someone more meek and submissive hanging around City Hall Friday at 4:45.

Me: I can only hope.

But it wasn't true. As I tucked my phone into my pocket and went out the back door, I realized the only place where I'd want her submissive was in the bedroom—but only after putting up a really good fight.

The idea of it distracted me all day long.

I brought her roses.

"What's this for?" Her expression was suspicious as she dipped her face into the bouquet and sniffed.

"You're welcome," I said, entering her condo and slipping my coat off and hanging it in the front hall closet.

"Sorry. Thank you—they're beautiful." She led the way into the kitchen and pulled a vase from the pantry. "It just surprised me, that's all."

"Why should it surprise you? I know how you love fresh flowers, and I know white roses are your favorite. Plus, it was a good opportunity for people to see me doing something romantic. I parked sort of far away from the florist so everyone would see me walking down the sidewalk carrying the roses." I sat down at the island and tapped my forehead. "I'm always thinking."

She laughed as she cut the stems down. "Ah, so it was for show."

"Isn't everything? Smells good," I said, glancing at the pot on the stove. "What are we having?"

"Meatball sandwiches."

I grinned. "*My* favorite."

"I know. Want to pour some wine?" she asked, filling the vase with water. "There are a few bottles in the rack."

"Sure." I chose one and opened it. "I'll even get the glasses down from the high cupboard for you. Hey, I should put that in my vows."

"What do you mean?"

"Well, I talked to Judge Reinhart today, and he said the

official part of the ceremony is pretty quick and impersonal, so if we wanted to add any personal vows, we could." I pulled two glasses down and poured the wine.

"And *you* want to add *personal vows*?" She paused her flower arranging and tossed a surprised look over her shoulder.

"I thought it might be more convincing that way," I said defensively.

"You might be right." She finished with the flowers and set the vase on the island. "Thanks again for the roses. I love them."

"You're welcome." I handed her a glass of wine. "I also talked to my father today."

Her eyes widened. "Oh yeah? What did he say?"

"He said he's having paperwork drawn up to name me as his successor."

"Cheers." She touched her glass to mine, took a sip, and set it down. "Want to make the sandwiches while I put together some antipasto?"

"Sure."

"The broiler is ready. I usually stick the rolls in there with a few slices of provolone before I—"

"I *know* how to make a sandwich, Bianca."

She smiled. "Do your thing."

Working side by side, we got dinner together and sat down to eat. "Did you tell your family about Friday?" I asked.

She nodded. "My mother cried."

"Mine too." I took a big bite of my sandwich—it was delicious, just like everything she made. "By the way, our reception begins at six."

"Nice," she said. "Where is it?"

"The Bulldog Pub. We rented out the back room."

Her nose wrinkled. "My wedding reception is at the Bulldog Pub?"

"Listen, princess, we had to call in a favor to get it, so don't complain."

She sighed. “Fine. The Bulldog it is. I need to figure out what I’m going to wear.”

“Same.” I took another gigantic bite. “This is really fucking good, by the way.”

“Thank you. I think you should wear a black suit.”

“Okay. What color tie?”

She took a bite and thought about it while she chewed. “Red.”

“Done.”

“I guess I’ll get a white dress.”

I shrugged. “Sounds good to me. Do you want another ring? Like a wedding band or something?”

“Nah,” she said. “One ring is good enough. You want a ring?”

I shrugged. “I’d wear a ring, I guess.”

“Okay. I’ll get you one. What about food?”

“I talked to the Bulldog owner. We’re working it out. If you want to take over the menu planning, be my guest.”

She nodded. “I’ll go over there tomorrow. We’ll keep it simple. Open bar?”

“Probably easiest.”

“So who’s coming to this party? Did you invite anyone today?”

“Griffin. Cole. Beckett. My family.” I shrugged. “I told my mother no aunts and uncles, no cousins. She claimed they were never going to speak to her again.”

Her eyes were wide as she reached for her wine glass. “What did you say?”

“I said, ‘You’re welcome.’”

She burst out laughing, and it made me feel way too good.

After the dishes were rinsed and put in the dishwasher, we sat down with pen and paper and tried to come up with vows, but neither of us could think of anything.

"What the hell? It's like we're not in love or something," she joked.

"Maybe we should just let the judge do all the talking." I leaned back in the chair and stretched.

She shook her head and pushed her glasses up her nose. "No, I like the idea of personal vows. I think you're right about it being more authentic."

"Maybe we should write them for each other," I suggested.

"What do you mean?"

"I mean, you get to come up with a couple things you want me to say, and I'll do the same."

A slow smile crept over her lips. "And we *have* to say what the other person has written?"

"Sure. Just don't make it too long."

"I'll keep it short and sweet," she promised.

"But not too sweet." Suddenly I was afraid of that smile on her face. "Don't make me sound ridiculous."

"I won't," she said, laughing. "I'm just going to make you sound in love with me. You can do the same thing. It'll be fun."

"Fun?"

"Oh come on." She thumped a hand on my leg. "What if this is the only wedding either one of us ever has? Don't we deserve to hear our soul mate say nice things about us?"

"But it won't be real. It's made up."

She shrugged. "It's what we've got."

I tried to think of an argument but couldn't.

That night when we said goodbye at her door, she hugged me. "Thanks for the flowers. I appreciate them."

"Thanks for dinner," I said, trying to conceal my shock at the fact that she wanted to get close to me without an audience.

"Any time." She released me and stepped back. "I like cooking for people who love to eat. My ex was always on a health kick—didn't eat carbs, didn't eat dairy, didn't eat sugar."

I made a face. "What's the point of living?"

She laughed. "Right?"

"Well, goodnight."

"Night."

I walked over to my car and got in, started the engine and turned on the heat. But I didn't leave right away. I sat there, staring out at the harbor in the dark, wondering about the strange tightness in my chest. What the hell was it? Second thoughts? Guilt? Dread? Nerves? It actually felt like a weird combination of all of the above. I took a deep breath, hoping the tension would ease, but it didn't.

I could still smell her.

The following evening, I went over to Cole and Cheyenne's house to help him paint the living room. Cheyenne was making dinner in the kitchen with Cole's daughter Mariah, who was chattering excitedly about a science project she'd just gotten an A on.

"They still do that volcano project?" I asked, shaking my head as I rolled on the paint.

"Yep. And it makes just as big a mess as when we did it." He glanced over at me. "Bet you'll be doing that same project in ten years."

I swallowed hard, focusing on the color going on the wall. "Maybe."

"What's wrong?"

"Nothing." I cleared my throat and took my roller over to the tray. "Just a lot going on this week."

Cole laughed. "No shit. You're getting married in two days. I had to trade my Saturday off in order to be there."

"Sorry."

"Hey, I was joking. You know I don't care about the day off." Cole's tone was concerned now. "What's going on?"

I shrugged, working the foam roller into the paint. "It's not a big deal. Bianca just said something yesterday that put me in a funk."

"Don't let it get to you. You guys know exactly how to push each other's buttons."

"It's not that."

"Then what is it? What did she say?" Cole stopped painting and faced me.

"We're writing each other's vows—don't ask, it was my stupid idea, which I now regret—and when I warned her not to go overboard, she said something like, 'What if this is the only wedding either one of us ever has? Don't we deserve to hear nice things about ourselves?'"

Cole nodded slowly. "Okay."

"And it just made me, I don't know, sad or something. She's throwing away her one chance to hear someone say why he wants to spend his life with her on me."

"So say nice things about her."

I frowned. He didn't get it. "But I won't mean them."

"So? It's what she wants."

"Something about it doesn't feel right," I insisted stubbornly.

Cole started to laugh. "Moretti, you are *marrying* this girl on Friday afternoon. Not because you love her, but so that you can inherit your family business. And you're worried about the three-minute vows?"

"When you put it that way, I guess it does sound kind of stupid," I admitted.

"I don't think it's stupid that you don't want to say things you don't mean—I think it's admirable. But realistically, you are faking this relationship. It always involved a measure of dishonesty, right?"

"Right."

"And you're not lying to *Bianca*."

"No. We're open about everything. We know exactly what we're getting into." Although lately, I wasn't positive that last bit was true. The ground felt a little less firm beneath us.

"Then you have to trust each other. She chose this too, after all. She picked you to have a *child* with." He lowered his voice, glancing over his shoulder toward the kitchen. "That's a big fucking deal."

"Yeah." I was silent for a moment, still staring at the roller in the paint tray. "Did you tell Cheyenne?"

"I did. I don't keep big stuff from her. I hope that was okay."

"It's fine." I swallowed hard. "Does she think it's crazy?"

"Yes. But she's weirdly happy about it." He laughed, scratching his head. "I think she just likes weddings."

"This one should be interesting." I closed my eyes. "I cannot *imagine* what Bianca is going to make me say about her during those vows."

Cole laughed. "What are you going to make her say about you?"

"I have no fucking idea." Shaking my head, I started to laugh. "But don't worry, I'll make it good."

Six

Bianca

"That's it. That's the one," my mother said, dabbing at her eyes when I stepped out of the dressing room at the bridal shop late Wednesday afternoon.

"Mom, you've said that about every dress she's tried on so far," my sister pointed out. They were seated next to each other on a pink velvet settee, watching me study myself in a three-paneled mirror.

"I kind of like this one," I said, turning to check out the back. It was ivory lace, knee-length and full-skirted, with an illusion neckline revealing a sweetheart bodice, and short lace cap sleeves trimmed with scalloped edges. The fitted waist was emphasized with a satin ribbon belt, and the billowing lace skirts were also trimmed with a scalloped edge. It had a slightly vintage feel that I loved—it actually reminded me of something Lucy Ricardo might have worn, which made me laugh to myself. Best of all, it wasn't too expensive or too long, which was basically a miracle at my height.

"That's a great choice for a bride your size," said the saleswoman, whose name tag read Anita.

"Sorry I'm late!" Blair Dempsey, a friend from my book club who was recently married to Enzo's friend Griffin, rushed into the shop. I'd asked her to come because she had beautiful taste, and I wanted a non-family opinion. She stopped short when she saw me and put her hands over her mouth. "Oh my God."

"What do you think?" I turned to face her.

"I *love* it." She clasped her hands over her heart. "It's sweet, it's elegant, it's fun, it suits your personality." She nodded. "It's perfect."

"I like it too." I faced the mirror again. "But is it too formal?"

"Not at all," Blair said confidently.

"Honey, this is your *wedding* dress," my mother said. "It should be formal."

"But I'm getting married at City Hall, Mom. And my reception is at the Bulldog Pub. We'll be eating sliders and fries and drinking boxed wine."

"And it's going to be amazing," Blair said, coming closer to me. She studied my reflection in the mirror. "It doesn't even need to be altered, which is a sure sign from the universe."

"Then I guess this is the one." I smiled, feeling triumphant. "Unzip me?"

"Wait, you're not even going to try on any of the other ones?" Anita was shocked. "You've only tried on three. Most brides try on at least a dozen."

"She's not most brides," said my sister with a snicker.

I glared at her over my shoulder.

"Still. Are you sure?" Anita was concerned, her hands knitted together.

"I'm sure. My wedding is on Friday, so I don't really have a lot of time."

"That's true," she admitted. "And this *is* stunning on you. Should we try a little veil?"

"No," I said firmly. "No veil."

"Just a short one?" Anita snapped her fingers. "Give me one minute. I have the perfect thing. It just came in."

While we waited, Blair sighed again, placing her palms on her cheeks. "The dress is so beautiful, Bianca. Enzo is going to lose his marbles when he sees you."

I laughed. "Thanks. Nothing I like more than making Enzo lose his marbles."

"It's just amazing the way you two fell for each other," she said, her eyes soft and dreamy. "To think, you've known each other almost your entire lives."

"Isn't it romantic and old-fashioned?" my mother said, rising from the settee to come closer and fuss with my hair. Her eyes filled again.

"Stop, Mom." I swatted her hands away. Her tears made me feel bad. Frankly, so did Blair's sweet words. Or maybe it was the sinking feeling in my stomach that I wasn't doing a very good job keeping my feelings for Enzo in the right place.

"This one!" Anita came rushing back into the fitting area carrying a sparkling headpiece with a pouf of French netting attached. Standing behind me, she settled it on one side of my head, and I had to admit it looked perfect with the dress. "It's called a birdcage veil," Anita explained. "It's a vintage style, but very trendy again."

"Oh, Bianca," Blair gushed. "It's so beautiful with your red hair."

"What do you think?" I turned around and faced my sister, and to my chagrin, she teared up too.

Then she nodded. "It's perfect, B."

I looked at my reflection again and took a deep breath, trying to keep my shit together. But all the tears were making it difficult—even Ellie was crying, and she *knew* this whole thing was fake.

I knew it too. So why was my throat so tight?

"Anyone up for a glass of wine after this?" I asked. "I have to go over to the pub to finalize the menu."

"I am," Blair said enthusiastically. "I want to hear the whole proposal story from start to finish. Griffin was absolutely useless on the details."

"I wish I could, but I have to get home and feed your father," my mother said.

Ellie declined too. "Sorry, I have to get home too."

After I'd changed back into my regular clothes and said goodbye to my mom and sister, I purchased the dress and headpiece with Blair looking on wistfully.

"I wish I could get married all over again," she said.

"At City Hall? With your reception at the Bulldog?" I teased, trying to keep the mood light.

"Yes! I wouldn't care. Don't get me wrong, I loved my wedding at Cloverleigh Farms, but it won't matter where you are, Bianca." She linked arms with me as we headed up the street. "The only thing that will matter is hearing Enzo promise to love, honor, and cherish you for the rest of your life. And getting to make the same promise right back."

I bit my lip. "Yeah."

When we reached my car, I carefully laid the dress across my backseat and placed the box with the headpiece in it on the passenger seat. After sticking a couple more quarters in the meter, we headed for the pub.

Inside, we sat at the bar and ordered a couple glasses of wine. The manager came over with the chef, and we finalized the menu—Enzo and I had decided we might as well fully embrace our pub-themed wedding, so appetizers included fried pickles and mozzarella sticks, entrees were sliders and fish and chips, and when I begged for a vegetable of some kind, the manager scratched his head, but the chef assured me he could do some delicious crispy Brussels sprouts.

"I'll take it," I said. "Done."

The other details were in place as well. Blair, who owned her own bakery, would bake our wedding cake. We'd use the vintage jukebox for music. Ellie's girlfriend Sierra was a photographer and had offered to take photos as a wedding gift. And Griffin, who owned a 1955 Chevy pickup truck, would come pick me up and drive me to City Hall in style.

I couldn't have asked for more from our family and friends—except that all of it was adding to the pit in my stomach.

When all the catering details had been finalized and we were alone again, Blair picked her wine glass up and touched it to mine. "Cheers. I'm so happy for you, honey. I don't blame you one bit for not wanting to wait to get married. When you know, you know. Now show me that ring."

I held out my hand, and she gasped at the diamond on my finger. "Oh, Bianca," she said breathlessly. "It's beautiful. The stone is big but not ostentatious, it's a classic setting, and yellow gold is so stylish right now."

I couldn't stand it anymore.

"It's not real," I blurted.

"What?" Blair blinked at me. "You mean it's a fake diamond?"

"It's a fake *engagement*."

"I don't understand. You're not really getting married?"

"No, we're getting married. That part is real. And as far as I know, the diamond is real." I took a breath. "But everything else is fake."

"But . . . I don't understand."

"Drink some wine," I said, picking up my glass for a sip. "You're going to need it for this story."

And she did. While I explained the situation to her, outlining the reasons we were getting married and what each of us would gain from it, Blair not only finished her first glass of wine but got halfway through a second. She nearly fell off her barstool when I showed her the engraving on the ring.

"So you're not in love?" She looked so heartbroken I had to laugh.

"No, we're not." I slipped the ring back on my finger. "I think we might *like* each other a little better at this point, but we are definitely not in love."

She sighed dejectedly. "This is so depressing."

"Not really," I said, trying to perk her up while also keeping my emotions in line. "We're doing this *for* one another. We're going to get exactly what we want in the end. No one is going to get hurt."

"But *I'm* hurt." She looked miserable for a moment, then she perked up. "Maybe you'll fall in love for real once you're married!"

"Good God, I hope not," I said, making a face.

"Why not?"

"This plan works specifically because we're *not* in love. Phase three would be a disaster if one of us had real feelings." *A huge, flaming dumpster fire where my heart used to be.*

"Phase three?"

"The plan has three phases," I said, sitting up taller and taking a sip of my wine. I'd been talking so much, I was still on my first glass. "We're in phase one right now—that's the engagement and wedding. The marriage and getting pregnant is phase two. The breakup is phase three."

"But if you really fell in love, you wouldn't have to break up," she said brightly.

I shook my head. "We will not be in love, Blair. We're not like you and Griffin. This is a business arrangement."

"But maybe—"

"No," I said with more vehemence than intended. "I don't think you understand—I don't want to fall for Enzo. I was in love with someone in Chicago for five years, and it was toxic and terrible and tore me apart. It took me a long time to feel whole again, and now that I do, I don't plan on giving anyone that kind of power over me, especially not Enzo Moretti."

She nodded and spoke hesitantly. "I'm really sorry about the bad relationship. I didn't know."

"I don't talk about it much. And it doesn't matter now." I softened my voice. "Sorry I got testy. I don't love discussing my romantic past. But I'm never going to be hurt like that again. Because I realized I don't need a man for what I really want—to be a mom. To raise a child. There is nothing between Enzo and me except some bad blood and a contract—which, by the way, I have just violated by telling you the whole truth."

"My lips are sealed," she said. "I won't even tell Griff if you don't want me to."

I bit my lip. "I hate asking you to keep a secret from your husband."

"In this particular case, I don't think he'd want to know the truth," she said. "So we're okay."

"Thanks." I finished my wine, set the glass down, and asked her the question I wasn't sure I wanted the answer to. "You think this is a mistake?"

She sighed and swirled her wine around in her glass. "I don't know. My gut reaction was shock, but honestly I feel like people have probably gotten married for worse reasons. At least you two are being completely honest with each other about things."

"We are."

"Then who am I to judge?" She lifted her shoulders. "I think women have to be bold sometimes to get what they want. Be adventuresome. Think outside the box. I know I had to. And it wasn't easy for me—I'd been raised to do what I was told, what was expected of me. Instead, I struck out on my own and did things my way. And look at me now."

"I'm looking," I said warmly. "And I've always admired your independent spirit. Someday, I hope to feel that way too—like I can look back without regret on the day I became Mrs. Enzo Moretti."

"Excuse me," said a voice from behind the bar. "Did you say Mrs. Enzo Moretti?"

I looked up and saw a very pretty, very *young* woman

with long, straight dark hair and flawless makeup application. Instinctively, I knew it had to be Reina, Enzo's previous girlfriend—the one he'd proposed to the night we'd agreed on the plan. I had to think fast.

"Yes." I beamed at her. "You must be Reina. I've heard so much about you. I'm Bianca."

She looked totally confused. "Are you his—so you're like—did you *marry* him?"

I laughed. "Not yet. We're tying the knot this Friday."

Her eyeballs nearly popped out of her head. "*This Friday*?"

"Yes. I know, it seems fast. We only reconnected after the two of you stopped seeing one another. But years ago, we were deeply in love. High school sweethearts, in fact. We only broke up when I left for college. When we started up again, it was like no time had passed." I snapped my fingers. "Instant rekindling of the flame."

"He wanted to marry me too," she said, looking annoyed that Enzo had moved on so quickly—not that I really blamed her. She glanced at my hand. "In fact, he proposed with that very same ring."

"Well, thank *God* you don't know a good thing when you see it, or else I wouldn't be marrying the love of my life in two days, right?" I tossed my head back and laughed. "Well, I should get home—he's got dinner waiting, and I'm starved. Although he's such an animal, he probably won't even let me eat before he starts tearing my clothes off."

"He tears your clothes off?" Reina asked, crossing her arms over her chest.

"Constantly. The man is *insatiable*." Enzo had told me Reina had found it odd that he wasn't interested in her sexually, so I couldn't resist torturing her a little. If she wasn't such a knockout, I might have felt bad, but the girl was a *solid* ten, maybe even an eleven. Enzo was nuts. "Could we get our bill please?"

"I've got this, Bianca." Trying to keep a straight face, Blair pulled a credit card from her wallet. "You go on home to your insatiable fiancé."

"Thanks, Blair." I kissed her cheek. "I'll talk to you later. Lovely to meet you, Reina! Maybe we'll see you here Friday night."

"I'm not working Friday night."

"What a bummer! Well, maybe we'll see you around. Ta!" Then I got the hell out of there before I did any more damage.

But I cracked up all the way home.

Later that night, I lay in bed and texted Enzo.

Me: Ran into your ex today.

Immediately he called me. "What the hell? You mean Reina?"

"Yes." Smiling, I settled back against my pillows. "She's super hot. Why didn't you want to bang her again?"

"I just didn't, okay? What did she say?"

"Well, she overheard me talking about the wedding, and she was confused, since you had proposed to her so recently."

Enzo groaned.

"Don't worry, I made it all work. I told her how we'd been high school sweethearts back in the day—I figured she was in diapers that long ago, anyway—and thank goodness she rejected your suit, because that opened the door for our magical reunion and now all is as it should be."

"And she bought it?"

"As far as I know. I'm pretty sure she was too busy being offended that you never touched her but you can't keep your hands off me."

"What the fuck? Who told her that?"

"I did," I said, laughing. "And it was really fun."

To my surprise, he started to laugh too. "I bet she was pissed."

"I think baffled is a more fair assessment. I could see the wheels spinning, like she was trying to figure out what I have that she doesn't."

"Ha."

"Seriously, Enzo. The girl is stunning. Why didn't you want to bang her?"

"I don't know." He sounded a little defensive. "She just didn't do anything for me."

"Oh." I couldn't help being pleased.

"Or maybe I was too preoccupied to think about sex, worrying about how I was going to get my dad to change his mind."

"Problem solved," I said triumphantly.

"Not really. I just traded one problem for another one."

"How do you mean?"

"Well, I'm meeting with my dad and his lawyer tomorrow to sign all the paperwork transferring majority ownership of Moretti & Sons to me, but I'll be celibate for at least a year."

"Oh. *That* problem." I pulled a decorative pillow onto my stomach and played with its fringed edge. "Well, it's a problem we'll share, at least."

"Will you even miss it?"

"Sex?"

"Isn't that what we're talking about?"

My skin warmed beneath my blankets. I had to take one leg out to cool off. "Yes. But hopefully I'll be pregnant soon."

"What does that have to do with it?"

"My body will be . . . otherwise engaged," I said. "I'll be too busy growing a human to worry about satisfying selfish needs."

"Is that really what you think? That sex is a selfish need?"

"You don't think there's something selfish about sexual gratification?"

"No. Because I always make sure whoever I'm with is gratified first and fully before I think about myself."

I took the other leg out. "Oh."

"Sex isn't selfish, Bianca. *People* are selfish. And it sounds like you've only been with selfish people."

"There haven't been that many," I said. I'd only been with two guys before Tate, and neither experience had wowed me. Tate had wowed me at first, but maybe I was just young and inexperienced. And after a while it didn't seem like I excited him that much anymore, which was probably why he'd sought excitement elsewhere.

"Whatever. I'm not one to judge someone for their sexual behavior—no, I take it back. I judge those assholes you were with who made you think sex was a selfish act."

"Maybe it's my old Catholic guilt talking," I said with a sigh. "When you spend all those years being taught by nuns, you grow up associating sex outside marriage—or even taking pleasure in it—with sin and shame. It took some time for me to unlearn that stuff and be okay with enjoying myself."

"Clearly I did not attend Catholic schools."

"Well, I think it's something they mostly emphasize to girls. I used to think you could get pregnant if you lay down next to a man in bed, even if you were fully clothed."

"Jesus. We're not sending our kid to Catholic schools, are we?"

The question took me by surprise. "I'm not sure. I haven't thought that far ahead yet."

"Yeah, I guess we don't need to worry about it now."

"What we *do* need to worry about is when I'm moving in with you. People are going to think it's weird if we get married and I still live here alone."

"Right."

"JJ is all set to move in here. My parents love the idea because they're so sick of him living at home. They even offered to pay half his rent. If he'd quit all the stupid trips to Vegas and betting on sports, he'd be able to afford a place of his own."

Enzo laughed. "Yeah, some guys are like that. Okay, so why don't we move you in Saturday?"

"Okay." A shiver moved up my spine, and I pulled the covers over my body again. "We'll be married then."

"You're right. We will."

Silence, during which both of us imagined it. Would we share a bed? The thought of it—scandalous yet thrilling—quickened my breath. As if he'd read my mind, Enzo spoke again.

"You can have your own bedroom here. I'll clean out the guest room."

I tried not to feel let down. Of *course* we'd have separate rooms. "Is that . . . is that okay?"

"Sure. I don't have many guests anyway. Will you need an office?"

"I can get along without a home office," I said.

"Should I rent a truck or do you think we can get everything here in cars?"

"I don't think we'll need a truck. It will mostly just be clothes and books. I'll leave my furniture and kitchen stuff for JJ."

"Great. So Saturday, then."

"Saturday." I thought for a moment. "What are we going to do about the, um, wedding night?"

"Oh yeah. That." Enzo exhaled. "Maybe you should plan on staying over here that night. I don't want people to see me dropping you off at your condo."

"Right. Okay. I'll—I'll pack an overnight bag."

"Sounds good."

Another silence, but it wasn't uncomfortable. I realized I didn't want to hang up yet. "So have you written my vows?"

"I worked on them a little," he said. "What about you?"

"I wrote a few things down." Then I giggled. "I really cannot wait to hear you say them."

He groaned. "Please remember that my guy friends are going to be there. Don't emasculate me."

"I wouldn't dream of it." The mention of his friends

reminded me of what I'd done earlier tonight, and I felt compelled to confess. "But I have to tell you something."

"What?"

I took a breath. "I broke a rule."

"Let me guess. You told someone else."

"I'm sorry!" I said, sitting up taller in bed. "It just came out!"

He groaned. "Who was it?"

"Blair."

"Oh." He actually didn't sound that upset. "Is she going to tell Griffin?"

"She said she wouldn't. She said he probably wouldn't want to know anyway."

"Yeah. I could see that."

"Anyway, I apologize. If you want to tell one more person to make it even, you can."

"Nah. The fewer people that know this isn't real, the better."

I picked at a loose thread on my comforter. "Right."

"And Cole told me Cheyenne knows. So we're even, I guess."

"Cheyenne knows? What does she think?"

"She has a twisted mind. She thinks it's romantic, like two people getting married so one of them can stay in the country."

I laughed. "I suppose it's similar."

Enzo yawned and groaned like he was stretching, and I pictured it—muscles straining at clothes. Unless he was naked and in bed already. My breath caught, and I crossed my legs, squeezing my thighs together. My nipples tingled.

"Well, I guess I'll hit the sack," he said. "Night, Lucy."

I smiled. "Night, Ricky."

I ended the call, set my alarm, placed my phone on the charger and my glasses next to it on my nightstand. Switching off my lamp, I lay in the dark on my back, covers tucked beneath my armpits, willing the hum beneath my skin to subside.

As much as I hated to admit it, Enzo's voice had the power to turn me on. His face too. And his body. Those lean, sculpted muscles. Would I get to see him naked? Could I walk in on him changing? Getting ready for bed? Accidentally sneak a peek while he was in the shower at some point? What if he was, you know, diddling himself in there? Wasn't that where guys jerked off the most? In an attempt to be sexier, I'd once tried to surprise Tate in the shower but he'd just been annoyed by the invasion of his privacy, and whatever mood I'd hoped to put him in was totally ruined. I'd apologized, grabbed a towel, and retreated.

Something told me if I tried that with Enzo, things would go down a lot differently.

Immediately I scolded myself for even thinking it. I had no proof Enzo wanted me like that. And wasn't it better if he didn't?

Business partners should not have sexual affairs, and that's all we were.

Still, I fell asleep with the words *gratified first and fully* shooting through my mind like fireworks.

On my wedding day, I woke up early.

As soon as I sat up, I looked over at my closet door where my wedding dress hung. On the floor were my shoes, satin peep-toe pumps in a gorgeous shade of chili pepper red a couple shades darker than my hair. I'd been to the salon yesterday for a trim and some fresh color, a mani-pedi, an eyebrow wax, and lash extensions. Blair and my sister had also talked me into getting some other strategic waxing done, just in case, and even though I did it, I assured them no one was going to appreciate it but me.

"Then do it for *you*," Blair said. "Not everything has to be for a man. Pamper yourself!"

"I heartily agree," I said, although a bikini wax wasn't really my idea of pampering.

But I did it.

Beside my shoes was the bag I'd begun packing last night for my sleepover at Enzo's house. Nothing too exciting, just some flannel pajamas I wouldn't be embarrassed to walk around in, some jeans and a sweater, socks and sneakers. Later, once I was ready, I'd toss in my makeup bag and a hairbrush.

At the foot of my bed were boxes full of clothing and other personal items, ready for the move to Enzo's house. I'd packed up my bedroom, office, and bathroom over the last two days. JJ was beyond thrilled about his good luck, and my parents thanked me repeatedly for giving him a good deal on the rent. I just hoped the place wasn't in shambles by the time I had to move back in.

Grabbing my glasses from my nightstand, I stuck them on my head and ran a hand through my hair. My phone buzzed with a text, and I looked at the screen.

Blair: HAPPY WEDDING DAY!!!!!!!

Smiling, I grabbed it and texted back.

Me: Thanks.

Blair: How do you feel?

Me: Good, I guess?

Blair: You guess? Come on, it's your wedding day! Get happy!

Me: Blair, it's fake.

Blair: LALALALALALA I'm not listening! It's still your wedding day, and I'll be over at one sharp to help you get GORGEOUS.

Me: You're the best. Thanks.

I'd given up trying to convince her all this fuss wasn't necessary—she refused to listen and was treating this like a real wedding day. Ellie was the same. She was picking up our flowers and bringing them over along with lunch at noon.

At four, Griffin would come by for Blair and me. Ellie would go with my parents, brother, and Grandma Vinnie. Enzo's parents, siblings, and nephews would all be there as well. Neither he nor I had wanted a crowd at the ceremony, but try telling that to two Italian families. Not to mention the parents of Enzo's closest guy friends, who'd known Enzo so long he felt like another son to them. That courthouse was going to be jam-packed.

It all felt a little out of control, but I'd made up my mind to just go with it. It made me feel good that so many people wanted to celebrate Enzo and me—it meant we were loved.

Just not by each other.

Shaking my head, I swung my legs over the side of the bed and put my pedicured feet on the floor. Studying my ruby-painted toenails, I smiled. It *was* my wedding day, and if it was the only one I ever got, I was going to enjoy it.

I went into the kitchen and made myself a cup of coffee, then settled on a stool at the island with the vows I'd handwritten for Enzo. Grinning, I sipped my coffee and read them over, picking up a pen to tweak things here or there. By the time I'd finished a second cup of coffee, I was satisfied.

Reviewing them one last time before typing them up, I started to laugh uncontrollably. Enzo was probably going to smother me with a pillow tonight in my sleep, but at least I'd get to hear him say these ridiculous things.

Worth it.

Seven

Enzo

I REDID THE KNOT IN MY TIE FOR THE FIFTH TIME AND studied myself in the full-length mirror on my bedroom wall. Frowning, I smoothed the crimson tie down my chest and grabbed my suit jacket off the bed.

After slipping it on, I buttoned the top button and adjusted my cuffs. Brushed a speck of dust from my lapel. Straightened my collar. Turning this way and that, I checked my reflection from all angles. Glanced at my shoes to make sure they were polished. Moved closer to the mirror to examine my face, ensuring my jaw wasn't too scruffy, my eyebrows weren't unruly, and my lips weren't dry. Running a hand over my hair, I wondered if I'd used too much product—I didn't usually worry about it, but I felt a little off my game today. I was looking for anything that made me feel a little more in control, even if it was just taming my hair.

Satisfied, I stepped back.

Over at my dresser, I added my dress watch, a classic white pocket square, and sprayed some cologne. Then I turned around and studied the room, double-checking it was fit for a woman's critical eye. Why, I don't know. It's not like Bianca was going to see it. I'd spent hours yesterday cleaning out the guest room for her. Emptying dresser drawers and storing my summer shit in boxes in the attic. Washing the bedding and making up the bed. My housekeeper had been here Wednesday, so everything was dusted and vacuumed, but I'd run a cloth over all the furniture anyway. Then I went out and bought some white roses and put them in a silver vase on the nightstand.

Maybe it was overkill, but after those vows I was going to make her read, she was probably going to shut herself in there and scream at me through the locked door just like my mother had done to my father for thirty-six years.

The thought of it actually made me smile. Maybe we wouldn't have sex on our wedding night, but we'd probably have a good, loud fight.

Where Bianca was concerned, it was the second-best thing.

A distant second, but second.

At two that afternoon, Cole, Griffin, and Beckett came over to my house to give me shit and drink a couple shots of whiskey. There hadn't been time for a bachelor night, so this would have to do.

Beckett arrived first, dressed in a dark blue suit and carrying a brown paper bag from which he pulled a bottle of bourbon from Journeyman Distillery. "How do you feel?" he asked.

"Okay. I'll feel better after a few sips of that." I grabbed four glasses and set them on the island, which was topped with black stone. If Bianca had never been here before, I might have worried that she'd find my taste in interior design too masculine—I liked dark neutrals, metals, leather, and clean lines, as opposed to her preferences for warm colors, white cabinetry, and soft, feminine textures. But she'd come over a few times in the last month and had nodded approvingly at my choices, even if she did find them a bit "monochromatic and somewhat cold." She'd probably bring over a suitcase full of fluffy pillows and blankets and start putting them on every surface.

Cole arrived next, wearing black like I was, although his tie was blue. "Shit," he said. "Was I supposed to wear a red one?"

I shook my head and handed him some whiskey. "No dress code. You're good."

Griffin let himself in a minute later, wearing a charcoal gray suit without a tie at all. "Is this okay?" he asked. "I wasn't sure how dressy we were supposed to be, and Blair wasn't home to ask."

"It's fine," I assured him. "This really isn't a formal thing."

"It's still your wedding," Beckett said. "That's a big fucking deal."

"No shit." Griffin swiped the unclaimed glass of whiskey. "I'm still trying to wrap my head around it. You sure you didn't knock her up?"

They all laughed, and my stomach muscles clenched. Suddenly I knew how Bianca had felt when she let the news slip to Blair. I wasn't in the habit of keeping shit from my friends, and these guys had been there for me for twenty years. We'd met in middle school and had been tight as brothers ever since.

"For fuck's sake, Moretti. I was kidding." Griffin grinned at me. "Lighten up. Married life isn't so bad."

"It's not that," I said, worried a confession was on the tip of my tongue. I pressed my lips together, a dam against the confession rising in my throat.

Beckett raised his glass. "Let's toast," he said. "To Moretti finally meeting his match."

We all tossed back our shots and set the glasses down.

"It's fake," I blurted.

My friends stared at me.

"Huh?" Griffin's blue eyes narrowed.

"Fake?" Beckett looked at the whiskey bottle, like maybe he'd purchased counterfeit bourbon.

Cole's eyes were steady on me, but he said nothing.

"This wedding. The relationship. Bianca and me. It's just an act."

"What? Why?" Griffin asked.

Beckett put it together first. "Your dad," he said. "The company."

I nodded.

"Shit," Griffin said. "Really? You're marrying her just to get the business?"

My chest puffed up a little. "I have to. It's worth it to me."

"Does *she* know it's fake?"

Again I nodded. "It was her idea."

"What?" Beckett's square jaw dropped. "Why would she—"

"Because she wants a baby."

Cole reached for the whiskey bottle and poured a second round of shots.

"Holy shit," Griffin said, shaking his head. "So she *is* pregnant."

"No, she's not. Not yet, anyway. But we're going to try as soon as we're married." I didn't feel like getting into the details, so I left it there.

Beckett picked up his second shot and threw it back. We all followed suit. Once the empty glasses were on the table again, it was silent. Obviously, no one knew what to say.

"I'm sorry, you guys. I wanted to tell you all right from the start, which was only about a month ago, but Bianca and I promised each other we'd keep it to ourselves. As you can imagine, it's not something we want getting out. Especially to our parents. I only got to tell one person, and I drew Cole's name out of a hat."

"I'm glad you said something to everyone," Cole said, looking relieved. "And if this is what you want, then we support you."

"Fuck yes, we do." Griffin recovered some of his usual unflappability. "Sorry if I was a little taken aback."

"It's okay," I told him. "I know it's fucking crazy. But it's what we both agreed to do to get the things we want. And I *have* always wanted to be a father. That part is real enough."

"And the marriage will be real?" Beckett asked.

"Yes. It's more of a business arrangement than anything else—we're just friends—but we are really getting married." It was the first time I'd ever referred to Bianca as my friend. It felt nice, actually.

"Well, then." Beckett poured one more round of shots and picked up his glass. "To friendship."

Cole raised his shot. "And fatherhood."

Griffin lifted his glass. "And fuck the Mavs."

"Fuck the Mavs," the rest of us chorused, and my heart felt free. I breathed easier.

For about an hour.

Right around four that afternoon, I stood on the sidewalk in front of City Hall as Griffin's old red pickup pulled up with Bianca in the passenger seat. Immediately I felt that vise start to cinch around my lungs again. It was hard to see through the window, but my pulse picked up anyway.

I went to the truck and opened her door, and when she smiled at me, it took off in a full-on gallop.

She was *stunning.*

In a complete stupor, I offered my hand to help her down, and she put her palm in mine before carefully attempting to place one red heel onto the running board—but she was too short.

She looked at me. "Um, remember that time you said you'd help me reach the things I couldn't reach? How about when the thing is the ground?"

Grinning, I put my hand around her tiny waist and lifted her out of the truck, setting her gently on her feet. "How's that?"

She laughed and gave me a little curtsy. "Thank you, kind sir."

I let my eyes sweep over her from head to foot, lingering briefly on her ruby lips. Gooseflesh rippled my skin beneath my suit. "You look beautiful, Bianca. I mean it."

"Thank you. You look very handsome."

"Thanks." I offered her my elbow. "Shall we get married?"

She laughed. "We shall."

Everyone who'd gathered in front of City Hall—mostly our family and closest friends, but also a few strangers who happened to be wandering by—applauded and cheered as we made our way up the steps. I opened the glass door for Bianca and followed her inside. The courtroom, where the ceremony would take place, was upstairs.

"We have a few minutes," she said. "Do you think we should rehearse our vows?"

I tried to speak but words didn't come. Her face was knocking me out. Had she done something different with her eye makeup? Her eyes just looked so sweet and pure and blue. How had I never noticed the tiny smattering of freckles across her nose? Or the way one eyebrow arched higher than the other? And those lips—they nearly matched the satin color of her shoes, but they didn't look sticky, like her lipstick would come off on me. They looked soft and delicious, like a ripe red cherry. What would they taste like? We'd kissed a couple times for show, but there'd never been any tongue involved.

Now I wanted to put my tongue in her mouth. What the actual fuck?

"Enzo?"

Oh shit. She'd asked a question about the vows, hadn't she? "Uh, let's not rehearse them. I feel like it will be more fun to surprise each other."

"Okay." She glanced around the lobby. "Should we find somewhere to wait? So we can make more of an entrance upstairs?"

"Yeah." Composing myself, I took her hand. "Come with me."

Our options were limited, since this was a municipal building, not a wedding venue, and most of the offices were occupied. But at the end of the hall was a stairwell, and we ducked into it.

Facing her again, I took a small box from inside my jacket pocket. "I have something for you."

Her lower lip dropped. "Enzo! I don't have anything for you!"

"Just open it."

Frowning, she handed me her bouquet of white roses. "Hold these, please."

I took them from her and gave her the little leather box, which was new, although the jewelry inside was not. She opened its hinges and gasped at the small diamond earrings twinkling in white velvet. Her face lit up. "Oh, Enzo, they're beautiful!"

"They were my mother's," I said. "My father gave them to her on their wedding day. They were his mother's before that—a gift from her father, the original Enzo."

"Oh my goodness, I'm going to cry." She fanned her face with one hand. "It's too much."

"Do you want to wear them? You don't have to," I said quickly. "I figured you'd be wearing jewelry already, but—"

"Of course I want to wear them." Quickly, she pulled the backings off the small gold hoops she had on. "These are no big deal. But can I put them in your pocket? Blair has my purse."

"Sure." I took the tiny hoops from her and tucked them into my pocket, watching as she put on one diamond stud, and then the other. Inside the small, confined space, the scent of her perfume was even more beguiling.

"What do you think?" she asked, turning her head slightly so I could admire them.

"Beautiful." But I hardly looked at the diamonds.

Her eyes filled. "Thank you, Enzo. I really love them, and I promise to give them back when—when—" But she couldn't finish her sentence and those tears were dangerously close to falling.

I squeezed her shoulder. "Let's not worry about that today, okay? Today, they're yours."

"Okay." She composed herself with a couple deep breaths. "Okay."

I handed her bouquet back and reached into my inside jacket pocket once more, pulling out a piece of white paper folded into a square. "Here are your vows."

"Oh! Let me get yours." Bending down, she slipped one shoe off and took what appeared to be a large white index card folded into fourths from the sole of her red high heel. Straightening, she said, "Sorry. I had nowhere else to put them. I typed everything out and taped them to the card."

"Okay." We exchanged written vows, and I tucked the index card into my pants pocket. "And you'll go first, right?"

"Right." She wrapped the folded paper around the stem of her bouquet and laughed. "Why am I so nervous?"

"I am too. But we'll be fine." Our eyes met. "And listen, I just want to say thanks for doing this. It means a lot to me. I know you don't really want to be my wife."

She seemed surprised. "You're welcome. Thanks for agreeing to be my child's father. I know it isn't what you'd have chosen."

"That doesn't matter anymore," I said firmly. And then more words started coming out before I could stop them. "I'm going to take care of you, Bianca. And the baby. I want you to know that."

She opened her mouth to say something else, but right then, the door to the stairwell swung open, and Bianca's sister Ellie appeared, Cole right behind her. "What the hell, you guys?

We didn't know where you went. Judge Reinhart says you're up. Dad's waiting for you out here, B. Everyone else is seated up in the courtroom already."

"Okay, sorry." Bianca looked up at me. "Ready?"

I nodded, swallowing hard. "Ready. See you in there."

Ellie opened the door wide enough for me to pass her, and Cole and I hurried down the hall and up the wide stone steps. "Still doing okay?" he asked me.

"A little sweaty."

He laughed. "I think that's normal. I guess I meant, are you still sure you want to do this?"

I thought of Bianca—her teary eyes when she'd put on the earrings, her impish grin when she'd asked for help getting out of the truck, the scent of her perfume.

And okay, her meatball subs.

"Yes," I said.

Except my reasons were getting all jumbled up in my head. I was doing this for myself, wasn't I? For the company? As Cole and I made our way into the courtroom, past rows of benches on either side of the aisle toward the judge, I forced myself to focus on the task at hand: securing my future at Moretti & Sons. Marrying Bianca was just a means to an end, that's all.

Nodding at the judge, a stout sixty-something man with a fringe of salt-and-pepper hair and a large belly under his black robe, I took my place at the front of the room and turned around. Cole stood behind me. Quickly, I scanned the room—my parents and the rest of my family in the front two rows. Beckett, Blair, Griffin, and Cheyenne right behind them. On the other side of the aisle was Bianca's family, including old Grandma Vinnie in the front row, sizing me up like she knew I was a fraud. I had to look away. Italian grandmothers were known to have the powers of the Malocchio, or the evil eye.

You did not mess with the Malocchio.

At the back of the courtroom, the door opened and Ellie

slipped inside, pausing a moment to grasp her flowers with both hands. Then she made her way up the aisle, her heels clicking on the wood floor.

And then, without any music or fanfare, Bianca and her father appeared in the courthouse doorway and began to walk toward me. Everyone rose to their feet, and a murmur of admiration moved through the crowd. I didn't blame them—Bianca was exquisitely beautiful.

For a moment, I felt a genuine rush of affection for her. Not love, exactly, but warmth and appreciation, fondness and friendship. She smiled as she approached me, offered her cheek to her father, and watched as her dad shook my hand, clasped me tightly and thumped me on the back several times, then took his seat next to her mother, who was already wiping her eyes.

"Hey," I whispered as we faced each other.

"Hey," she whispered back. Her smile was confident and bright.

But her bouquet shook in her hands.

The judge began the ceremony, which, true to his word, was very quick. Actually, I barely recall any of it. I put a ring on Bianca's finger. She put one on mine—a simple gold band. We solemnly declared that we knew not of any lawful impediment to our marriage, blah blah. It was all a blur to me—I couldn't stop thinking about those trembling roses. They made me want to sweep her into my arms and carry her out of there, take her somewhere private and hide out from the world, just the two of us. No pressure and no business deal and no bullshit. Just her and I, together.

My chest was tight. Or maybe it was my collar. Either way, I was finding it tough to breathe. I wiped the sweat from my forehead and tried to focus.

"Now, I'm given to understand the two of you have written some personal commitment vows?" the judge asked.

"Yes," Bianca said. She turned around and handed her flowers to Ellie, then unfolded the vows I'd typed up.

For a moment, I felt bad about what I'd written for her—it was pretty fucking stupid and she was going to hate me for it. In fact, her cheeks were beginning to match her shoes as she glanced at the first few lines. But then she started to read, and all the weird tension inside me eased. It was so fucking funny, I decided I had no regrets whatsoever.

"My dearest Enzo," she said, clearly trying not to clench her teeth. "You are the best thing that ever happened to me. I don't know why I was so mean to you when we were kids. I think now I was afraid of the way I felt for you. I had never met anyone so good-looking and awesome at baseball before." She paused for a breath and hitched her weight over to one foot. "I can't wait to spend the rest of my life ironing your shirts and cooking your favorite foods and watching you win the Allegan County Senior Men's Baseball Championship year after year. It is my dream come true. P.S. I won't even care if you snore because it is such a manly sound. I love everything about you and always will."

She looked up from the page, and I swear to God I thought smoke was going to puff out of her ears.

"That was beautiful, sweetheart," I told her, unable to keep a grin off my face.

"Your turn," she said, her smile laced with venom.

Oh, shit.

I pulled the piece of paper from my pocket, unfolded it, and began to read.

"My sweet, brilliant, beautiful Bianca, what can I say but that my life before you was a meaningless, shallow void—in the words of the immortal Edward Cullen, it was 'an unending, unchanging midnight.'" I paused here to give her a look—who the fuck was Edward Cullen?—and cleared my throat before continuing. "You have brought light into the egotistical and immature darkness that was my soul. I see now that you were always my one true love, and I was just too wrapped up in myself to commit to anyone else. But no longer. To sum up, again I quote Edward Cullen: 'No measure of time with you will be long enough, but we'll start with forever.'"

I dropped the hand holding the page to my side and gave her an incensed stare, my nostrils flaring with anger.

She smiled triumphantly. "That was lovely, Enzo. Brought a tear to my eye."

"Well, then," said Judge Reinhart briskly. "By the authority vested in me by the State of Michigan, I now pronounce you husband and wife. You may kiss the bride."

The last thing on earth I wanted to do right now was kiss the little witch, but what choice did I have? Leaning forward at the waist, I planted my lips chastely on hers, and she placed a hand on my shoulder. A sigh echoed through the courtroom.

We parted, glaring at each other as the judge began to speak.

"Ladies and gentlemen, I present to you Mr. and Mrs. Enzo Moretti."

Our families and friends jumped to their feet, applauding, whistling, and shouting. I offered the witch my elbow and she slipped her hand through it as we made our way back down the aisle and exited the courtroom, followed by our guests.

Out in the hallway, we were swarmed by people wanting hugs and handshakes, so there was no time to give Bianca any shit for those stupid vows. My mother and sisters were crying. My father was bursting with pride. Mr. and Mrs. DeRossi both told me how happy they were—I was the answer to their prayers for their daughter. "Take good care of her, son," Bianca's dad said, clapping me on the shoulder.

"I will, sir." I glanced over at my new wife, who was currently being embraced by all my sisters at once, and felt slammed with guilt. Was this man going to hate me in a few months? Was he going to think I was the sort of man that broke such a promise?

Then it got worse.

"Please. Call me Dad," he said, thumping my shoulder several more times. "We're family now."

"Okay." I swallowed hard. "Dad."

This whole thing felt a little out of control.

A few minutes later, we all made our way downstairs and took photos in the lobby and on the courthouse steps, and I tried to smile. In one picture, I had to pick her up and cradle her like a baby, and through my teeth, I whispered, "I'm tempted to drop you."

She whispered right back, "I'm tempted to kick you in the balls."

Finally, it was time to head over to the Bulldog for the party. Telling everyone we'd see them there, I grabbed Bianca's hand and tugged her down the street toward my car. When we reached it, I opened the passenger door for her, slammed it shut, and stomped around to the driver's side.

As soon as I was behind the wheel, I turned on her.

"Egotistical and immature? What the hell was that all about?"

She put up a hand. "Please. It was not worse than having to say all that nonsense about how mean I was, or how good-looking and awesome at baseball you are. Or that it's my dream come true to iron your shirts and attend your games."

"Who the fuck is Edward Cullen?"

"He's only the most romantic character ever written," she said heatedly.

Rolling my eyes, I started the engine. "Let me guess—a teenage vampire."

"Well, technically he's over a hundred years old," she retorted. "But yes, he appears to be a teenager. And Cheyenne and Blair thought it was very sweet that you quoted my favorite book during your vows."

"*You* quoted your favorite book," I muttered, pulling away from the curb.

"Will you relax? Everything went fine, Enzo. We pulled it off."

"I guess."

"We're married, aren't we? Boom—phase one complete."

I drove in silence for a minute or so, rubbing a finger beneath my lower lip.

"What's wrong?" she asked.

I frowned. "Nothing."

"Something is wrong. You're doing the thing with your finger on your chin, and that vein is popping out on your forehead."

I glanced over and saw she'd scrunched up her face in an exaggerated imitation of me, complete with finger beneath her pursed red lips. Smiling a little, I focused out the windshield again. "It was something your dad said."

"What? That you couldn't return me? I'm final sale?"

"No. He called me *son* and told me to take good care of you."

"Oh," she said soberly.

"I said I would. And then he said to call him Dad." I shook my head, my stomach roiling.

"Well, that was nice."

"Yeah, but it's all bullshit, Bianca. I'm thinking like, in a year, this man is going to despise me. He's going to think I'm not a man of my word. That bothers me."

Bianca sighed in exasperation. "Good grief, Enzo. You need to relax. This isn't 1955. I don't need a man to take care of me. My dad's just old-fashioned. And when we split up, I'll make sure he understands that."

"Still doesn't feel right."

She started laughing. "Well, it's too late now. We're married, Ricky."

I frowned again, even though I knew that vein in my forehead was popping out.

"Hey," she said as I parked in a lot not far from the pub. "We knew what we were getting into when we made this deal. I know it's not conventional, but what is marriage anyway? Maybe it's just an illusion perpetuated by Disney movies and romance novels. Maybe it's just a piece of paper. Maybe it's just an antiquated idea that reeks of misogyny and sexism—I mean, the bride's dad *gives her away* like she's a piece of property!"

I turned off the car and looked over at her. "That seems kind of harsh."

"Don't get me wrong, I bought into the fantasy all my life. I was waiting for the handsome prince to decide on me, but he didn't. He didn't, Enzo. So *I* decided on me." She was all worked up now, color in her cheeks, defiance in her eyes. "But I need your help."

"I need your help too." I tried to shake off the anxiety, running a hand over my hair. "Sorry, I don't know what my problem is."

She let out a breath. "It's okay. Look, it's been a crazy week. Things happened fast, and our heads are spinning. You probably haven't gotten much sleep—I know I haven't. So let's go in and have a few drinks, eat some fried pickles, and celebrate our partnership with our friends and family. So what if it's not exactly the kind of partnership they all think it is?"

"Uh, about that." I cringed. "I kind of let the truth slip to my friends."

"Enzo!" She pressed her lips together. "Who?"

"Cole already knew, so really just two more people—Griffin and Beckett."

She nodded, accepting it. "They know to keep it to themselves?"

"Yes. And I trust them with my life."

"Then I will too." She smiled. "So let's go face the music and dance."

Eight

Bianca

"YOU DID WHAT?" I LOOKED DOWN AT THE envelope in my hands and across the table at my parents.

"We got you a night in the honeymoon suite at the Bellamy Creek Inn." My mother beamed. "It's your wedding present."

Enzo and I exchanged a *what-the-fuck-do-we-do-now* glance, the first one of the night.

Our party was in full swing around us, and everyone was having a great time, myself included. The jukebox was loud, the food was tasty, the crowd was rambunctious, and there was nothing formal or stuffy about the occasion at all. More than one person had told me it was the most fun they'd ever had at a wedding reception.

We'd only done one or two traditional things—we'd cut the cake, Griffin had made a quick toast, I'd thrown my bouquet—so mostly it just felt like a fun night out with friends. Enzo and I had even danced together (our song was officially "Witchcraft" by Frank Sinatra, chosen by Enzo, of course) and smashed cake in each other's faces. Every once in a while, someone would start clinking a fork on the side of their glass, and soon the room would fill with the sound. Enzo and I dutifully joined lips each time, but our kisses were always closed-mouthed and quick. It seemed like we'd get through the night without any trouble.

And then my parents called us over to their table and handed us a great big wrench in the shape of a gift certificate for the honeymoon suite.

"We—we hadn't really planned on a honeymoon or anything," I said. "We're both so busy with work."

"I know, that's why this is perfect. It's just for the night." My mother sighed. "You'll love it. The package includes champagne and chocolates, breakfast in bed . . . I know you said you didn't need time away, but you're newlyweds! You need at least *one* special night."

"Gee, thanks." I forced a smile. Next to me, Enzo squirmed in his seat. "We'll, um, enjoy this. But you really didn't have to."

"Well, you guys insisted on paying for your own wedding," my father said. "It was the least we could do."

"Right." I tucked the envelope into my bag and finished my wine. "I'll be right back. I'm just going to get another glass of Prosecco."

"I'll join you," said Enzo, rising to his feet. "Thank you very much for the gift, Mr. and Mrs. DeRossi."

"Ah ah," my father said, his tone a warning.

Enzo straightened his tie and tried not to wince. "I mean Mom and Dad."

My parents glowed.

As we walked to the bar, Enzo put a hand on the small of my back. I'd noticed it was something he did often, and I had to admit I sort of liked it. It was an intimate gesture without being suggestive. Deep down, I hoped it wasn't just part of the act.

Everyone smiled at us as we made our way across the room, and I felt an odd surge of pride that I was his wife—or at the very least, that people *thought* I was the one he'd chosen. He was so handsome and charming and well liked. He could have had any woman he wanted, and he'd picked me.

He did not pick *you,* scolded a voice in my head. *This is all one big act. And you better not get caught up in it.*

We reached the bar and ordered two more drinks—another Prosecco for me and a beer for Enzo. "So what are we going to do about this honeymoon suite thing?" I turned to face him. "That's one I didn't see coming."

"Me neither." He shrugged. "You could go stay there, I guess."

"By myself?" I laughed, shaking my head. "Do you know how fast it would get around town that I was staying in the honeymoon suite at the Bellamy Creek Inn alone on our wedding night?"

"True." Enzo frowned, and it struck me how unfairly handsome he was, even when he was brooding about something. He looked fantastic in his suit and tie too. Several times tonight, I'd imagined what it would be like to take it off him, piece by piece. Run my hands through that thick dark hair, messing up his perfectly styled waves. Jump up and wrap my legs around his torso. Bite his bottom lip.

Our drinks arrived, and I took a much-needed sip. "But I feel bad. I don't want it to go to waste."

Enzo tipped up his beer and took several long swallows. "Fuck it. Let's use it."

"Use it?" I looked at him in surprise. "Like stay there together tonight?"

"Yeah." He shrugged. "Might as well."

"What about the bed situation?"

"What about it?"

"I think we need some additional rules," I said as heat rose from the bodice of my dress and crept toward my face.

Enzo looked amused. "Okay."

"If there's a couch, one of us sleeps on it."

"Why? You don't trust yourself to share a bed with me?"

I glared at him. "Very funny."

"Bianca, if you want me to sleep on the couch, I will. But I assure you, even if we shared the bed, your virtue would be safe. I *can* keep my hands to myself."

"Well, I can too."

"So then we'll share a bed for a night." He raised his beer bottle to his lips again.

"Fine. We'll share the bed." I pointed my finger at him. "But no funny business. You stay on your side and I stay on mine."

"Are you going to draw a line down the middle?"

"I might." I took a drink. "And no sleeping naked."

"Now you're just being mean."

"How is that mean?"

"What if I always sleep naked? You're making me feel ashamed. And the human body is nothing to be ashamed of, Bianca. In fact, mine is quite nice. I think you'd enjoy seeing it naked."

"I'm sure you do."

"I might even enjoy seeing *yours* naked." He shrugged. "Just putting that out there."

"Ha! Not a chance."

He shook his head. "I had no idea how repressed you were."

"I'm not repressed just because I wear pajamas to bed, Enzo. You're just trying to trick me into letting you see me naked."

"Is it working?"

"No."

He took another drink. "The least you could do is walk around topless or something, considering that I just began a yearlong dry spell for you."

"I think you'll live," I told him, patting his arm.

"Easy for you to say. You're a woman."

"This again?" I rolled my eyes. "Contrary to what men might think, Enzo, women crave sex just as much as they do."

"I had no idea you were craving sex with me, Bianca." Enzo gave me the eyes and slipped an arm around my waist. "But don't worry, I know how we can solve this problem."

I laughed, beating one fist against his solid chest. "Don't even think about it. And get your paws off me."

But instead of letting me go, I felt his lips—and then his *tongue*—brush my temple. Then he released me. "Frosting," he said, licking his lips. "Don't worry, I got it."

I touched the spot he'd licked, my heart hammering in my chest, heat pooling between my legs. Taking a step back, I attempted a cool expression as I smoothed my hair. "You made a mess shoving that cake in my face. Is it anywhere else?"

Regarding me silently, he took another sip of his beer. "No. You look perfect."

I gulped some wine and tried to calm down.

But as our party wrapped up, I couldn't stop thinking about sex with him, picturing him naked, imagining his body moving over mine. What was it going to be like sharing a bed with him? Would I even be able to sleep?

This is ridiculous, I kept telling myself. *You can't break the no-sex rule. You were the one who put it in the contract to begin with. Fine, this isn't the wedding night you once dreamed of, but remember why you're doing this in the first place.*

But my body was having a hard time letting my mind stay at the wheel.

"Everything okay?" Enzo asked me on the ride over to his house. We were going to drop off the wedding presents we'd received, and he needed to grab a few things for the overnight stay at the inn.

"Fine," I said, careful not to look at him.

"You seem quiet all of a sudden."

"I'm just tired."

"Me too." He yawned. "Getting married is fucking exhausting."

"Having a baby will be worse."

"True." He paused. "Speaking of which, when do we go in for the first attempt?"

"I have an appointment with the fertility specialist next week. Because I don't ovulate normally, I'll have to take some preliminary steps to make sure we know exactly when it will happen, and then time the insemination right. There's a drug I have to take."

"What do I have to do?"

"Not much. Show up and get off."

"I prefer provide a sample, please," he said haughtily. "Don't cheapen it."

I laughed, in spite of everything. "Just make sure it's a good one. We need the gold-medal swimmers."

"How dare you imply I have any other kind?"

"Speaking of which." I shifted in the passenger seat to face him. "What are you going to think about?"

"When?"

"While you're, you know, providing the sample. What will you think about?"

He frowned. "Jesus, Bianca. I don't know."

"Porny stuff?"

"Probably. Am I supposed to think about the Holy Ghost or something? Because I don't think that will result in my best work."

"It doesn't have to be religious," I said. "Just not anything too . . . you know, skeevy."

"What if your definition of skeevy isn't the same as mine? We've never hooked up, so I don't know if you're totally vanilla or like a little kink."

"What kind of kink?" I asked, curious.

"Any kind. Bondage, blindfolds, role play."

"I've never done anything like that," I confessed. But now I was thinking about it. Would I let him blindfold me? Tie me up? Would I trust him not to hurt or humiliate me? I wasn't sure.

"I'd be happy to test your limits—all in the name of research, of course."

"You know what? Never mind," I said, crossing my legs a little tighter. "Think about whatever you want. It's really none of my business."

I stayed silent after that. What the hell was wrong with me, anyway? I needed to stop allowing my hormones to make this thing between us into something it wasn't.

My limits already felt tested.

Around ten o'clock that night, Enzo unlocked the door to the Bellamy Creek Inn's honeymoon suite. He pushed it open and looked back at me. "Want me to carry you over the threshold?"

I rolled my eyes and dragged my suitcase into the room. "So you can threaten to drop me again? That won't be necessary."

He let the door close behind him, dropped his leather bag on the floor, and yawned.

I ditched my heels and flopped back onto the king-sized bed, which was decorated with faux rose petals and two giant pillows that said MR. and MRS. on them. Over on the table by the window was an ice bucket holding a bottle of champagne, two glasses, and a box of chocolates.

Enzo wandered over to it. "Oh, look. They left us a note. 'Congratulations, Mr. and Mrs. Moretti. Please let us know if there's anything we can do to make your stay more enjoyable. Cheers to your future.'"

I propped myself up on my elbows. "Everyone's so happy for us. It's making me feel bad."

"I know." Loosening the knot in his tie, he came over to the bed, where he flopped onto his back beside me in a sea of fake rose petals, some of which fluttered around us like confetti. "But it's done."

I sighed. "It's done."

He looked over at me. "So now what do we do?"

"I don't know."

"The bar downstairs is already closed."

"I'm too tired to go back out anyway."

"Same." He yawned again. "Should we just go to bed?"

My bare toes curled. "I guess."

"I can't wait to get this suit off." He got up and walked over to the dresser.

I watched him yank off his tie, shrug out of his jacket, and remove his cufflinks. Which was all fine—I enjoyed it, actually—except then he began unbuckling his belt.

"Enzo!" I scolded. "Not in here!"

"Why not?"

"Because *I'm* in here."

"So go in the bathroom or something."

"*You* go in the bathroom!"

He laughed, pulling his belt from the loops and setting it on the dresser. "This is my room too. And I don't have any hang-ups about my body. If you don't want to see it, close your eyes or something."

But I couldn't. I was mesmerized by the sight of his hands in the mirror, unbuttoning his white dress shirt and then peeling it off. He tossed it aside and whipped his undershirt off, grabbing it from the back and yanking it over his head. I didn't know where to look first. At his sculpted arms? His strong back? His rippling abs? His bare chest, golden and broad and showing some hair? For some reason, the hair surprised me. I'd figured Enzo was the kind of guy to manscape his whole body. But I liked that he hadn't shaved it—it was masculine and sexy. I caught my bottom lip between my teeth as I stared at his reflection.

And he caught me staring. His lips curved up on one side, although he said nothing. Just held my gaze as his hands dropped to the button and zipper of his pants.

I sprang off the bed, bolted for the bathroom, and slammed the door behind me. "Fine! Be that way!"

Inside the bathroom, I leaned back against the door and squeezed my eyes shut, breathing hard. I felt hot and sticky beneath my dress, and my stomach would not stop jumping. Were his pants off yet? What about his underwear? Would he put something else on? What was I going to do if I walked out and he was naked? And was he expecting me to take off my dress in front of him?

Opening my eyes, I looked around the bathroom. Towels were folded like swans on the marble vanity. Two fluffy robes hung on wooden hangers from hooks on the back of the door. The tub was huge—definitely big enough for two. In the mirror, two crimson splotches had appeared on my cheeks. My neck was flushed as well. Even my legs looked a little pink.

I fanned my face, willing my skin to cool off and my hormones to settle.

A knock on the bathroom door made me jump.

"Yes?" I called, my voice cracking.

"You can come out now. I'm decent."

"Define decent."

"All the scary man parts are covered."

"I'm not *scared* of your man parts, Enzo."

"Oh no? Then why'd you hide out in the bathroom the moment I unzipped my pants?"

"To give you some privacy!" Angry, I swung the door open to find him standing there in heather gray lounge pants, tied *very low* on his waist with a white drawstring. I was briefly distracted by the tops of the V lines appearing on either side of his abdomen, but I pulled myself together and looked him in the eye. "But if you don't want privacy, fine. I'll come out."

He grinned as I brushed past him, careful not to let our bodies touch. "Want help getting out of that dress?"

"No, thank you," I said, grabbing a hanger from the closet and wheeling my suitcase into the bathroom. "I'll just be a minute."

"Suit yourself." He shut the door for me.

Alone again, I realized right away I should have taken him up on his offer. There was no way I could reach the zipper on the back of my dress. I tried for several minutes before giving up. Sighing, I opened the door and went out into the room to find him pouring champagne.

"Hey," I said. "I do need help."

He set the bottle down and came over to me. "Turn around."

I presented my back to him, and he slowly pulled the zipper down to my waist. Expecting him to make a joke or put his hands on me, I was surprised when he didn't. "Thank you."

"No problem." He went back to pouring champagne, and I returned to the bathroom.

See? He's not really interested. He didn't even touch you.

I tried not to feel disappointed about it.

Behind the closed door again, I slipped out of my dress and hung it with the robes. After trading my white lacy panties for more comfortable pink cotton boy shorts, I tugged on my navy plaid flannel pajamas, took out my contacts, put my hair up in a scrunchie, and scrubbed off my wedding makeup.

When my face was clean, I put my glasses on and studied my reflection in the mirror. I was still wearing the diamond earrings he'd given me. I touched them both, my belly fluttering. It meant something to me that he'd given me a family heirloom. Then I looked down at my ring, which still said *Love Always, Ricky* inside it. It made me smile. Enzo had asked me if I wanted the engraving removed, but I'd said not to bother. It suited us.

And it served as a good reminder.

I left the bathroom, pulling my suitcase behind me, and hung up my dress in the closet. Then I went over to the bed, where Enzo was leaning back against the MR. pillow, legs stretched out in front of him, bare feet crossed at the ankle. In his hand was a glass of champagne and next to him was the box of chocolates.

"Hey," I said, climbing onto the MRS. side of the bed and sitting cross-legged.

"Hey." He reached toward his nightstand for a second glass of champagne and handed it to me. "For you, Mrs. Moretti."

"Thank you, Mr. Moretti." I laughed and we clinked glasses. "To the successful completion of phase one."

"Salut."

We both drank, and then it was quiet in the room. I studied the chocolates and picked one out, taking a bite. "This probably isn't what you pictured on your wedding night, huh?"

Enzo chose one and ate it too. "Honestly, I don't think I ever pictured my wedding night at all."

"Seriously?"

He shrugged. "I take it you did?"

"All the time. Since I was a little girl."

"Are you implying it didn't look like this?" He spread his arms.

I laughed, shaking my head, and picking out another chocolate. "No. It did not."

"So what did it look like? Wait, let me guess." He took a sip of champagne and then continued. "A tall, strapping, dark-haired vampire carried you to his lair and penetrated you hard and deep with his steely fangs."

He was spot on—at least where my teenage dreams were concerned. But I pretended to be offended. "*No*, that's not what I pictured, you jerk."

He smiled. "So tell me."

"When I was little, he was Prince Eric from The Little

Mermaid. As a grownup, I thought I'd marry my ex-boyfriend," I said, carefully skipping over the vampire years.

"Oh, right. What was his name again? Taint?"

"Tate."

"Whatever. And what was it that Taint was going to do to make the night memorable for you?"

I sighed, sipping my champagne. "You know what? I can't even name anything specific. It was just going to be the most magical night of my life."

"Magical? Well, fuck. You were doomed to be disappointed, babe. There's no such thing as a magical dick."

I rolled my eyes. "It wasn't his *dick* that was going to feel magical. It was the night itself. It was the things he'd say. It was the *mood*."

"Are you implying," he said with mock offense, "that the honeymoon suite at the Bellamy Creek Inn lacks mood? We've got champagne. We've got chocolates. We've got swans in the bathroom and pillows that say MR. and MRS. What could possibly be more romantic than that?"

Laughing, I lifted my shoulders. "I don't know."

"See, I happen to think this is perfect. I never pictured anything, so I'm not disappointed." He thought for a second. "Except for the no-sex rule. That's definitely a bit of a letdown."

"Well, I imagined sex too. And even if my groom didn't have a magical dick, he would at least know how to use it."

"Oh yeah?" Enzo looked amused. "Tell me all about it."

"No, you'll laugh."

"I swear, I will not laugh." He went to get the champagne bottle, pouring me some more before topping off his own glass. "I want to hear your innermost fantasies."

After another sip, I gave in. "He'd take one look at me and be completely unable to resist. He'd want to ravage me completely. He'd say—"

"Sorry, I have to interrupt for a moment. In this fantasy, are you wearing *those* exact pajamas?" He gestured toward my navy plaid flannels.

I glared at him and pushed my glasses up my nose. "You know what? Just forget it."

"No, no. I'm sorry, go on. I'm listening." He took another sip and watched me with a glint in his dark eyes. "Tell me what he'd say."

I sighed, knowing I was *asking* to be made fun of, but unable to keep my mouth shut. Damn this champagne and his smooth talking. "He'd say I was his one and only love. He'd say nothing would ever come between us. He'd say he couldn't wait to spend the rest of his life with me."

"Did he say, 'You complete me?' Because I saw that in a movie once and I thought it sounded like something a chick would like."

I narrowed my eyes at him. "Just when I think you're not a pig."

"I'm sorry," he said, laughing. "It's just that women and men fantasize very differently."

"Okay, so tell me *yours*," I demanded. "What would your wife say to you on your wedding night to get you all hot and bothered?"

"Easy," he said. "It's all one-syllable stuff like, 'oh, yes, God, right there, just like that, you're so big, don't stop, fuck me, harder'—I guess that's two syllables. But you get the gist."

Not only did I get the gist, but just hearing Enzo say those words was enough to arouse me. Beneath my flannels, my nipples tightened, and blood rushed between my legs. But I had to pretend I wasn't turned on. "*Oink*. Also a one-syllable word."

His grin was slow and seductive. "You don't like talking in bed?"

I shrugged, hating how hot my face felt. I knew it had to be candy-apple red. "Not much."

"See, I think a woman *should* talk in bed. I think she should say exactly what she wants and how she wants it. Otherwise, how's a guy supposed to know how to please her?"

"I don't know."

"Most guys probably figure if she says nothing, it all just feels good. And I bet that's not the case."

"That is not the case," I confirmed. "Can I have the last chocolate?"

"It's all yours. That's why you have to talk," he went on. "Tell the guy what feels good and what doesn't. He's not a mind reader."

"But what if I'm shy about it?" I said as I chewed caramel and chocolate.

"You? Shy? Come on." He gave me a look that said *no way*. "Maybe as a kid, but not anymore."

"But I still find it difficult to be vocal about what I want in *that* particular situation, okay?" I licked my fingers.

"So how do you let the guy know what you like?"

"I just sort of think really hard about it and hope he gets the message."

"That's ridiculous." Enzo finished his champagne, got out of bed, and set his empty glass on the table. "No amount of wishful thinking is going to bring you some kind of fairy-tale magic-wand dick that just *knows* how to make you come. Even I like a little direction. You want more champagne?"

Agitated, I shook my head. What I wanted was his fairy-tale magic-wand dick inside me, making me come without my having to ask for it. Why couldn't he find me so alluring he couldn't resist?

"I'll be right back." He went into the bathroom, and as soon as I heard the door close, I pulled my pajama top away from my body repeatedly, trying to cool off. Then I chugged the rest of my champagne. I was going to melt lying next to him all night.

When he came out of the bathroom, I went in and brushed my teeth. By the time I came out, he'd turned off all the lights, and I had to feel my way toward the bed. Reaching it, I turned back the covers and slid beneath them. Facing away from him, I set my glasses on the nightstand and curled up into a ball.

My heart was pounding. My head was buzzing from the champagne. When I inhaled, I could smell his cologne. Squeezing my eyes shut, I willed my senses to shut down and let me sleep.

But I couldn't. I was too tipsy. Too hot. Too bothered.

Too curious.

I kept thinking about what Enzo had said. *I think a woman should talk in bed. I think she should say exactly what she wants and how she wants it.*

I rolled onto my back and whispered into the dark. "Hey."

"What?"

"I can't sleep."

"Me neither. I was about to jerk off, but I thought you might be mad about it."

I bit my lip. "What if I wasn't?"

"Huh?" He sounded more alert. "That was a joke."

"But what if I wasn't mad about it? Would you do it?"

"Hold on a second." He sat up, turned on the lamp, and looked over at me. "What the fuck are you even saying right now?"

I was surprised how rattled he was. "I don't know. I guess I was just trying to do what you said—talk in bed. Say what I want. You never said it didn't count if I only wanted to watch."

Enzo glared at me, his jaw clenched. "That's not funny."

"I'm not joking."

"Yes, you are, and it's not funny." Suddenly he jumped out of bed, taking the pillow that said MR. on it with him, and holding it in front of his crotch. "You're just fucking with me, trying to make me hard so you can call me a pig again."

"I am not!" I sat all the way up and noticed his legs were bare. "Did you take your pants off?"

"I was fucking hot," he snapped. "But I left my underwear on and I wasn't anywhere near you. I stayed on my side."

"I'm not accusing you of anything!" I stared at that pillow. "Did I really make you hard?"

"No."

He was lying. It gave me a kick. "Me? In my plaid flannel pajamas?"

"*No,*" he insisted.

"I don't believe you." I grinned at him and got to my knees on the mattress. "Give me that pillow."

"Stay back, Bianca."

"Come on, just give me that pillow." I crawled onto his side of the bed and made a grab for it.

He backed up. "Quit it!"

"What's the big deal, Enzo? All I want is the pillow."

"Well, you can't have it."

"Why not?"

"Because you don't want what's behind it."

My eyes wandered over his chest and arms and abs. I licked my lips. "Maybe I do."

"Then prove it."

"How?"

He lifted his chin, his eyes challenging me. "Take off your pants."

I hesitated.

For about three seconds.

Nine

Enzo

SHE FUCKING DID IT.

Right in front of my eyes, Bianca quickly wriggled out of those flannel pants and tossed them aside. And then, as if her bare legs weren't tempting enough, she got back on her knees, and undid the top two buttons on her shirt.

"Shit!" My dick got even harder. "I thought you were bluffing."

"Well, I'm not." She undid two more buttons and let the shirt slip off one shoulder. "I'm into this, Enzo. For one night. Are you?"

"What about the contract?"

She shrugged. "How about we draft a . . . a verbal exceptions clause?"

"Like a wedding night exception? Where we suspend the rules?"

"Exactly."

"And tomorrow it expires?"

"Sure. I think one night should be enough to satisfy our curiosity."

I cocked a brow. "Is that what we're calling this?"

"Isn't that what it is?" She touched her chest. "*I'm* curious about what you're hiding behind that pillow. And *you're* curious about how far I'll go to get it."

She was right. Part of me still thought she was bluffing. But on the slim chance she wasn't . . . "Your shirt. Off."

She undid the rest of the buttons, slipped the shirt from her shoulders, held it out to the side and dropped it. "Done."

My eyes locked onto her breasts with laser-like focus, and I salivated like a fucking teenage boy. They were small but perfect, with adorable apricot-colored nipples I could practically feel beneath my tongue.

"Now you," she said.

I tossed the stupid MR. pillow aside and stood there with my cock bulging obviously inside my briefs. Her eyes dropped to it, and her lips opened. I couldn't resist stroking myself through the fitted cotton, balls to tip. Her eyes widened slightly. Her neck and chest flushed pink as the panties she wore, which I wanted to rip off with my teeth.

"Should I keep going?" I asked, sliding my thumb inside the waistband.

She met my eyes and my challenge. "Yes."

I slid my underwear down my legs and stood up, naked as the day I was born. My cock was thick and veined and hard, curving away from my body and up toward the ceiling. I wrapped my fist around the base of my shaft and slowly worked my hand up and down its length. "So now that you know what was behind the pillow, what else are you curious about?"

She opened her mouth to say something, then closed it, like she'd lost her nerve.

I shook my head. "Uh uh. Not tonight, Mrs. Moretti. Tonight you have to say exactly what you want."

"And you'll make it happen?" she asked. "You'll do whatever I say?"

"If it's humanly possible and it will make you feel good."

She swallowed and chewed the tip of her thumb, but those blue eyes on my cock told me to push further.

"Say it," I demanded. "Tell me what you want, or this ends now."

She dropped her hand, and the words tumbled out in a rush. "I want to know what you'd feel like inside me. I want to know what it's like to be with someone who puts me first. I want to feel beautiful, irresistible, like I'm worth someone's forever, like he'll die if he can't have me, like he'll lose his mind if I don't—"

"Lucy." I grabbed her beneath the arms and tipped her onto her back. "Take a breath, okay? Let's start at the beginning."

She sucked in her breath as I tugged her underwear down her legs and dropped them to the floor.

My heart was beating hard in my chest as I got on my hands and knees and moved up her body until my face hovered over hers. Her blue eyes were darker than usual, her face flushed. "Now let me think," I said, brushing her hair back. "What were my lines again? Oh, right." I kissed her lips, gently teasing them open with my tongue this time. "You're my one and only love."

I felt her smile, heard her start to laugh, and I moved my mouth over her jaw and down her throat. "Nothing will ever come between us."

Inhaling the warm, slightly floral scent of her skin, I kissed my way across her collarbone and back up the other side of her neck. "And I can't wait to spend the rest of my life with you—or at least the rest of tonight."

She laughed harder, threading her hands into my hair. "You paid attention."

"Of course I did." I teased her earlobe with my tongue, which was how I discovered she was still wearing the earrings I'd given her. Not only was it sexy that she had on nothing but diamonds, but I liked that she hadn't taken them off. It meant something to me—something that tightened the wrench around my heart.

I ignored that feeling and focused on the woman beneath me, settling my hips above hers and letting the length of our bodies meet skin to skin for the first time. Bianca moaned softly, opening her knees and pulling my head up to meet my lips with hers. She kissed me differently this time, sucking my tongue into her mouth, tightening her fingers in my hair. Her heels dug into the backs of my legs, and her hips began to rock underneath mine.

By no means was I inexperienced, but something about being with Bianca for the first time was making me anxious. I wanted this to be perfect for her. I wanted her to remember this as the best night of her life. I wanted her future asshole boyfriends—and they'd all be assholes, she clearly had terrible taste in men—to be haunted by the specter of me giving her the kind of pleasure she'd only dreamed about.

With that in mind, I was more attentive to her than I'd ever been to anyone. I went slow. I buried my own urges and stayed in control. I was aware of her every breath and sigh, her every arch and gasp. I discovered she liked it when I put my tongue on her throat, she loved it when I took her nipple between my teeth, and she moaned loudly when I reached between her legs and stroked her clit with soft, gentle circles.

"Oh God." She gripped my shoulders. "That feels so good. I love your hands on me like that."

I took my mouth off her breast for a fraction of a second. "Wait until you feel my tongue."

She sucked in her breath as I kissed a meandering path down her rib cage, across her belly, over one hip, her skin like satin under my lips. Moving down between her legs, I gently pushed them apart and put my mouth all along her limbs . . . her thigh, the inside of her knee, her calf, her ankle. I took my time, working my way down one leg and up the other, before settling between her thighs and letting her feel my breath on her skin.

"Yes," she panted.

"Yes, what?"

"Yes, I want you to do that. I thought you stopped to ask permission."

I smiled, rubbing my lips lightly against her. "Did you? That's cute."

"Enzo." Her voice was weak. Her hands curled into the bedding. "Do it."

"Do what?" I teased her with one tiny, shallow caress, just the tip of my tongue.

"Put your mouth on me."

"Say please."

"*Please.*" A whisper. A *whimper.*

I rewarded her for saying what she wanted with several long, firm strokes up her center, moaning with pleasure at the velvet texture of her, the sweet scent, the honeyed taste. I was rewarded in turn by her blissful sighs, her clutching hands, her hips rising to meet my tongue. She was so responsive, I almost thought she'd been lying before when she said she was shy in bed. Then I decided she'd been telling the truth and it was me bringing this out in her.

The thought of it made my cock surge with need.

But she had to come first.

I performed every trick I knew, dazzling her with acrobatic feats of the tongue, astonishing her with nimble and dexterous twists of my fingers until she was bucking wildly beneath my mouth, her clit pulsing against my tongue, her body contracting around my fingers inside her. She let loose with all my favorite one-syllable words and even some multi-syllabic praise—*don't stop, yes, right there, oh God, you're fucking amazing, you're making me come, this is crazy*—and then I heard the words I never thought I'd hear out of Bianca DeRossi's mouth.

"Enzo," she rasped. "I want you to fuck me. Now."

Although I was dying to get inside her, I took my time, torturing her as I moved slowly up her body, kissing her as if I wanted to make sure my lips had been on every inch of her skin. Finally, she got impatient enough to reach beneath my arms and try to yank me up.

I laughed. "You're awfully impatient, Mrs. Moretti. I'm still working my way through the script. I think now is when I tell you—"

But then I struggled to speak, because she reached down and put her hands on my cock—both of them. She worked one up and down my shaft and used the other to tease the crown. It had been so long since someone had touched me that way, I was momentarily paralyzed by how good it felt.

And then—*and then*—she scooted down between my legs so that I was kneeling over her face. While I stared down at her in utter disbelief, she angled my dick toward her mouth and ran her tongue around the tip. I fell forward, bracing myself with two hands on the headboard. Thank *fuck* I'd turned on that lamp.

"I didn't know this was part of the show," I managed.

"I'm improvising." Her breath was warm on my skin, and my entire body shuddered with pleasure, with anticipation, with surprise.

Beyond stunned, I continued to watch as she licked around the crown, sucked on just the tip, ran her tongue up and down my length. My breathing grew heavy and fast as I battled for control, fighting the compulsion to shove my dick between those ruby-red lips I'd been obsessing over all day. All week. All month. Fuck it, ever since she'd moved back here and started messing with my head.

But soon she made it happen on her own, lifting her head to take my cock into her mouth, using her hands on my ass to pull me closer, take me deeper. I groaned from deep in my throat, agonizing over how good it felt, how hot it looked, how desperately I wanted to let go and fuck her mouth with total abandon.

Unable to stop myself, my hips began to rock slowly above her, my stomach muscles flexing. She flattened her palms on my hip bones and slid them up over my abs, moaning with pleasure. It was too much—her pale hands with those red nails, her lips wrapped around my cock, her tongue gliding against my thick, hard length. Even the ring I'd put on her finger turned me on.

She was mine.

Mine.

Mine.

My grip on control slipped away. My desire outpaced my manners. My hips moved faster, harder, my cock hitting the back of her throat. Bianca's noises grew more helpless and panicked, but she didn't push me away. Her eyes closed for a moment, and I watched her struggle to breathe, and it shouldn't have turned me on the way it did. I felt like a god and a monster at the same time. When she opened them again and looked up at me, I nearly exploded.

But if this was a one-time-only exception to our deal, I wasn't about to let it end this way. Pulling out of her mouth, I grabbed her and yanked her up again.

"You didn't let me finish," she said, wiping her mouth with the back of her hand.

"Because that's not how this ends." I slipped my fingers inside her again, finding her warm and wet. "Should I wear a condom?"

"Do you want to?"

I hesitated. Probably no guy ever really *wanted* to, but I was not into being reckless where sex was concerned. I always, always wore protection.

But tonight felt different.

"No," I said.

"Then don't." Those wet, red lips curved up. "If I got pregnant, it would save us time and money."

"I'm definitely into saving time and money," I told her, replacing my fingers with my cock. "But mostly I just want to know what it feels like to be inside you."

Her eyes closed again as I moved with long, slow strokes, each one deeper than the last. I couldn't believe how good it felt to be bare inside her and said a quick prayer I'd be able to last until she had at least one more orgasm.

"I want to make you come again," I whispered, my voice gravelly with need. "Talk to me."

"You're perfect," she said, her face buried in my neck. Her hands moved down over my ass. Her breathing was hushed and quick. "Don't stop. I love the way you move. I love how deep you are. I don't have words for what it's doing to me."

Gratified, I kept the rhythm steady and my body tight against hers. Despite the difference in our height, we fit together perfectly, and I loved the way she moved beneath me, like she wanted this as much as I did. Her fingers dug into my skin. Her teeth on my shoulder. Her breath on my skin. Her hips bucking. Her voice growing louder and more high-pitched. My name on her lips. Her skin sweaty and slick against mine. Friction. Tension. Need. Heat.

Then she was crying out, her body racked by convulsions that sent me spiraling over the edge, an animalistic groan erupting from my chest as I emptied myself into her in wave after wave of pulsing, throbbing bliss. It was so intense, I started to panic.

I can't breathe, I thought. *We burned up all the oxygen in the room. I can't breathe.*

Picking myself up off her, I gulped for air.

"Are you okay?" she asked breathlessly, placing her hands on my chest.

I nodded, but when I looked down at her, my heart felt like it might explode. Her face was familiar, but her expression was new—softer. Sweeter. More vulnerable. Like the show was over and now it was just us behind the curtain. No more acting.

The compressed sensation in my chest grew worse, like someone had wrapped a fist around my heart and was squeezing it like a lemon.

Bianca frowned. "Your heart is beating really fast. If you go into cardiac arrest and die, do I get the house?"

The pressure eased up, and I managed to laugh. "Trying to kill me?"

"Of course not. We haven't even gotten to phase two yet."

"Right." I dragged myself off her and flipped onto my back.

"I'll be right back," she said, putting her glasses on and heading into the bathroom.

While she was gone, I closed my eyes and concentrated on inhaling and exhaling in steady, even breaths. But it was difficult, because every time I thought about what had just happened, my heart tried to jump out of my chest again. What the hell? Why did sex with Bianca have to be that good? My idea had been to impress her so much that she'd be tortured by the memory and no one would ever live up, but now I feared the person who'd be tortured was me. What woman was ever going to surprise me that way again? Who could make me laugh one minute and growl at her the next? Was it because I'd spent so many years being mad at her that the sex was so hot? Was it really never going to happen again? But I had *ideas—so many ideas*—about things I wanted to do to her.

I frowned. Fucking Bianca was supposed to satisfy an urge, not create a bigger one.

The bathroom door opened and she came out. After setting her glasses on the nightstand again, she hopped back onto the bed. A few fake rose petals flew off.

"What's with the grumpy face?" she asked, stretching out on her side.

On my back, I put one arm behind my head and looked over at her. "I'm mad."

"About what?"

"That the sex was so good."

Her eyes lit up, and she reached over and slapped my chest. "Oh my God, same. I was just in the bathroom cleaning up and thinking how pissed I am at you."

"At me!"

"Yes. How dare you have the magic-wand dick!"

I had to laugh. "As much as I would like to agree, there was no magic involved, Bianca. You told me what you wanted."

She rolled her eyes. "I said like three things."

"They were enough." I hesitated. "I also think we just had some good chemistry. And there was a lot of . . . tension built up."

She sighed. "Yeah. That was the best sex I've ever had. But I shouldn't tell you that—you'll get smug."

"I was already smug from the magic-wand dick thing."

She narrowed her eyes at me. "No more compliments for you tonight."

"Hey, I earned them. Didn't I do a good job with my lines?"

"Yes," she admitted. "A-plus work going off book."

"Speaking of A-plus work . . ." I paused reverently.

"What?"

"That blowjob."

She grinned. "You liked it?"

"Um, yeah."

"Good." She fell onto her back and put her hands behind her head, closing her eyes.

"Now who's smug?" I teased, rolling to my side next to her.

Her eyes closed, but her smile remained. I couldn't resist tracing her lips with my fingers. She started to laugh. "What are you doing?"

"I don't know. I just like your mouth."

"I bet you do. I let you put your dick in it."

"Hey, I liked it before that." I nudged her side. "I just never said anything about it."

She opened her eyes and looked at me. "Why not?"

"I don't know. Things just aren't like that with us. We trade insults, not sweet nothings."

"True." She sighed and closed her eyes again.

Unable to resist, I moved my hand to the far side of her hip and pulled her closer to me. "So that whole exceptions clause thing. When exactly does that expire?"

"I don't know. Midnight?"

I glanced at the digital clock on her nightstand. "Guess what? It's only eleven-thirty-five."

She looked at me in surprise. "You want to do it again?"

"Why not?"

"I don't know. Because we already satisfied our curiosity."

I shook my head. "Sorry, but my curiosity is not nearly satisfied."

"No?"

"No." Taking her by the waist, I hauled her on top of me so she straddled my hips. "For instance, I'm very curious about what you look like as a reverse cowgirl."

The smile that crept onto her lips sent a bolt of lust shooting straight to my cock. "Saddle up, Ricky. Yeehaw."

"If you could have a superpower, what would it be?" Bianca looked at me expectantly from across the tub. After a vigorous bout of rodeo sex, we were both sweaty enough to warrant rinsing off, and she'd talked me into a bath. We were sitting back against opposite ends, bubbles up to our chests.

"Easy," I said. "I'd want to read minds."

"Oh my God, that's the *last* thing I'd want."

"Why? It would make you so powerful. You'd be able to outsmart any opponent, win every argument, know every pitch that was coming at you before you had to take a swing."

She shook her head. "Life is not a baseball game, and some thoughts are meant to be private."

"Okay, so what superpower would you want?"

"Time travel," she said. "So I could go back and undo a bunch of stupid mistakes."

I studied her dripping hair, which was much darker when it was wet—almost burgundy. It made her skin look even more radiant. I liked her face without makeup too. And the fact that she was wearing diamonds in the bathtub. "Like bringing a book to that high school dance?"

She shook her head. "No. I stand by that decision."

Laughing, I reached for her, tugging her toward me. "Come here, selfish, I have to stretch my legs and you're taking up all the room at that end of the tub." Really, it was just an excuse to feel her skin on mine, but she didn't have to know that.

She floated over to me and lay with her stomach above mine, her hands on my chest. Beneath her hips, my cock stirred. I knew she felt it from the way she looked up at me. Expecting a joke, I was surprised when she didn't make one. In fact, the look in her eye—maybe I couldn't read minds, but I was getting pretty good at reading her—was practically an invitation.

"So," I said, sliding my hands down her back, over her ass. "It's definitely after midnight."

"It is."

I pulled her tighter against me. "I vote we extend the clause until sunrise."

"I second that vote."

"Then I believe it is unanimous, Mrs. Moretti."

She smiled, her eyes going wide, and whispered, "That is so fucking weird."

"I know. Are you actually going to change your name?"

"I guess. It might look suspicious if I don't."

"I think you should." I really did, and it wasn't just for appearances. There was something I honestly liked about the idea, although it would have been more fun if she'd hated it.

But she was being uncharacteristically agreeable right now. It was fucking with me.

She drew up her knees on either side of my hips and traced my collarbone with one fingertip, then played with the hair on my chest. "You know, all things considered, this has been a pretty good wedding night."

I grinned. "Oh yeah? Did I say all the right things?"

"I think so."

"You *think* so? Give me something else. I'll work it in."

She tipped her head to one side and pursed her lips. "Hmm. Give me a line from *Romeo and Juliet*. Not the one about dying, please."

"Okay. Let me think." I racked my brain, trying to recall a line she would find more romantic. I had a good memory, but it had been fifteen fucking years. "I've got it," I told her.

"I'm listening."

"O my love, I've been really trying. Trying to hold back this feeling for so long. And if, perchance, you feel like I feel, then come on."

"Enzo!" She splashed me again, her expression outraged. "That is not Shakespeare, that is *Marvin Gaye*!"

"But I changed it up a little," I said defensively. "Made it sound fancy and shit."

"You're the worst." She put her hands in my hair and pressed her lips to mine, her tongue slipping between them. "But you make me laugh."

"I'm about to make you do more than that," I said, reaching between us to touch her again.

She smiled against my mouth. "Let's get it on."

The sun peeked through the drapes the next morning, waking me up.

For a second, I forgot where I was, but as soon as I took a breath, I could smell Bianca's perfume. I glanced over at her side of the bed, disappointed to find it empty, and then gradually became aware of the shower running in the bathroom. I checked the digital clock on the nightstand—it was just after nine.

Absently, I ran a hand over the rumpled sheets where she'd slept. We'd both fallen asleep fairly quickly after round four, probably around three in the morning. I couldn't remember the last time I'd had so much sex in one night. Maybe never. But I hadn't been able to stop wanting her.

I'd had a hunch Bianca would be a firecracker in bed, and she was. Feisty, playful, attentive, generous. Even during sex, she liked to bite and tease and scrap, which was fine with me because the struggle only turned me on. And in the end she would always submit to me—why wouldn't she, when it would result in an orgasm that, in her own words, "made the earth quake?"

My dick began to perk up, and I frowned, flopping onto my back again. This was pointless. The sun was up, the clause was expired, and the contract was back in place. What the hell was I doing anyway, caressing the sheets like a lovestruck idiot? I didn't love her like that. I didn't love anyone like that, and I didn't want to. Love was confusing and messy and unpredictable. I wouldn't build a house on a foundation of quicksand, would I?

Bianca came out of the bathroom, one towel wrapped around her body, another wrapped turban-style on her head. Her glasses were slightly foggy. "You're up," she said.

"I'm up." Since I wasn't sure where we stood, I quickly tried to adjust the sheet so my morning wood wasn't obvious.

Too late.

"You're *really* up," she said, giggling at the tent my erection was creating.

"I always wake up this way," I said defensively, because I didn't want her to know thinking about her had me so hard.

"Don't worry, I'm not going to ask to play with your magic wand again," she said, going over to her suitcase and kneeling down.

Okay. So we were back where we'd begun. Fine with me, although I felt anything but fine about it. I felt angry and resentful.

But I wouldn't show it.

"Good," I said, carefully getting out of bed and taking the sheet with me. Wrapping myself up in it like a toga, I headed for the bathroom, trying not to notice the way her ass peeked out from below the towel.

Bianca rose to her feet with clothes in her arms, a smile on her lips. "You don't have to hide, Enzo. I've already seen what's under the sheet."

"I'm not hiding. I'm covering up. For *your* sake," I added.

Her eyebrows shot up. "*My* sake?"

"Yes. I wouldn't want you to get excited about something you can't have. It would be like putting your favorite dessert on the menu but saying you can't order it."

She snorted. "I think I'll be okay. I had enough dessert last night to last me a while."

"You're *welcome,*" I said, making a little bow before going into the bathroom.

Once inside, I had to stop and take a deep breath.

Getting through phase two with my dignity—and sanity—intact might be harder than I thought.

Ten

Bianca

As soon as the bathroom door shut, I sat down on the bed and exhaled.

Ever since I'd woken up and looked over at him asleep next to me, I'd been pretending.

Pretending he didn't make my heart pound faster. Pretending last night hadn't been the best night of my life—the hottest, the most romantic, the most fun. Pretending I could just go back to the way things were before.

But what choice did I have? It was what we'd agreed on. It was the deal we'd made. And I didn't want to be one of those women who confuses sex with love—he'd already warned me about that. He didn't like it when a woman said one thing and did another, or when she changed her mind about what she wanted from him.

But I hadn't, had I? Not *really*. It wasn't like I was in *love* with him, I thought, admiring him as he slept—all gorgeous and naked and sexy and tousled. I had a feeling if I moved closer to him, his skin would be warm. Would he let me snuggle up? Would he open his arms and wrap them around me? Would he hold me or push me away?

I couldn't risk the rejection. I just couldn't.

So instead of getting closer like I wanted to, I got out of bed and took a shower, scrubbing my skin raw, as if I could rub the memory of him off me. Wash away my feelings. Rid myself of the stupid idea that we could be something real.

When I came out of the bathroom, I'd forced myself to act the way I assumed he wanted me to—as if last night hadn't meant anything more than a good time. I smiled. I teased him. I laughed when he teased me back—and I laughed for real at the sight of him in that sheet, edging toward the bathroom, trying to hide his erection, which poked at the sheet like a sword.

He had no idea how badly I'd wanted to tear that sheet off him, toss my towel to the floor, and jump right back into bed.

But no. He couldn't know how I felt. How I was starting to care more deeply for him than I should. How I regretted insisting on the no-sex rule. How badly I wished that even just *one thing* he'd said to me last night had been real.

How scared I was that last night meant nothing to him.

No, that was stupid. I didn't need to be scared. I *knew* it meant nothing. I was just acting crazy—maybe it was all the hormones in my system. Orgasms released something that made you feel woozy and cuddly, right? After all the orgasms Enzo had delivered last night, my system was clearly on overload.

I just needed to wait for the hormones to dissipate, that was all. Remember my lines and keep up the act. Putting a hand over my stomach, I took a deep breath and let it out. I could do this.

Then I looked down at my ring.

Really, at this point in the game, I had no choice.

By the time Enzo came out of the bathroom, dripping wet with a towel slung low around his hips, I was fully dressed, sitting on the bed running a brush through my hair.

My insides tightened as he walked by me. "Did you take care of your problem?"

"I didn't have a problem, Bianca. I had a hard-on. It went away."

"All by itself?" I teased. Meanwhile, I squeezed my thighs together, trying to suppress the flutter between my legs.

"Yes," he snapped. With his back to me, he threw the towel to the floor and pulled a pair of boxer briefs from his bag.

I watched him step into them and pull them up, desire pooling at my center. God, he had a great ass. And were those red marks on his back from me? Gah, that was hot.

I tried to make my voice sound normal. "Are you hungry? I thought we could go down to breakfast in the dining room here before we check out. I'm assuming we don't want breakfast in bed."

"I'm good with the dining room." He stepped into a pair of jeans and hitched them up. "Unless you want to hang out in here and stare at my butt all day."

That's when I realized he could see me staring at his ass in the mirror. My face went red. "I wasn't staring at your butt!"

He grinned. "No?"

"No." Flustered, I stood up. "I just . . . *noticed* it, that's all. It was right at my eye level. But from now on, if you wouldn't mind not walking around naked, I would appreciate it. Despite what happened last night, this is still a business arrangement. I don't want us to blur the lines and get confused."

"Ten minutes ago you said I didn't have to hide behind a sheet because you'd already seen me naked." He put on deodorant, obviously amused.

It had been a long time since I'd watched a man get dressed—I'd forgotten how it could be just as intimate as watching him get undressed. I couldn't take my eyes off him. "I just want us to be clear that the rules are back in place."

"Don't worry. We'll have our own bedrooms at my house,

so my naked ass will not confuse you." He tossed his deodorant back in the bag and pulled a white T-shirt over his head.

"Are we still moving me in today?" I asked, watching his abs disappear beneath the cotton in the mirror, more than a little sad to see them go.

"Works for me."

"Good. I'm all packed up. Might take us a few trips, but everything is in boxes ready to go." I watched him tug a blue sweater over his head and realized I was still standing there gawking, so I turned and went for the bathroom. "I'll just blow dry my hair and then we can go eat."

In the bathroom, I shut the door, turned the blow dryer on cool, and aimed it at my face.

"So what are the chances that we actually, you know, did the thing last night?" Enzo took a bite of his omelette and looked at me curiously.

"That we actually what?" I asked, buttering a piece of toast.

"Saved time and money. Completed phase two."

I lowered my voice to a whisper. "Oh—you mean, what are the chances I got pregnant?"

"Yeah."

I took a bite of toast and shrugged. "I have no clue. Like I said yesterday, I don't ovulate normally. So I'm never sure what my fertile days are. But if I had to guess, I'd say slim to none."

"I don't really get that whole 'fertile days' stuff. So you can't just get pregnant any time? You have to wait for certain days?"

"I mean, I think it's technically *possible* to get pregnant at any time, but it's unlikely. Especially for me."

His expression was dubious, like he didn't believe me. "But we did it like *four times* last night. I feel like I hit the target at least once."

I laughed, reaching for my coffee. "This isn't like throwing darts, Enzo. It's not dependent on your skill level, impressive as it may be."

"You were impressed with my skill level, huh?"

"Maybe," I said coyly. "Certainly your stamina. Your enthusiasm. And the, um, size of your equipment. I definitely stand corrected on that count."

His smile was one of total self-satisfaction. "Thank you. I work well under a deadline."

I tilted my head, squinting at him. "So you're saying it was work?"

"Okay, I perform well under pressure. Is that better?"

"Marginally."

"Look, I was racing against the clock, that's all I meant. I kept thinking you were going to say time's up, clause is null and void, contract is back in place. I had to try to get my fill of you before you closed up shop."

"And did you?"

"Get my fill of you?" His eyes held mine, flickering with mischief. "Honestly, no."

My stomach flipped. I set my coffee cup down, and it rattled on the saucer. "What are you saying?"

"I'm not saying anything. I was answering your question."

Our eyes were still locked when our server, Shelly, appeared. "And how are my newlyweds?" she asked, refilling our coffee cups.

"Good," Enzo said.

I still couldn't speak.

"So are you heading off on a honeymoon?" Shelly smiled wistfully at us. "Somewhere warm and sunny?"

"No, Shelly, we are not." Enzo turned on the charm, reaching across the table to take my hand. "Believe it or not, I offered to take my beautiful bride anywhere she wanted to go, anywhere in the world, and you know what she said?"

"What?" Shelly was rapt.

Enzo looked at me and smiled disarmingly. "She said she didn't need fancy trips to exotic locales. Just being married to me was a vacation in itself."

"Oh." Shelly clucked her tongue and put a hand over her heart, looking at me like she was about to cry. "Is that really what you said?"

"It's close," I said, faking a smile as I stepped on Enzo's foot beneath the table.

Shelly sighed. "That's so romantic."

"Isn't it?" Enzo kissed the back of my hand. "What do you say, dumpling, should we finish up and get going?"

I glared at him. "Sure."

"Would you like to put this on your room charge?" Shelly asked.

"Yes, please." Enzo gave her one final smile. "Thanks."

When we were alone again, I took my hand from Enzo. "What was that all about?"

He shrugged. "Just keeping up the act. I thought hand-kissing was allowed."

"No, not that. The thing you said. About . . . about not getting your fill of me last night."

"Oh, that." Enzo picked up his coffee and took a sip.

"Yes, *that*. What did you mean?" My heart was racing.

"Exactly what I said. I didn't get enough. If you were anyone else, and this was any other situation, we wouldn't be down here eating breakfast right now. We'd still be upstairs bouncing fake rose petals off the bed." He set his cup down. "But rules are rules, and I understand why we have to put them back in place."

"You do?"

"Sure. It's like you said before, when my naked ass confused you, this is still a business arrangement. We don't want to blur the lines." He cocked his head to one side. "Right?"

"Right." I picked up my coffee cup and took a sip. "That's what I said."

After breakfast, we checked out of the inn and headed over to my condo. On the way, Enzo called Griffin to see if we might be able to borrow his truck. Griffin said it wouldn't be a problem and even offered to help with the move. He said he'd come over to my place around one o'clock, after he finished up a few jobs at the Bellamy Creek Garage, which he owned and ran as head mechanic. It was housed in an old fire station, and he and Blair lived in an apartment above it.

In the meantime, Enzo and I transported smaller loads in the back of my car and his SUV, then rode back to the condo together, leaving my BMW in his garage. We got in one more run over to Enzo's house before Blair and Griffin showed up together. Blair had brought sandwiches from the bakery, and we took a quick lunch break before loading up the back of the truck with the rest of the boxes.

Over at Enzo's house, everyone helped to carry my stuff inside. More than half the boxes went upstairs to the guest room Enzo had set aside for me, which was spacious and beautifully decorated. It held a queen-sized bed with a headboard upholstered in charcoal gray suede, a dresser painted black with a silver-framed mirror above it, and a black nightstand. The walls were painted a soft shade of pewter, and the white bedding looked surprisingly plush. There was even a vase of white roses on the dresser.

The sight of those roses made my pulse race—it was the kind of sweet, thoughtful gesture I was learning Enzo liked to perform. But that was just it—it was a performance.

I looked away from them.

Right across the hall, I had my own bathroom, sparkling clean, and stocked with fluffy white towels. He'd even purchased my favorite shampoo and conditioner, which he must have seen in my condo bathroom at some point.

Damn him. Why did he have to turn out to be so thoughtful? So generous? So good in bed?

It was *just like him* to aggravate me this way.

I mean, which was the real him, the cocky bastard who made me say all that bullshit during our vows or the nice guy who brought me flowers?

Blair came upstairs with me, ostensibly to help me unpack, but mostly she just wanted the scoop.

"So? How was the wedding night?" She sank down on the bed and wiggled her eyebrows at me.

The guys were downstairs, way out of earshot, but I still went over and shut my bedroom door. "It was good."

"Elaborate please. Were there shenanigans?"

I opened one box and began to put socks, bras, and underwear into drawers. "There may have been a shenanigan or two."

Behind me, Blair squealed. "I knew it!"

I spun around to see her on her back, kicking her feet in the air. "What do you mean?"

She sat up again. "After seeing you guys together at the reception, I bet Griffin fifty bucks you guys wouldn't be able to stay in the same hotel room without messing around."

"Seriously?" I laughed.

"Yes, except it was so obviously true that Griff wouldn't even take the bet."

"How was it obvious?"

"It just was. There's something between you guys that just, like, sizzles."

Leaning back against the dresser, I shook my head. "I'm not even sure how it happened. One minute we were arguing, as usual, and the next I was taking off my pants."

She giggled. "Sounds about right. So was it good?"

"It was amazing," I admitted. "The man knows what he's doing. And he's not selfish at all, like I thought he would be. He's patient and generous and highly, highly skilled."

"Wow. So was it kind of like hate sex?"

I thought about it. "No. We laughed a lot. It was really fun. Then after the first time, we both said how mad we were that it had been so good."

"Why would that make you mad?"

"Because we weren't allowed to do it again. But we did." I felt heat in my cheeks. "Three more times."

Her jaw dropped. "Even Griffin and I only managed to do it once on our wedding night."

"That's different. You guys had done it before, and you knew you'd have all your lives to do it again—as many times as you want to. Enzo and I just had the one night."

She looked confused. "I don't understand. You're married. Why would you only have the one night?"

"Because sex isn't part of our arrangement." I turned around and started filling drawers with clothes again. "We agreed on that. We just sort of gave ourselves a wedding-night free-for-all. Now it's back to the rules."

She let that sink in. "So are you saying you'd turn him away if he knocked on your door tonight?"

"He's not going to knock on my door." But at the thought of it, my entire body warmed.

"But if he did," she pushed. "What would you do?"

"Hmmm. Is he wearing clothes?"

"Let's say he's shirtless."

"Damn. Is his hair doing that thing in the front?"

"Definitely. And he smells good. Like, really good."

"Ugh, that's so annoying." I sighed. "Ideally, I like to think I'd be strong enough to be the first female in his life to resist him." Turning around, I faced her. "Realistically, though, I'd probably think about it for two seconds, then jump his bones."

She cackled with glee. "I knew it."

Blair and Griffin stayed for dinner, and I cooked my first meal in Enzo's kitchen—Italian wedding soup and bruschetta on toasted sourdough. Enzo volunteered to go to the grocery store for ingredients, so after checking his pantry and fridge, I sent him on his way with a list. Griffin tagged along, and Blair helped me unpack the rest of my things and then reorganize Enzo's kitchen. He probably wouldn't be able to find anything easily for a while, but my system made a lot more sense for a cook. He actually had a beautiful kitchen, with high-end appliances, gorgeous finishes, and pricey copper cookware. I loved cooking in it.

After Griffin and Blair left for home, Enzo and I finished the dishes and cleaned up the kitchen. When the sink was empty and the counters gleamed, I felt like a cup of tea. My nerves were a little frayed, and I didn't think more alcohol was a good idea. The closer we got to bedtime, the more anxious I became. Was Blair right? Would he knock on my door?

I took a plain white mug down from the cupboard and found a box of herbal tea I'd brought from my condo in the pantry. "Want some?" I asked Enzo, who stood at the island looking at his phone.

He glanced up. "No thanks." Then he returned his attention to the screen and frowned.

"What's wrong?" I used the insta hot to fill the cup.

"My mother wants us to come for Sunday dinner tomorrow after church."

"Okay." I paused. "Is that a problem?"

He met my eyes. "Father Mike is coming. I think she's going to push us again about having the marriage blessed."

"Oh." I bobbed the teabag in the hot water. "I still feel weird about that. Since this isn't a real marriage."

"Same." He set his phone aside and rubbed his face with both hands. He hadn't shaved today, and his stubble was dark and thicker than usual. "I'll think of some way to put her off. Want to watch a movie or something?"

"Sure."

I took my tea over to the smaller of the two couches and sat at one end, my legs stretched out across the cushions. After grabbing a beer from the fridge, Enzo joined me, settling on the opposite end of the same couch, even though there was another one—a bigger one—adjacent to it with just as good a view of the large TV screen. Neither of us reached for the remote to turn it on. Enzo seemed distracted as he took a sip of his beer.

"Everything okay?" I asked, wrapping both hands around my warm mug.

"Yeah. Just thinking."

"About the priest?"

"About my parents, actually."

"What about them?"

He rubbed that spot beneath his bottom lip he always rubbed when he was fretting about something. "Their relationship is a big reason why I've never really looked forward to marriage."

I took a sip of tea. "Tell me."

"Basically, here's what I grew up thinking about being married to someone—it's noisy, frustrating, and sometimes destructive. There's a lot of yelling, and the things you yell loudest are the things you know will piss the other person off the most. You never let something go that might be used to pick a fight. And if you're not getting your point across with volume, just slam a door, throw some dishes, or threaten to leave."

"Wow." My eyes were wide. "I had no idea your parents fought so much."

"They don't do it in public. And maybe it's not as bad as it used to be, but growing up, it was bad enough that I could not imagine why anyone would choose to get married if they didn't have to. It's like you're handing another person instructions on exactly how to make your life a living hell, a map detailing where all of your buttons are and how to push them."

"Well, they must have had *some* good times. They're still together."

"Yeah. They're good at two things. Fighting and sex."

I couldn't resist poking him with my bare toes. "Sounds like another married couple I know."

He laughed, lifting his beer again. "Please. We are *not* my parents."

"No, we're not. And we're not my parents, either." I was quiet a second, taking another sip of tea. "My mother is completely subservient to my dad. She's never stood up to him a day in her life, even when I know she disagrees. It always drove me nuts. And I think . . ." I hesitated before admitting this. "I think that's why I get so mad about my last relationship. I ended up going along with what he wanted for way too long, just to hang on to him. Not that my father ever betrayed my mother—that I know of—but I never wanted to be that way. Timid and deferential."

He gave me the side-eye. "Princess, you did not inherit a single subservient or deferential gene."

I poked him with my foot again, and he grabbed it. Then he looked at me. "Why are your feet so cold?"

"Sorry." I pulled up my knees. "My socks got wet earlier, and I meant to go put on a new pair and forgot."

He got up and grabbed a throw blanket off the back of the longer couch, brought it over and covered my legs with it—not only that but when he sat down again, he lifted my feet onto his lap and rubbed them with one hand while he kept talking. "I guess my point was that I'm glad we're doing things our way. I was always afraid of turning into them. It didn't seem like a nice way to live."

"Same," I said, my insides warming right along with my toes. "Our marriage might be a sham, but at least it's not dysfunctional."

"Right." His hand stilled on my feet, and he looked down at it. Then slowly, he slid it up my shin.

I held my breath.

But a moment later, he cleared his throat and reached for the remote control. "What should we watch?"

We decided on a few episodes of *Schitt's Creek,* which made us both laugh and eased the tension in the room. But it ratcheted up again when we turned off the TV and headed to bed, Enzo following me up the darkened stairs.

I held my breath, hoping to feel his arms come around me. Feel his body warm and solid behind me, holding me close. Hear his voice whisper my name, tell me he didn't want to sleep alone.

When it didn't happen by the time I reached the second floor landing, I turned left, heading straight for my bedroom.

"Night," he called softly.

"Night," I said without turning to look at him. Inside the room, I leaned back against the closed door and listened. When I heard his bedroom door shut, I exhaled.

Guess he wasn't going to test me tonight.

I should have been glad about it.

Eleven

Enzo

I got ready for bed and angrily tossed the covers back. After sliding between the sheets, I jerked them up to my waist and scowled at the ceiling in the dark.

I wanted her. I fucking wanted her, and she was right there on the other side of the wall. This was ridiculous.

What was she thinking? How would she react if I knocked on her door?

But what reason would I have for doing it? The rules were back in place, and it was no longer our wedding night. There was no pretense under which I could safely hide. If I went to her room, she would either think I was a pig who just wanted sex, or she'd suspect I had feelings for her.

I wasn't sure which was worse.

If only I could think of a valid *reason* to violate the terms of the contract again, it would be okay. Turning onto my stomach, I punched my pillow a few times before burying my face in it. The moment my eyes closed, she was there—unbuttoning her pajama top, daring me to touch her. Slipping down between my thighs, taking my dick in her mouth. Putting her hands on my ass, pulling me deeper, my bare cock buried inside her. I groaned into my pillow, remembering how good it had felt.

And it hit me—the reason we should do it again. It was fucking genius!

I was up and out of bed in a heartbeat, moving down the darkened hall, knocking on her door.

"Yes?" she called.

"Can I come in?"

"Okay."

As soon as I pushed the door open, she turned on the lamp on the nightstand. Then she sat up in bed.

"What is it?" she asked, eyeing my bare chest.

"I was just thinking."

"About what?"

"About saving time and money."

She blinked at me. "Huh?"

I went over and sat on the bed at her side. "Saving time and money on the inseminations, like you said. Instead of paying for just one shot each month, we could just keep trying at home for free, as often as we want." I put my hand on her leg, above the covers. "Since we've already done it and all."

"But . . ." Her gaze dropped to my hand. "What about the rules?"

"I've got it all figured out. What if we mutually agreed to *suspend* that particular rule in the interest of, uh, increasing our chances of success in phase two?" As I talked out of my ass, I slid my hand up her thigh. "I feel that phase two deserves a strong, proactive commitment and an innovative approach in order to . . . maximize opportunities for conception."

She laughed. "That's why you're in here right now? To maximize opportunities for conception?"

"Of course. What other reason would there be?"

"I don't know." She folded her arms across her chest. "You tell me."

We eyeballed each other.

It was clearly a standoff, and I didn't want to lose.

But I also didn't want to leave.

"Okay, *maybe* I can think of another reason," I hedged.

Her satisfied smile gave me the confidence to kiss her, but when I leaned forward to do it, she put two fingers over my lips. "First you have to tell me what it is."

I sat back, annoyed. "Look, I'm offering you my superior genetic material—which is why you married me, after all—for *free*, whenever you want it. What's the problem?"

She shook her head. "That's not how this is going to work."

I exhaled noisily. "*Fine*. I had a good time with you last night."

"And?"

"And I want to do it again."

"Because?"

"Because it felt good."

"Buuut"—she shrugged—"you could make yourself feel good all by yourself in your room. You don't need me for that."

"Fine." I scowled at her. "I enjoy making *you* feel good."

That smile appeared again. "Why? Do you like me?"

"Goddammit, Bianca," I seethed. "You're such a pain in the ass! I want you, okay? Is that what you want to hear? I knocked on your door tonight because I was lying in bed alone and I couldn't stop thinking about you. Now you can tell me to fuck off if you want to, but quit playing games! Do you want me or not?"

Instead of answering, she grabbed my head and crushed her lips to mine. "Yes, I want you," she whispered. "But I like playing games."

I slid beneath the covers, stretching out above her and claiming her mouth. "You drive me fucking crazy," I told her, pressing my cock between her legs and pinning her wrists to the mattress. "Like honest to God, you make me feel like I'm losing my mind."

Laughing, she buried her face in my neck and inhaled. "God, she was right. You *do* smell good."

"Huh?"

"Never mind. I have decided I like your proposed amendments to our earlier agreement," she said, wrapping her legs around me. "Also your sizable assets and your willingness to be flexible. Shall we just call the orgasms a value-added experience?"

I grinned down at her. "Now that's more like it."

I spent the entire night in her bed, and this time when we woke up the next morning, she was still wrapped in my arms. Rain drummed softly on the roof. I inhaled, taking in the scent of her hair, and rested my lips briefly on the top of her head.

I liked her like this. Warm. Sweet. Soft. Not talking.

The thought made me chuckle, and she stirred. But she stayed where she was, her cheek on my chest, one arm and leg draped across me. In the past, I'd have found being clung to like that suffocating. And I'd have made my exit from bed long before sunrise. This morning, with Bianca, I was already thinking about being inside her again.

Talk about witchcraft.

"Think we're expected at church?" she asked, her voice sleepy.

"Probably. And then at my parents' for dinner."

She sighed. "Oh yeah."

I stroked her back, trailing my finger down each vertebra. "I suppose we could skip out. I don't think anyone would begrudge us a little honeymoon weekend."

"But the priest is coming for dinner."

"All the more reason to absent ourselves. My mother will probably try to make him bless us right over the chicken parm."

"Good point. Let's play hooky."

"What should we do instead? What does your perfect Sunday look like?"

"Hmm." Her hand wandered down my abdomen. "This is a pretty good start."

"I agree."

"And then there would be food. Waffles or something. Then I'd probably curl up on the couch with a book and a blanket and some coffee." She looked up at me. "Am I boring?"

"Yes."

She smiled. "What would *you* do with a rainy Sunday?"

"Honestly, I'd probably get under the blanket and try to take your pants off."

"Aren't you tired of getting my pants off yet?"

"Is that a real question?"

"Yes."

I flipped her onto her back and set my hips on hers, my erection caught between us. "Does it feel that way to you?"

She poked my chest. "You said yesterday at the inn you were always hard in the morning. You said *specifically* it wasn't about me."

"That was a lie. It was definitely about you." I kissed her jaw, her neck and her collarbone, then picked up my head again. "Did *you* tell any lies at the inn?"

"Hmm." She thought for a moment. "Yes. I lied when I said I wasn't staring at your butt. I was definitely staring."

"I definitely saw that."

"I couldn't help it." She grabbed my butt with both hands. "You've got a great ass."

"The feeling is mutual," I said. "In fact, I once had this dream where I was chasing you through the house and you were only wearing an apron."

She giggled. "Did you catch me?"

"Uh huh."

"What happened next?"

"I don't know. I woke up and had to jerk off."

She grinned. "Next time we'll give it a better ending."

We eventually made it downstairs, and I made waffles for her. She watched me from her perch on the island, wearing an old Detroit Tigers sweatshirt of mine that was gigantic on her and a pair of tiny little shorts beneath it I couldn't even see. Her hair was a mess—she'd put it up in a ponytail on top of her head but half of it had escaped and hung around her face.

"What the hell?" I complained, opening drawer after drawer. "I can't find anything. Where is the rubber spatula?"

She laughed and pointed. "Try the drawer to your left there. I had to rearrange some things yesterday."

I gave her a look. "You *had* to?"

"I wanted to. Your system made no sense."

"It made sense to *me*," I grumbled, but I found the spatula in the drawer she'd indicated.

She hopped off the island and wrapped her arms around me from behind. It felt ridiculously good. "Sorry. Want me to draw you a map of where everything is?"

"Never mind. I'll figure it out." I watched her refill her coffee cup, admiring her bare legs. "You know, I don't think I've ever made breakfast for someone in my kitchen before."

"No?" She leaned back against the counter, her hands wrapped around her cup.

"Not like this. I've never been big on sleepovers, especially at my house."

"I'm *shocked*."

I stirred my waffle batter. "Be nice, or I won't say the cute thing I was about to say."

She laughed. "What's the cute thing?"

"That I am genuinely enjoying having you here." I looked over at her. "Brace yourself—I think I like you."

"Ewwww." She made a face like she was disgusted.

"I know, right?"

"I suppose it could be an okay thing." She lifted her coffee to her twitching lips. "Since we're married and all."

I glanced at the wedding band on my finger. It was still kind of a shock to see it there—but I didn't hate it. In fact, I thought it was sort of cool.

"Hey, do you think we should adjust our written contract to reflect the eighty-sixing of the no-sex rule?" Bianca asked.

"Um, I'm not likely to forget sex is now on the menu. Are you?"

She laughed. "No. And you were right—the more times we try, the better our chances."

"I'm always right, babe, so get used to it." I paused to enjoy her eye roll. "And just to let you know, I was *really* focused on the task this morning."

"I thank you for your professional dedication, but do you have to call it a *task*?" Her nose wrinkled.

"Sorry. I'll call it target shooting—that's more like a hobby, right? Or a sport? An enjoyable leisure activity?" She stuck her tongue out at me, and I had to laugh. "You know, if anybody had told me a year ago I'd be married to Bianca DeRossi and trying to have a baby, I'd have asked him what he was smoking. But here we are."

"Here we are."

"And you know what else?" I checked the waffle iron to make sure it was hot. "Since we're friends now, I'm going to tell you a secret."

"Oooh!" Her eyes lit up. "Yes, tell me a secret."

"I thought I'd hate being married, but I kind of like it. It makes me want to do . . ." I pumped a fist in the air. "Drastic and manly things."

She burst out laughing. "Drastic and manly things? Like what?"

"Well, now that you laughed at me, I'm not going to tell you," I said haughtily, pouring some batter on the iron.

"No, come on. Tell me. I really want to hear this."

I shut the lid and faced her. "Okay. So ever since we said *I do,* sometimes when I look at you, I get this caveman instinct to throw you over my shoulder and growl at any asshole who tries to get close. I know it sounds possessive and sexist and horrible, because you are not my property, but you *are* my wife." I shrugged. "And you can call me a pig, but I can't help it if being a husband brings out that side of me."

She grinned mischievously. "If I told you I kind of like it, are you going to beat your chest and make ape noises?"

"I might." I pretended to scratch my armpit like a monkey.

She shook her head like I was a hopeless case. "So, hitting the target . . . This is one of your drastic and manly things?"

"Yes." I couldn't help grabbing her waist, setting my hips against hers. "Which means my ego is involved now, and when that happens—look out."

"Then this is one time when I actually hope to make your ego even bigger." Then she looked at the ceiling. "God help me."

On Tuesday after work, I met up with Beckett at the pub for a couple beers. We texted Cole and Griffin to join us, but they were both busy—Cole had to take Mariah somewhere, and Griffin was making dinner for Blair.

"That's a new one," Beckett said as we waited for the bartender to pour. "I didn't even know Griff could cook."

"I think Blair might have taught him some things." I shook my head. "But I agree, he's definitely more domesticated than ever before."

"What about you?" he asked as two tall glasses of Bulldog Pale Ale were set in front of us. "How's married life?"

"It's good, actually."

"Yeah?" Beckett cocked a brow at me.

"Yeah." I shrugged and took a drink. "Turns out, I don't hate it as much as I thought I would."

He laughed. "Maybe because it's only been four days?"

"Maybe." I lifted my glass. "But it's probably because she gave up the no-sex rule."

"Wait a minute. There was a no-sex rule? How the hell were you guys going to have a baby without having sex?"

"Don't ask." I took a drink. "She wanted to make it all complicated and do an insemination at a fertility clinic, but I convinced her it would be much more convenient, less expensive, *and* more likely to work if we just went about it the old-fashioned way."

Beckett laughed and shook his head. "Genius."

"Right?"

"And you're going to split up after the baby is born?"

"Yes."

"That might be tough. Don't you think?"

"I think we'll be able to stay friends," I said, stretching my torso. I had a stitch in my side or something, or maybe I'd pulled a muscle at the gym this morning. "We're really getting along now."

"I meant on the kid."

"Oh." I glanced at Beckett. His mother had abandoned his family when he was really little—he'd been raised by his father and older sisters. He'd never talked about his mom growing up, and outwardly he'd been so damn successful—straight A's, Varsity athlete, Ivy League scholarship, MBA from Yale, high-stakes Wall Street career, which he'd willingly given up to come back and run his family's cattle ranch—that it was easy to forget he'd endured such a hardship. "I'm going to raise the baby with her," I assured him. "He or she will definitely have two involved parents."

"That's good." He took another drink of his beer.

"How's your dad?" I asked. Mr. Weaver had been showing signs of dementia for the last couple years, and each time Beckett talked about him, the stories got worse.

"Don't ask," he muttered.

"I'm sorry, man. Is it that bad?"

"It's pretty bad." Beckett drank again. "And over the winter I was around more to keep an eye on him, but pretty soon the days will get longer, and I'll be out of the house from sunup until sundown. He'll need constant supervision, whether he likes it or not—and he will not."

"I thought you hired someone."

"I've hired *three* people," Beckett said, pinching the bridge of his nose between his thumb and index finger. "He fires them all as soon as I leave the house. And even when I tell the caregivers he doesn't have the authority to do that, he's such an asshole, they want to quit. He just has no filter anymore. He told one she had a face for radio."

I laughed. "Sorry, I know it's not funny."

"He also thinks he's a Major League ball player now. He's always talking about having to get to his games."

"Well, that seems harmless enough."

"Not to me, it doesn't. I'm trying to keep him grounded in reality. And all he does is fight me, lie to me, or accuse me of stealing his things."

"What things?"

"Oh, you name it. His baseball uniform, his money, his car."

"Can I do anything to help?"

"Nah. I'll figure it out. I just have a lot to deal with right now." He was silent a moment. "You remember Maddie Blake?"

I grinned at him. "The one that got away?"

He frowned. "Fuck off, we were just friends."

"She was *always* at your house."

"Because she lived across the road and we had classes together. We did *homework* at my house, asshole."

"Fine, but you still wanted to bang her."

"Yeah, well, she had a jerk boyfriend."

A memory surfaced from our last year in high school. "Didn't you kick his ass at the prom afterparty?"

The color in Beckett's face darkened. "Yeah."

"Dude, that's the maddest I've ever seen you get. I thought for sure you were gonna knock that guy's teeth out."

"I should have." He shook his head. "He was such a dick to her. But he was so drunk, it wasn't even fair. She begged me not to bust up his face."

"I can't even remember what started it."

Beckett shrugged. "She asked me to drive her home because he was drinking so much. I was walking her out when he came after me."

"Oh yeah. Now I remember." I hadn't seen the start of the fight but everyone at the party had raced from the backyard bonfire to the driveway in front where Beckett was standing over the guy he'd just punched in the face and shoved to the ground. I remembered Maddie crying and pleading with Beckett to stop, recalled the guy's bloody nose, and the way Beckett's hands were clenched into fists as he screamed at the guy to *get the fuck up and say that one more time.*

Cole, always a peacemaker, had put himself between Beckett and the bleeding guy, but it had taken Griffin and I both to pull Beckett away and make sure he didn't kill anyone with his bare hands. It had been so shocking—despite his size and strength, Beckett was normally quiet, calm, and even-tempered. "That's the only time I ever saw you get in a fight."

"Wasn't much of a fight." Chest puffed up, Beckett took a drink of his beer.

"True. So you've kept in touch with Maddie?"

"For a while, when we first went away to college. Then her mom died, and out of nowhere, she dropped out of school and got married. I didn't hear from her for a while." He paused and took another sip. "But while I was living in Manhattan, she came and stayed with me for a few days."

"Really?" I stared at him, surprised. "Did anything happen between you?"

He shook his head. "She was still married. And actually, she was pregnant. She ended up going back to him, even though I tried to talk her out of it."

"Why'd you do that?"

His jaw ticked. "Because he didn't deserve her."

"Was he abusive?"

"Not physically. He was just a jerk. They ended up getting divorced about a year ago."

"So now she's a single mom?"

"Yeah. She's got a six-year-old son, Elliott."

"Huh." I tried to picture Maddie Blake. "Does she live around here? I don't think I've seen her since high school."

Beckett shook his head. "She lives in Ohio, but she's coming up here in a few weeks to sell the house she grew up in. Her mom left it to her, and she's been renting it out. Actually, I was going to ask a favor of you."

"Sure. What is it?"

"Could you maybe take a look at this house and give her an estimate on some improvements? The property manager neglected to do any maintenance, and it's been vacant for a while." He winced. "I've looked at it from the outside, and it's in pretty bad shape."

I sipped my beer. "I can do that. No problem."

"I don't know how much money she has," Beckett said, rubbing the back of his neck.

"I'll take a look and see what we're dealing with. Don't worry, I'll give her a good price."

"That's what I told her." Beckett sounded relieved and picked up his beer again. "Thanks, man."

"Is she going to stay there until it's sold?"

"Actually, she's going to stay with me."

I looked at him in surprise.

"She was going to stay there," he went on quickly, his tone slightly defensive, "but that place is a wreck. I don't think she realizes how bad it is. We've got plenty of room, and she said her son is really excited about visiting a farm."

"Well, there you go, you can finally bang her," I joked.

He rolled his eyes. "Fuck off, asshole. I'm just doing something nice for an old friend."

I decided to lay off him, since he was obviously under a lot of stress right now—but I remembered the way he'd looked at Maddie Blake in high school, even if he'd never admitted how he really felt about her. "She'll be here in a few weeks, you said?"

"Yes, as soon as Elliott is out of school for the summer. I'll let you know as soon as I hear from her."

I sipped my beer. "You *do* have a lot going on."

"Tell me about it. I'm gonna wake up with white hair one of these mornings, just like my dad."

"My advice is to get a fake wife and have lots of sex. It's excellent stress relief."

He laughed. "A wife is the last thing I need, fake or otherwise. I've got enough people to take care of right now, not to mention a herd of cattle, some goats, chickens, horses, a dog—"

"Okay, okay." I held up one hand in surrender. "You win. No wife. How about I buy the next round?"

Beckett nodded and finished off his beer. "Sold."

Later that night, when Bianca and I were curled up in bed after a round of target practice—I made sure to call it that—I thought about Beckett again. "Hey, if I ever lose my mind and start wandering around town babbling nonsense, don't let our kid feel responsible. Put me in a home or something. Just make sure they have good food."

Bianca picked her head up off my chest. "What?"

"Beckett's dad has dementia, and Beckett has to deal with it." I told her about Mr. Weaver's erratic behavior, and how Beckett was struggling to keep him safe while running the ranch on his own.

"Poor Beckett," Bianca said, laying her head down again. Her bare legs were twined with mine, and she was playing with the hair on my chest.

"Yeah, I feel bad for him."

"When did his mom die?"

"She didn't die—that I know of, anyway. She just took off when Beck was really young. He never talked about it."

"Poor thing. Does he have siblings?"

"He has two older sisters, Mallory and Amy. But they don't live close enough to help out every day."

"Does Beckett ever date?"

"I think he had a girlfriend for a while in New York, but since he moved back here, there hasn't been anyone serious. He's always so busy with the ranch, and now with his dad." I played with her hair, letting soft auburn strands slide through my fingers. "In high school, he was always hung up on this one girl—Maddie Blake. Not that he'd ever admit to it."

"Yeah?"

"She lived across the road from the ranch and they had classes together, so she hung around his house a lot, although he claims they only did homework."

Bianca snorted. "Which you cannot imagine doing, if *you* were alone with a girl in high school."

"Precisely." I tugged a lock of her hair. " But actually, I believe him. She had a boyfriend, and Beckett was not the kind of guy to go after someone else's girlfriend."

"What was he like back then?"

"Pretty much the same as he is now. A workaholic. Crazy smart. An awesome athlete. Busy all the time. When he wasn't at school or practice, he was working. He used to get up at fucking five a.m. and milk cows before coming to school."

"He never had a girlfriend?"

"Not really. I think he was always hung up on that Maddie girl."

"And he never told her?"

"Nope. Not his style."

"What was she like?"

"She was nice. Pretty, but not in a super showy way. Kind of quiet." I thought back. "Everyone liked her, but she only dated losers—I never understood it."

Bianca sighed. "You never know what's going on in someone's head."

"I guess. Anyway, Beckett said she eventually *married* a loser and had a kid with him. But she's divorced now, and she'd coming back here in a couple weeks to sell the house she grew up in." I told her that Beckett had asked me to give an estimate on some improvements, and I'd agreed to give her a good price.

"Aww. Of course you did." She kissed my chest. "You're a good friend."

"Beckett's a good guy."

Bianca was silent a moment. "Hard to believe a mom could just abandon their child like his mother did, but . . . I guess it happens."

"Yeah."

"As intense as our parents can be, we're lucky we grew up the way we did."

I was about to agree with her, when it struck me *our* child would not grow up the same way.

That twinge in my side returned, and I frowned. "Let me up for a second," I told her. "I need to stretch."

She sat up and I leaned over, stretching one arm over my head, hoping the pain would alleviate.

"You okay?" she asked.

"I'm fine. I must have hurt myself at the gym this morning." The pain eased up slightly, and I switched off the lamp. When I leaned back again, she returned to my side, and I put my arm around her, listening as her breathing slowed.

"Do you think we're going to fuck up our kid?" I blurted.

"What? No." She sat up. "Why would you say that?"

"Because we're not going to raise it together."

"Yes, we are."

"You know what I mean—in one house."

"Oh." She was silent a few seconds. "No, I don't think we're going to fuck up our kid. Plenty of children grow up in two different households. The important thing is that they know they're loved."

What she said sounded good, but something wasn't sitting right with me tonight.

"Are you—are you changing your mind about having a baby?" she asked nervously.

"No." I rubbed my face with both hands. "No, I'm still good with the plan. Sorry, I think I'm just worried about Beckett, and it's fucking with me."

"That's okay. I understand." She lay down on her side of the bed and pulled the covers up to her shoulders, facing away from me.

"Hey. What are you doing over there?"

"I don't know. I'm giving you some space."

"Well, I don't want it. Come here."

She rolled over toward me, and I gathered her into my arms. "I just want you to know, and I mean this with one hundred percent sincerity, I'm not sick of you yet."

Her laughter made the ache in my side disappear. "I'm not sick of you yet either."

"Okay. Good." I kissed her once more and went to sleep.

Twelve

Bianca

CHEYENNE HOSTED BOOK CLUB ON THURSDAY NIGHT, and after everyone left but Blair and me, the three of us sat in her living room talking.

"I'm dying to catch up," Cheyenne said, pouring herself some more wine and settling into the L of a cream-colored sectional sofa I'd helped her and Cole choose. "How are things going?"

"Good," I said.

"I noticed you're not drinking wine," said Blair, who sat on the corner opposite from me, a suspicious smile on her face.

I took a sip of my tea. "Nope."

"Does that mean you're already pregnant?" Cheyenne's eyes popped.

"No," I said, laughing. "Just trying to be."

Blair sat up ramrod straight. "Wait a minute. You told me before that the first insemination wouldn't be until late April. It's only mid-March."

"About that." I took another sip of tea. "We, um, decided to try it the old-fashioned way."

Both my friends stared at me.

"Are you serious?" Cheyenne asked.

"Yes."

"I knew it!" Blair thumped her hand on the couch. "I said to Griffin when we left your house on Saturday that you guys would not be able to stick to that ridiculous no-sex rule."

"You were right," I confessed. "We couldn't."

"I'm so confused," Cheyenne said, placing a palm on her forehead. "Are you guys actually a couple now? Or is everything still fake?"

"I think we're something in between," I said. "Not a couple, but not entirely fake either. More like friends with benefits."

She continued trying to understand. "But you're still planning to break up eventually?"

"Yes. After the baby is born, if I get pregnant. Sooner if I don't."

"Like how soon?"

"We said we'd give it three months." My stomach felt a little funny when I said it out loud. Three months didn't seem nearly as long as it had when we first signed the contract.

"Wow." Cheyenne blinked. "And you'll be able to just walk away?"

"Sure," I said with confidence I didn't fully feel. "That part of the plan hasn't changed. From the very beginning, we agreed on an expiration date. We just adjusted things to have a little more fun in the meantime."

"But what if you really like each other by then?" Cheyenne pressed. "Don't you think it could work?"

"No way," I insisted, before that voice in my head saying *well, maybe . . .* could make itself be heard. "The reason I chose Enzo is because I knew there would be no possible way I'd ever fall for him. In fact, he made me put that in the contract."

"He did?" Cheyenne rolled her eyes. "What an asshole."

"I know." I laughed, shaking my head. "And at the time, it

seemed ludicrous that he'd even think it. But he claims he's been in this situation before, where someone says she's okay with casual fun but then she falls in love with him."

"But you're not that girl," Blair said. "This is not that situation."

"No, it's not. And it never will be." I sat up a little taller. "Look, I appreciate his honesty. I spent years in a relationship letting myself be strung along with empty promises. At least Enzo is being up front about it. He's never going to love me. I'm okay with that."

Blair gasped and looked at Cheyenne. "She sounds just like you."

"Huh?" I glanced back and forth between them.

"I said that too, about Cole." Cheyenne smiled knowingly. "That he was never going to love me."

"Oh." I tilted my head this way and that. "Well, that was a different situation. You guys had a different history. Different circumstances."

"So did Griffin and I," said Blair. "There isn't one path that leads to love, Bianca. All we're saying is that we don't think you should completely close yourself off to the idea of finding something real with Enzo. It could happen, even though neither of you expects it."

"Neither of us *wants* it," I insisted, growing a little agitated. I wasn't them, and they weren't me. Why did I have to explain this again? "We're in this for something else entirely. And because I'm a mature, self-aware woman who has learned from her mistakes, I'm being one hundred percent careful this time not to get sucked into the fantasy. Yes, we're married. But it's just a piece of paper for us. Yes, the sex is great. But it's just sex. Yes, Enzo is hot and funny and maybe slightly less irksome these days. But I'm on a mission, and I know what it is—and what it's not."

Blair sighed dramatically and looked at Cheyenne. "We can't have nice things, Chey."

Cheyenne shook her head. "Nope, we sure can't."

"You guys are ridiculous," I said, laughing as I rose to my feet. "And I'm leaving before you get any more carried away. Enzo and I are not a love story. *Period.*"

Friday afternoon, I texted Enzo while we were both still at work.

Me: Anniversary dinner tonight? I'll cook.

Enzo: Sounds good. Meatball subs?

I laughed at the row of kissy-face emojis that followed.

Me: Again?

Enzo: I'm a simple man.

Me: Home by six?

Enzo: I'm at a site this afternoon but I should be able to make that happen.

Me: See you then.

I left work a little early, hit the grocery store on the way home, and had everything prepped by five-thirty. Then I went upstairs, took off every stitch of clothing, and put on the apron. I'd bought it earlier this week—it was a vintage style, red and frilly with little cherries on the skirt. After tying the bow in the back, I put on my highest heels, added some perfume and red lipstick, and went back downstairs.

In the kitchen, I put on some Frank Sinatra, poured two glasses of wine, and turned the oven on.

At about twenty after six, I heard his key in the lock. The door swung open, and I quickly turned to face the oven, giving him a view of my naked backside beneath the apron's perky bow.

The door closed, and I heard a few footsteps before they stopped suddenly. "Jesus Christ."

I peeked at him over one shoulder—he was staring at me and clutching his chest with one hand. In the other, he held a bouquet of white roses.

"Am I dead?" he asked, his eyes wide. "Is this heaven? Because this is exactly what I imagine it looks like and sounds like and smells like."

I scowled at him. "You're late."

"I'm sorry. We're behind on this project, and I had to make sure the tile guys didn't fuck off and leave before the job was done. Then I stopped at the florist." He set the roses on the counter.

I pouted for show, even as my heart fluttered that he'd brought me flowers again. "You chose the tile guys over me?"

"*No one* would choose the tile guys over you." He came closer, his eyes dark and hungry.

I scooted around the island, putting it between us. "You said you'd be home at six o'clock. It's six twenty."

He followed me. "I'll make it up to you."

"I don't know if I'm interested anymore." I kept backing around the island, Enzo in slow but steady pursuit.

"No?" He pulled off his black, collared Moretti & Sons work shirt, taking his T-shirt with it. "How about now?"

My insides tightened at the sight of his bare chest and abs. But I sniffed. "Meh."

"Meh?" His eyebrows peaked as he tossed the shirts to the kitchen floor. "Last night you said my body looked like it was sculpted by Michelangelo. But tonight it's *meh*?"

Giggling, I moved a little quicker to keep him from grabbing me. "Last night you weren't late for our anniversary dinner."

"I said I was sorry. I brought you roses. Can't you forgive me?"

"No. Because then you'll think it's okay to be late all the time. In order to teach you a lesson, I think I should—"

He lunged for me, and I squealed, ducking his reach and racing around the island into the living room.

Enzo chased me, hurtling over the couch to beat me to the stairway, which he blocked.

"No fair," I said, huffing and puffing. "I'm in heels. You're in boots, you can run faster."

"What are you gonna do about it?" he asked, his head cocked to one side.

"Hide somewhere else." Spinning away from him, I ran for the first-floor bathroom, struggling not to break an ankle in my Jimmy Choos.

When he chased me, I managed to pivot on a dime and rush toward the stairs again. But I wasn't even two steps up when he caught me around the waist as I shrieked and squirmed in his arms.

"Tell you what," he said low in my ear. "Since I'm a nice guy, I'm going to give you a head start. I'll let you get to the top of the stairs before I come after you. That's fair, isn't it?"

"No," I said, struggling to get out of his iron grip.

"On your mark, get set, go." He loosened his vise-hold on me and I escaped, dashing up the stairs as quickly as my heels would allow. I hadn't even reached the top before I heard him coming up behind me, two steps at a time, his work boots making big heavy sounds on the steps.

"You cheated!" I squealed, racing toward his bedroom, which we'd been sharing since my second night here. "You said you'd give me until the top of the stairs!" I moved as fast as I could, but I still couldn't manage to slam the door shut behind me—Enzo easily caught it with his forearm and swung it open.

"I didn't cheat. I lied. There's a difference."

Breathing hard, I backed toward the bed, my hands out in front of me. "You once told me you never lied."

"That was before you put on the apron. Before you ran away from me." He came toward me slowly now, his dark eyes on fire, his tone menacing. "Do you think that was nice to do to your husband? Torture him? Make him mad? Turn him into a monster?"

The backs of my legs hit the bed just as he grabbed my forearms. "What are you going to do to me?"

"I'm going to punish you."

My heart was pounding. "How?"

Without answering, he spun me around, put his hand on my back, and forced me forward at the waist. The next thing I heard was his belt being undone. The next thing I felt were my wrists being bound behind my back. The next thing I knew, he was leaning over me, his fists braced beside my shoulders, his voice teasing in my ear. "Come on, Lucy. Fight me."

I struggled against the leather strap, but it was too tight—and he still hovered right over my back so I couldn't stand up. I huffed and puffed and writhed, but I gave up the effort in less than ten seconds.

"Do you surrender?" he asked, his breath tickling my skin, his lips brushing the back of my neck. His chest was hot and solid against my back, and my body was burning up for him.

"Never," I hissed.

"Then I guess you leave me no choice." He straightened up and delivered a loud, hard slap to my ass. "What about now?"

I yelped—because yes, it fucking stung—but then I laughed. "No! Is it too late to change my mind about marrying you?"

"On our anniversary? You heartless wench." He smacked the other side of my ass, then covered both cheeks with his palms, pressing gently.

"I didn't sign up for this abuse!"

"This isn't abuse, babe." He knelt behind me and kissed my burning flesh. "This is revenge."

"For what?" I breathed. His soft, full lips moving over the skin his hands had just marked, made my legs tremble.

"For making me want you this way." One of his hands slid up between my thighs, his fingers probing inside me. "For teasing me. For tempting me."

My pulse was firing rapidly, my insides were melting at his touch. "You deserved it."

"Maybe I did." He slipped his fingers in deep, then withdrew them, rubbing them over my clit in slow, rhythmic circles. "But you're still a wicked little girl."

"You like it," I whispered as he pushed my heels farther apart and buried his face between my legs, fucking me with his tongue.

My mouth fell open and my eyes squeezed shut. Was this real? Enzo Moretti—cocky, high-and-mighty, self-absorbed Enzo Moretti was kneeling between my thighs, worshiping my body with his arrogant mouth and his insolent tongue and those beautifully rugged hands?

In no time at all, my legs were nearly numb with pleasure. My insides were knotted so tight, I cried out with the need for release. My swollen clit hummed as he licked and sucked and teased it. But any time I got close to orgasm, he always backed off—and I knew he was doing it on purpose, because I'd hear the low chuckle in his throat and feel his breath on my warm, wet skin. He knew my body so well already.

"Enzo," I begged, near tears. "Please."

"Please what?"

"Let me come."

"Say you're sorry."

I was done with games. "I'm sorry. I surrender."

He laughed. "So fucking easy."

But he did what I asked for, pushing his fingers deeper and working his tongue faster, and inside a minute, my body was pulsing and spasming, my insides contracting in sweet relief.

My body was still buzzing with bliss when Enzo sank his teeth into my ass and growled. I cried out in pain, although secretly I couldn't get enough of the way he seemed so out of control tonight.

He rose to his feet, and I heard the zipper of his jeans go down. A second later, I felt his cock sliding back and forth along the crack of my ass. "Yes," I whispered, arching my back in invitation.

"Have I told you," he said in a gravelly voice, "how much I fucking love this outfit? You should wear it every day."

I laughed, still trying to catch my breath. "Would we ever leave the house?"

"No," he answered, pushing inside me with slow, deep strokes.

"You'd lose your company."

"Fuck my company." He gripped my hips, pulling me back as he drove forward, making me gasp with every deep, aggressive thrust. "All I want is you. All I fucking want is you."

He sounded mad about it.

Then I couldn't talk anymore, because he was moving inside me too hard and too fast, raveling me up into that tight, high spiral, taking me to the brink where pain and pleasure were nearly indistinguishable, and all I wanted was more. With my hands still bound behind my back, I was completely at his mercy, but there was no mercy in him tonight. He fucked me hard and rough, as if he really were furious with me for the way he felt, for the way he wanted me.

His breathing was ragged and heavy, his pace brutal, his cock hitting me viciously deep. When I wasn't sure I could take any more, he dropped down onto one forearm and slid the other hand beneath my apron between my legs. Working his fingers over my clit, he buried himself deep within me and I felt the thickening stillness and then the surge as he began to throb inside me again and again. His release pushed me over the edge, and my own climax crashed through me, my body contracting around him.

I could feel his heart pounding against my back as he collapsed above me, one arm still looped beneath my hips, the other braced over my shoulder.

"Fuck," he said in a low, hoarse voice. "You okay?"

"I'm fine," I said, still breathing hard, my chest pressed into the mattress.

He lowered his lips to my temple then rested his forehead against it. "Can I put in a request for more nights where I come home to meatball subs and you wearing only an apron?"

"Are you going to be on time?" I teased.

"Never. Because I fucking love it when you're mad at me. I'm beginning to understand why my parents fought all the time. I think it was foreplay. No wonder they had six kids."

Laughing, I wriggled beneath him. "I'd settle for one. Can I get up now? I think my arms are dead."

"Yes, but before we move, I would just like to say, I *really* think I did it this time. Because I was like next level deep. Intergalactic deep. Deep Space Nine." He pulled out and straightened up, removing his belt from my wrists, rubbing them gently. "Wow. Your ass has two giant handprints on it."

Lifting myself halfway up, I tried to peer at it over one shoulder. "Does it really?"

"Yes. It looks like a kindergarten art project I did once." Grinning, he hitched up his jeans and zipped them. "But this was a lot more fun."

I glared up at him. "Next time, *I* get to be rough with *you*. I'm going to etch my name on your back with my fingernails."

"Stop it, you're turning me on." He reached to help me up.

"No, wait," I said, turning onto my back. "Let me just rest here a minute. Maybe it will help."

He nodded and grabbed me by the ankles, swinging my legs up onto the bed. "There. Want me to tip you upside down or something?"

"No. But I just realized the oven is on. There's nothing in there yet, but maybe we should turn it off?"

"Fuck no, I'm starving. I'll go down and get the sandwiches together. What else can I do?"

"Nothing. I'll be down in a minute or two."

"You're not going to put clothes on, are you?" he asked accusingly. "I'll get mad at you all over again."

I laughed. "Maybe just some pants. You can take them off later."

"I suppose that will have to do."

"Hey," I called when he was nearly out the door. "Was this a better ending than waking up from your dream?"

He looked confused for a moment, and then he laughed. "Babe," he said, shaking his head. "It's not even close." As he went down the hallway toward the stairs, I could still hear him talking. "Not. Even. Close."

When I came downstairs in one of Enzo's T-shirts and some pajama pants, he had the candles lit, the meatball subs in the oven, and the island set for two. I laughed when I saw him—over his bare chest and jeans he had a black apron on that said THIS IS A MANLY APRON FOR A MANLY MAN DOING MANLY THINGS WITH MANLY FOOD.

"Cute," I told him, patting his stomach on my way to the fridge to grab the salad.

"Thank you. My sister Cat got it for me for Christmas last year." He grabbed my arm. "You sit down. I've got this."

"I was just going to—"

"You're just going to sit down and relax. I poured you some more wine, and"—he looked alarmed for a second—"wait, can you have wine?"

"A few sips are okay," I said.

"Good. Then you sit down right there while I get dinner on the table. You've done enough."

"At least let me put the roses in a vase."

"I will permit that," he said, like he was doing me a big favor.

While I trimmed the stems and filled a vase with water, he moved around the kitchen, singing along to "Witchcraft," and occasionally cursing me when he couldn't find something. When dinner was ready, Enzo took off his apron and we sat down to eat next to each other at the island.

"There's a house for sale I'm thinking of buying to flip," he said, picking up his sub. "The agent called me today. Huge price reduction."

"Oh yeah?"

"Yeah. It's in the Historic District. Center Avenue."

"I love Center Avenue!"

"Want to go look at it tomorrow? It would be a pretty big project. It's old as fuck, has some water damage, and hasn't been redecorated since Star Wars was in theaters, but it would be a cool project." He shrugged. "If you were interested."

"Like . . . we'd do it together?"

"That's what I was thinking. I've got some extra cash right now—my dad gave me a wife bonus, so thanks—and you're really good at what you do. I think we'd make a good team."

"I think so too." I took a sip of wine, flushed with pleasure at his compliment. "Sure. Let's go look at it."

The next morning, Enzo called the agent who had the listing, and he agreed to meet us at the house at noon. Enzo was right—it was a big old thing, a hundred and twenty years old, and my sister Ellie would have refused to go in it because she'd have insisted it was haunted. But I loved its Victorian charms—the steeply pitched roof, the asymmetrical façade, the wraparound porch, the picturesque turret. Someone had painted it white long ago, but the paint was flaking off now so it looked more gray than anything.

We went inside, and even though the smell was moldy and the surfaces dusty, Enzo and I were able to see past the shabbiness due to age and neglect. Ugly eighties wallpaper could be removed, warped floors could be refinished, crumbling plaster could be repaired, cracked windows could be replaced, and the kitchen and bathrooms could be modernized while retaining its character. Both of us were thrilled that the gorgeous dark woodwork hadn't been covered in glossy white oil paint over the years.

But it would be a massive, time-consuming renovation. In the back of my mind, I couldn't help thinking that this project would probably last longer than our marriage.

When we were done, we thanked the agent for meeting us, and went for lunch at the diner, where I dug my notepad and a pen from my bag and we began brainstorming ideas for the exterior, the interior, and the landscaping. Enzo knew someone he could consult about original Victorian paint colors, and I had a friend in Chicago who ran a company that reproduced historic wallpaper patterns. I scribbled four pages of notes before my pen ran out.

"Hey, you know what this kind of reminds me of?" I asked him, tucking the pad of paper back in my bag. "The night you first came to dinner at my place. When we sat at my island and drew up the contract."

"Oh yeah. You're right, it does." He paused and smiled. "I like this better."

"Same," I said, wishing my heart wasn't beating so fast as I looked at him across the booth from me. I dropped my eyes to my notepad. "So, this is a pretty big restoration job."

"Biggest I've ever tackled, that's for sure."

"It's going to take a while, don't you think? Like maybe four to six months?"

"Sounds about right."

I met his eyes. "That's . . . that's potentially longer than phase two, depending on our luck."

He shook his head. "You have no faith in my skills."

"Enzo, I'm being serious."

"So am I. Look, I happen to have a good feeling about phase two, but even if I'm wrong and your sorry pessimistic ass is right, I don't see a reason why we shouldn't be able to work together on the house."

"People might think it's weird."

"Fuck people. I don't care what they think." He reached across the table and took my hand. "I want to do this together. Do you?"

"Yes," I said without thinking twice. "The house has tons of potential, it will be an excellent investment for you, and it will be a fantastic marketing tool for me. I'd love to document the entire renovation on social media and then hold a big open house once it's complete."

"Okay. Then let's do it."

I smiled, linking our fingers. "Let's do it."

That afternoon, he took my car for an oil change at Griffin's garage while I got some work done at home and did laundry for both of us. I even ironed a couple of Enzo's shirts, laughing as I recalled my wedding vows.

That night, we met up with friends for pizza, and I heard him telling Cole about a bunch of my ideas for the new house. "She's so fucking talented," he said. "This could be huge for her."

When we got home, we barely made it into bed before going at each other again. I tore at his clothing like it was on fire. I fisted my hands in his hair. I grabbed and pulled and begged and dug my heels into the backs of his thighs, coming undone beneath him as stars exploded behind my eyes.

Afterward, as I brushed my teeth and washed my face in the bathroom, I was starting to think I'd landed in some kind of alternate universe.

"Hey, say something to bug me," I told him as I climbed back beneath the covers. "We've been getting along so well all day, I feel like I'm losing my grip on reality. Or like maybe you've been kidnapped by aliens and I'm going to give birth to something that looks like Baby Yoda."

He laughed. "Don't say that. What if he can hear you?"

"Who? Baby Yoda?"

"No, *our* baby."

"We don't have a baby."

"You don't know that." Rolling onto his side, he pointed at my stomach. "He could be in there right now, listening to us. Or what if it's a girl? You're giving her a complex about her looks already." He patted my belly. "Don't listen to her, sweetheart. You're beautiful."

I laughed, swatting his hand away. "Even if she was in there, she doesn't have ears yet. Now stop jinxing us. All I wanted was for you to say something annoying."

"Okay." He propped his head on his hand and looked at me. "I think it's weird that you cut your pizza with a knife and eat it with a fork. As if you're too fancy to pick it up like a normal person. How's that?"

"That's good."

"And why do you have so much shit in your car? And in your purse? What are you, a homeless person?"

I sighed. "That'll do."

"You sure? I've got more."

"I'm sure. Turn off the light."

He did, then gathered me close to him again. "Night, Lucy."

"Night, Ricky."

A week later, I got my period.

I was disappointed, but it wasn't like I hadn't been expecting it. I'd known what the odds were. I'd had them explained to me plenty of times. I couldn't even be sure I'd ovulated during my last cycle. And yet I still found my eyes blurry with tears and my throat lumping up as I reached beneath the bathroom sink for the box of tampons. Enzo had gone to the gym early, and right from there he went over to the Moretti & Sons office, so I didn't tell him right away. It wasn't the kind of thing I wanted to say on the phone or in a text.

I was lying in bed finishing a good twenty-minute ugly cry when I heard him come in around four that afternoon. After fixing up my face, I went downstairs with slow, heavy steps.

He was in the kitchen looking at his phone, but he glanced up when I came in. Right away he noticed something was wrong. "What?" he asked, his dark eyes concerned.

"It didn't work," I said, my throat constricting. "I'm not pregnant."

Immediately he set his phone aside and wrapped me in his arms. "I'm sorry. Are you okay?"

"I'm okay." His warm, solid chest was a comfort. "This month was a long shot anyway."

"I'm going to refrain from making jokes about my awesome long shot."

I laughed in spite of the desperate urge to cry.

"So what's next? When can we try again?"

"Well, I'm going to start Clomid on Monday. Then I think we can try again about ten days after that."

"Okay. In the meantime, let's focus on getting that house, okay? How about we put in a lowball offer and see what happens?"

I nodded.

"Hey." Releasing me, he tipped my chin up, forcing me to look him in the eye. "In ten days, we can try again. And by this time next month, we'll be celebrating. I know it."

"I hope you're right."

"I'm always right. Remember?"

I managed a shaky smile. "How could I forget?"

"I don't know. You're not too bright sometimes. Come here." Grabbing me around the neck, he pulled me into his chest and rubbed his knuckles against my scalp before embracing me again. "Let's go out for dinner tonight. I'll even let you choose the place."

"Okay." Swallowing back more tears, I let him hold me and rub my back. I breathed in his scent. I listened to him tell me everything was going to be okay.

And I felt the ground giving way beneath me.

Thirteen

Enzo

I HAD NO IDEA HOW SHITTY I'D FEEL THAT BIANCA HADN'T gotten pregnant. I felt like I'd let her down.

She cheered up when we went out for dinner, and she kept a smile on her face afterward when we met up with Griffin and Blair for drinks, but I could tell she wasn't completely herself. For one thing, she hardly ripped on me at all, even when given the opportunity. And when I poked fun at her, she didn't poke back or even give me her mad face.

I was actually really worried by the time we got home, but I didn't want to bring it up again, in case she was just trying to forget it and move on.

"Want to watch TV or anything?" I asked her.

"Nah. I'm tired," she said. "I think I'll just head up to bed."

"Okay. I'll go up too." I followed her up the stairs, but when she reached the top, she stopped moving, and I bumped into her from behind. "Whoa. You lost or what?" I took her by the shoulders and steered her into the bedroom. "It's this way, Columbus."

"Well, I wasn't sure where I should sleep."

"What? Why?" I let go of her and started unbuttoning my shirt.

She appeared flustered. "Well, because we can't—we don't need to—there won't be sex for a while. So I thought maybe I should sleep in the other room, the one I was supposed to use. Most of my clothes are still in there and everything."

Our eyes met, and I peeled off my shirt. "Do you *want* to sleep in the other room?"

She opened her mouth. Closed it again. Looked away from me. Fidgeted.

I laughed, grabbing my undershirt from behind and yanking it over my head. "It's an easy question, Bianca."

"No, it isn't," she said, her eyes on my chest.

"What's so difficult about it? Do you want to sleep in here with me or alone in the other room?"

She blushed and folded her arms over her chest. "It's not really fair of you to ask me that question when you're shirtless."

I smirked. "No?"

"No. It clouds my judgement."

"What about when I do this?" I flexed my biceps and arranged my face in a sexy, brooding pout. "Or this?" I turned sideways and struck a different pose, giving her the Moretti smolder over one shoulder. "Can you think now?"

Shaking her head, she started to laugh. "You're ridiculous."

"I know. But you can't resist me."

Her eyebrows shot up. "Oh, I think I can. In fact, goodnight."

She went for the door, but I darted in front of her, scooped her up and tossed her over my shoulder before depositing her on the bed.

"You're the one being ridiculous." I braced myself above her. "Just stay in here."

"Do you *want* me to stay in here?" she asked craftily.

"I don't know. Maybe you should take off your shirt and ask me again."

She laughed. "Listen, I'm just trying to stick as close to the original arrangement as possible. I feel like we've mucked things up so much already."

I was about to argue with her but realized she was right. What we were doing looked nothing like what we'd planned on. The no-sex rule, the separate rooms, the whole pretending to like each other—it had all gone out the window somehow.

But I liked things the way they were, and I didn't want them to change. And if I couldn't manage to get her pregnant, she was going to be gone in two months anyway.

I didn't want to think about it.

"I still think you should just stay in here," I told her. "It seems stupid for you to go back and forth. Plus I like sleeping next to you."

"You do?" She looked surprised.

"Yes. Sleeping Bianca is my favorite. She smells just as good as Awake Bianca, but she never rolls her eyes and she doesn't give me any lip."

"Sleeping Enzo is nice too. All of the muscles, none of the attitude. Although, he does snore, so it's a bit of a tradeoff."

I grinned down at her. "So will you stay?"

She sighed, like the whole thing was such a hardship for her, but then she smiled. "Yes. I'll stay."

"Good." I stood up and went over to the dresser, where I unbuckled my belt and pulled it from the loops.

"Enzo."

I looked up, meeting her eyes in the mirror. She got off the bed and came up behind me, wrapping her arms around my waist and resting her forehead on my back.

"Thank you," she said.

I put my hands over hers.

The vise tightened around my heart.

I told myself to give Bianca the days she needed to recover without pestering her every day about when we could have sex again. I didn't want to pressure her, and I didn't want her to think I was some kind of animal—even though I kind of felt like one around her.

Which was probably why I made it exactly five days after she started the Clomid before I asked her if it had been ten days yet.

"No," she said, laughing at me. She was propped up on pillows in bed, wearing her glasses, her nose stuck in a book, just like I'd imagined. "It's only been five."

"But it's Friday."

"So?"

"So usually we do fun things on Friday nights."

"We did do a fun thing. We made homemade ravioli."

"Yes, and while that was more fun than I thought it would be, it still does not compare to the kind of fun I am thinking of right now."

She gave me a look that said *not tonight, dear*—or maybe not *tonight, asshole*—and I was forced to accept my sexless Friday night fate.

Sunday night, I risked putting a hand on her leg. "How about now? Has it been ten days yet?"

"Nope. It's only been seven."

I rubbed her bare thigh, my dick growing harder by the second. She looked so cute in her little pink tank top and glasses. "Are you *sure*? Because I really think it's been at least ten days. Maybe even twenty."

"Yes, I'm sure." She removed my hand from her leg. "But I'm glad you're so eager to get back on the job. Your dedication is inspiring."

I harrumphed loudly and flopped onto my back. "Frankly, these workplace conditions are appalling. I'm suffering from some kind of work-related mental and emotional stress."

She giggled, set her book and her glasses on the nightstand, and turned onto her side. "How about some workman's compensation?"

I looked over at her. "What did you have in mind?"

Her hand wandered beneath the sheets and stroked my cock, which jumped at her touch. "I'm sure we can work something out."

"Are you serious?"

Instead of answering, she tossed the covers back, dragged my boxer briefs off, and knelt between my legs. "Do I look serious?"

"You look fucking *hot*," I told her, my stomach muscles tight with anticipation. "And this feels like Christmas morning."

She gave me a coy smile before dropping her head and running her tongue along the hard length of my shaft, making me groan with pleasure and anticipation.

Then I watched in utter ecstasy and delighted surprise as she went about giving me the best blowjob of my entire life. I don't even know for sure what it was that made it so damn good—the shock of it being her idea? The way she used her hands? The playful way she licked and stroked and sucked, like she was actually enjoying it as much as I was? The soft sighs and happy moans she gave me, as if my dick was the best thing she'd ever tasted and she couldn't get enough? The way she took my cock to the back of her throat, so deep she gasped for air? The way she let me fist my hands in her hair and control the pace as I fucked her perfect mouth so hard and quick I came before I wanted to, completely out of control, out of my mind, out of my skin with desire and need and appreciation for her?

I'd never felt like I didn't deserve an orgasm before, but seeing her lips on my cock as the orgasm thundered through me, then watching her swallow and sit up, drawing the back of her hand across her smiling mouth was nearly enough to make me weep and beg forgiveness.

"Oh my God," I said, barely able to catch my breath. "That was fucking incredible. Marry me."

She laughed. "We're already married."

"Oh yeah." I felt like I was having a strange, euphoric out-of-body experience. I was just looking at her—the messy hair, the proud little grin, the swollen lips, the blue eyes, the flushed cheeks—but it felt like I was running as fast as I could, like I was stealing second base, or maybe rounding third and preparing to slide into home in order to beat the throw. My heart was galloping wildly inside my chest, and something like adrenaline surged through my veins. There were things I wanted to say to her, but they were as foreign to me as another language—I didn't even know where to start.

She sat back on her heels and tilted her head to one side. "So how was that? Good enough to tide you over until Wednesday night?"

I nodded, because I didn't trust myself not to say something weird and ridiculous.

Something like, *I think I might be in love with you.*

But that wasn't true. It couldn't be true. I wasn't the kind of guy who fell in love—I was stronger than that. Smarter than that. It was the blowjob, that was all. It must have released those weird biological hormones that made ancient man want to, like, build a hut and hunt a woolly mammoth.

Quickly, I buried the thought and zeroed in on something more familiar. More comfortable.

"Tell me what I can do for you," I said as she lay down next to me again, facing her nightstand. I curled my body behind hers, wrapping my arm around her waist.

She hugged it to her. "Nothing."

"Are you sure?" I kissed her shoulder. "I'm really good with my—"

"I'm sure," she said, laughing as she reached for the lamp and switched it off. "I know you're really good with your *everything,* but I can wait. Technically, we just broke the rules anyway."

"What do you mean? We got rid of the no-sex rule," I reminded her as she settled her head on the pillow.

"We got rid of it for the purpose of conception," she said. "What we just did was fun, but it's not going to get me pregnant."

"True." I paused, looking down at her in the dark. "So you're saying that was fun for you?"

She laughed. "Yes, that was fun for me. But don't let it go to your head. I mostly did it so that you'd stop bothering me—until Wednesday anyway. Now go to sleep."

I curled up behind her again, feeling slightly off balance by what had just transpired, but unable to put my finger on exactly why.

One thing was for sure, though. I couldn't wait for Wednesday night. Just thinking about it made me smile.

I had a surprise for her.

Tuesday after work I went over to Cole's house to help him get an old refrigerator out of his basement. Afterward, he asked if I wanted to hang out and have a beer.

"Sure," I said, pulling my phone from my pocket. "Let me just text Bianca and let her know I'll be a little bit late."

While Cole grabbed two bottles from the fridge and popped off the caps, I sent Bianca a message apologizing that I'd be home later than I'd said and offering to pick up takeout on the way home. She responded that she'd worked late tonight anyway, so that sounded perfect.

"So how's everything going with you guys?" Cole handed me a beer and leaned back against the counter.

"Good." I took a sip of my beer and wondered what was okay to reveal to Cole and what wasn't. I didn't want to betray Bianca's confidence, but Cole had been one of my best friends for twenty years, and he was a father too. I didn't think she'd mind if I told him what was going on. "She didn't get pregnant last month, so she was upset about that, but other than that, it's been good. We're actually getting along pretty well. Much better than I thought we would."

"That's cool," he said. "Sorry about the other thing."

"It's okay." I shrugged. "She knew it probably wouldn't happen that fast. I don't know shit about that stuff—apparently you have to time it exactly right, and even then the chances aren't great."

"I don't know much about it either," Cole admitted. "Trisha got pregnant almost right away."

"Yeah, I guess some people just get lucky." It made me sad that Bianca wasn't one of them. "Unless I'm doing it wrong."

Cole laughed and lifted his beer. "It's not that. I remember it took my brother's wife a while too. Almost a year."

"A year? Shit." I shook my head. "She only gave me three months, and I'm down one already."

"Can't you give yourselves more time?"

I frowned and took a long pull on my beer. "I don't think that's an option."

"Why not?"

"We agreed from the start that this was temporary. We said three months, unless she got pregnant."

"You also said you wouldn't have sex," Cole pointed out. "If that part of your plan can change, why not the timeline?"

"I don't know," I said. "I just feel like that's a bad idea."

"Why?"

"I don't know. Like what if it still won't work, and month after month, we're just stuck with each other, no end in sight, and she starts to hate me for letting her down and I start to regret putting myself in this position, where I'm failing a wife I didn't even want in the first place, and all we do is fight and get on each other's nerves, and then she leaves, because we ruined everything, and we hate each other forever . . ." I set my beer down and rubbed my face with both hands. "Fuck. Just . . . fuck. No."

"When you put it that way," Cole said, "it's tough to argue with you." He paused. "But what if it went the other way?"

"You mean, what if she gets pregnant?"

"Sure, let's say she does. You'd still let her leave?"

Suddenly an anvil was on my chest. "I'd have to, if she wanted to go. It's what I agreed to. And why would I want to be with someone who didn't want to be with me?"

"But what if—"

"Okay, stop." I picked up my beer and held up the other hand, palm toward him. "You're making this complicated when it isn't. There's no sense in asking *what if* questions. If she doesn't get pregnant, we shake hands and get a divorce in two months. If she does, we shake hands and get a divorce in a year. That was the deal. It's the only way we don't end up hating each other."

The back door to their kitchen opened, and Mariah came in, Cheyenne right behind her, carrying a couple grocery bags.

"Hi, Daddy," Mariah said, taking off her shoes before rushing over to give him a hug. "Guess what? We're making pancakes for dinner!"

Cole laughed and hugged her back. "My favorite."

"Hi, Uncle Enzo." Mariah smiled at me.

"Hey, squirt." I returned the smile, noting that she looked even more grown up than she had the last time I'd seen her. Kids changed so fast. "You're getting so tall. Pretty soon I won't even be able to call you squirt."

She grinned even wider. "Good!"

"Hey, Enzo," Cheyenne said, setting the grocery bags on the counter before giving Cole a quick kiss. "Would you like to stay for dinner?"

"Much as I love pancakes, I can't, but thanks for asking. I'm bringing home dinner tonight."

"Such a good husband," she said, winking at me. "Who'd have guessed?"

I finished off my beer. "Alright, I'm out of here, before the abuse gets any worse. Bye, guys."

On the drive home, I thought again about how quickly Mariah was growing up—it seemed like only yesterday I'd gone over to the hospital to see her for the first time, and to both console and congratulate Cole, who'd lost his wife but welcomed a child in the span of only twenty-four hours.

He'd raised Mariah as a single dad for nine years, and he'd done such a good job. She was healthy and happy, outgoing and talkative, smart as a whip and sweet as cotton candy. Would I be as good a dad as Cole was? What would it be like to watch a child grow up right in front of me? Listen to him laugh for the first time, watch her take her first steps, feel a tiny hand in mine, hear a little voice calling me Daddy?

Suddenly I was choked up.

I'd always imagined doing rough-and-tumble things with my kids, but now I was picturing softer, sweeter things too—feeding a baby a bottle, putting a Band-Aid on a cut, reading a bedtime story.

And I realized how badly I wanted it all.

That night, I broke down and pestered Bianca again, kneading her hip with my hand. "Come on, it's so close. Can't we try?"

"No," she insisted. "It's not time. One more night."

"Is it me," I asked irritably, "or are these last couple days somehow way longer than twenty-four hours apiece?"

"They're not."

"Maybe we should at least *rehearse* tonight." I rolled up close to her. Kissed her shoulder. "You know, make sure we remember how to do it."

She shook her head. "Nope. We have to time this perfectly.

According to my predictor kit and the doctor's instructions, tomorrow is best, so we're waiting until tomorrow."

"But we can do it tomorrow too." I slipped my hand beneath her pajama top.

"No way." She removed my hand. "We can only do it every other day. Too much sex can decrease the number of gold medal swimmers."

I gave her a dirty look, and she gave it right back, her eyes steely behind her glasses. "Fine," I said. "I'll wait."

"Thank you."

"But it won't be easy. You've got this very angry librarian thing happening right now. It's turning me on."

That made her laugh. She pushed her glasses up her nose and nodded in satisfaction. "Good."

My secret seduction plans for Wednesday night nearly got derailed when my father fell off a ladder on a job site that afternoon and had to be rushed to the emergency room. As soon as I got the call, I raced over to the hospital, dialing Bianca on the way.

"I'll be right there," she said.

"You don't have to come," I told her. "They said he only lost consciousness briefly and just needs an X-ray. I'm sure he's fine, and it's in the middle of your workday. Don't you have meetings this afternoon?"

"I'm canceling," she said. "I'll be there as soon as I can."

She hung up on me before I could argue further.

Just under an hour later, I was in the waiting room listening to my mother fret and ask the same questions over and over again—why hasn't anyone been out here to talk to us? How long can it possibly take to get an X-ray? Those people came in after us, why did they get seen already and we haven't?—when Bianca rushed into the room.

"Because, Ma, they already told us, they're short a

radiologist today and it's taking longer to get results. They said it would be a few hours, and they're sorry for the delay. Those people brought in someone having an asthma attack who didn't need an X-ray." I smiled tiredly at my wife as she hurried toward us.

"Hey," she said, her face concerned. "Any news?"

I stood up, and she hugged me tight. I inhaled the scent of her perfume and took comfort in the softness of her body against mine. "Not yet."

She hugged my mother next. "How are you?"

"I'm angry," my mother said petulantly.

"At the doctors?"

"Yes, and at Carlo! He had no business being up on a ladder at his age!" She sat down in a huff.

Bianca smiled patiently. "Why don't I get us all some coffee?"

"Thank you, dear. That sounds perfect. We haven't wanted to leave in case one of these doctors decides we're worth his time and comes out to talk to us."

"I'll get it." She touched my arm. "I'll be right back."

"Thanks." I sank down next to my mom and watched Bianca leave the room and turn left.

"She's a gem, isn't she?" my mother asked.

"She is," I agreed.

I was still thinking about her and trying to tune out my mom, who was back to alternately praying for my dad's quick recovery and cursing him for acting like an idiot, when Bianca returned with a tray of coffees from Starbucks.

She sat down on the other side of me, and we waited another hour and a half, during which my mother hardly paused to draw breath. "He's trying to kill me, that's what he's doing," she insisted.

"By climbing a ladder?" I asked, laughing although I felt like I was nearing the end of my rope.

"By doing something I've told him a million times he shouldn't do! He knows damn well he doesn't have the balance anymore, and that he'll fall and cause me to have a heart attack when I hear the news!" She scowled at me. "Don't laugh at me. You know it's the truth. He does things like this on purpose just to make me mad!"

I leaned toward Bianca and whispered, "This is why."

Giving me a sympathetic smile, she patted my leg and took my hand. "I get it."

Eventually, the doctor came out and said my father was fine, nothing was broken, but because he'd lost consciousness and had elevated blood pressure, they wanted to keep him overnight. We ended up waiting another couple hours for him to be admitted. I told Bianca a hundred times she didn't have to stay, but she refused to go. We ate terrible hospital food for dinner and didn't even end up talking to my dad because he was asleep by the time we got to his room.

When we walked out of the hospital, it was late and dark and pouring rain. My head was pounding, and I figured Bianca's was too. I was parked closer, so I drove Bianca to her car, waited for her to get it started, and then followed her home.

Once we were back at our place, I set my keys on the counter and caught her around the waist from behind. "Hey. Thank you for being there today, it meant a lot to me. I'm sorry it was such a long day."

"Don't apologize. I wanted to be there." She turned around in my arms and put her hands on my chest. "And if—if you don't feel like trying tonight, I would understand."

"Hush." I kissed her lips. "You go upstairs and relax. Take a bubble bath or something. I'll be up in a little bit."

"Okay," she said. "But I mean it. No pressure."

"I heard you." I glowered at her. "Now go do what I said, woman."

She rolled her eyes and headed for the stairs.

I waited until she was out of sight, then went back out to the garage for the package I'd been hiding in the back of my SUV. In the house again, I listened for the sound of the bathtub running upstairs before grabbing a beer from the fridge.

Then I dumped the contents of the package onto the counter and cracked the fuck up. This day might have been stressful, but this night was going to be epic.

Fourteen

Bianca

Upstairs, I filled the tub and sank into the water scented with lavender bath salts. I closed my eyes and took deep breaths, listening to the thunderstorm outside, trying not to see it as a bad omen, and repeating all my positive affirmations, determined to get the universe on my side. Like attracted like, right? So if I wanted that good energy, I had to put it out there.

But it wasn't all woo woo—science was on my side too. Biology was a thing. And medical intervention. I'd followed all the instructions, used the predictor kit, and by all indications the timing was right.

Still, I was nervous. Nervous . . . and excited.

Like, beyond excited.

It had been *ten days* since I'd felt Enzo's hands on me, felt his body over mine, felt that deep, sharp twinge of pain before it melted into pleasure. I knew he was anxious too—for heaven's sake, he'd pestered me for sex almost every night—but I'd stayed firm in my resolve not to give in. If I could resist him, or at least sex with him, then I was still on safe ground. It didn't matter that my feelings for him were growing stronger and deeper each day, as long as I was still in control. Being able to say no to sex that wasn't for procreational purposes made me feel like those walls around my heart were still standing.

Actually, I'd sort of hoped he might act a little distant while we weren't having sex, or at least give my feelings a chance to ebb. But if I'd thought he wouldn't be interested in hanging out with me without the lure of an orgasm at the end of the night, I'd been totally wrong. He came home for dinner every evening. He brought groceries or takeout or offered to cook. If we watched TV, he let me choose what we watched, and he didn't complain—much—if I chose something girly and romantic. One night he even gave me a foot massage while we watched a movie.

He came with me to visit Grandma Vinnie at the nursing home, where we listened to her tell stories about my great-grandparents, the bootleggers, and about growing up on Detroit's east side. We looked at old photo albums and marveled at the resemblance between my great-grandmother and me. Grandma Vinnie even thought the name Enzo DiFiore, which was Enzo's great-grandfather's name, sounded familiar to her. We laughed and wondered if maybe they'd known each other after all.

He also went over to my condo and fixed the garbage disposal after my brother JJ broke it somehow. He rescued me when I got a flat tire on the highway, rushing right out to change it himself, instead of making me call for service. And at night, he insisted I still sleep in his bed.

How on earth was I supposed to keep my feelings neutral?

But I couldn't worry about that now. I told myself those warm, fuzzy feelings would come in handy when it was time to split up because it meant we'd be able to treat each other with kindness and respect. We wouldn't fight over stupid things. We'd never say cruel things about one another in front of other people—especially our child. And we wouldn't make our friends choose between us. Everything would be fine.

And tonight, I would be his.

I got out of the tub, dried off and rubbed lavender-scented lotion into my skin. I took my hair down, brushed my teeth, and even put on my diamond earrings—I hoped they would be my good luck charms. Leaving my bedside lamp on, I took off my glasses and slipped naked beneath the sheets, waiting for Enzo to come upstairs.

Five minutes went by.

Ten.

Fifteen.

Outside, the storm got worse, the rain coming down harder and the wind whistling against the glass. Thunder rumbled in the distance. The power flickered.

I was about to throw on a robe and go see what was taking Enzo so long when the power went out completely. I waited a moment for it to come back on, and when it didn't, I sat up and called out. "Enzo?"

No answer. But I heard someone coming up the stairs.

"Enzo?" I called, my voice a little shivery this time.

Then he appeared in the bedroom doorway, carrying a candle in his hands—and wearing nothing but a black, floor-length cape with the collar turned up. "Enzo is not here," he said in a dramatic accent, something between Dracula and Ricky Ricardo. The fangs he wore made it difficult to tell.

I burst out laughing. "And you are?"

"I am Edward Mullins, of course." He set the candle on the dresser.

"You mean Edward Cullen?"

"Yes, sorry. I have been in a deep slumber for so long, I forgot my last name. But when I smelled your blood, I grew very thirsty."

"You can smell my blood, huh?"

"But of course."

"That's—that's quite an outfit you've got on there, Edward."

"Do you like it?" He brought one side of his cape across the lower part of his face. "I wasn't sure if capes were still in fashion." Then he swung it open with a flourish. "Or do you mean this?"

I let my eyes sweep over his naked body. "I like it all."

"Good." He threw the covers off me, exposing my bare skin. Then he growled. "I have not seen such beauty in centuries. I must have you or die."

I squealed as he climbed into bed, growling like an animal, and attempted to bite my neck with the plastic fangs. "Ow! Can you take those things out please?"

"If you insist." He tossed them to the floor and nipped my throat with his teeth. "Ah, yes. Much better."

Laughing, I ran my hands over his shoulders. "Do you want to take your cape off too?"

"That depends." His mouth traveled down to my chest, and he stroked my nipple with his tongue, making it hard before taking it between his teeth. "Will you still want me when I look like a mere mortal?"

I arched beneath his tongue, opening my legs as his hand moved between my thighs. "Enzo, you have never looked like a mere mortal."

"In that case." He rose to his knees and ditched the cape, then covered my body with his, his bare skin warm against mine. "Yes, this is much better. God, I've missed you."

Our mouths came together, our tongues seeking, our hands skimming, our breath growing faster and heavier. I'd been a little worried that the sex tonight would feel mechanical or obligatory or awkward, and I'd sort of assumed we'd get right down to the business of trying to conceive—but I'd been wrong. If anything, Enzo was even more patient, more playful, more passionate than he'd ever been. I found myself forgetting that this was simply a means to an end and reveling in every stroke of his tongue and caress of his fingers and sweet, slow undulation of his body over mine. I wanted to stay in this place forever, where I wasn't worried about failure or success, about time running out, about what the future would bring, and why I shouldn't love him.

There was nothing fake about it—I just wanted to be with him.

"Enzo," I whispered as he moved inside me. "Say something real."

"What?" He slowed his rhythm but didn't stop.

"Say something real," I begged.

At first he didn't say anything, he just looked down at me, and I was terrified.

But then.

"I never stop thinking about you," he said, his voice low and serious.

"Keep going," I whispered, the walls around my heart beginning to crumble.

"No one has ever made me feel the way you do. Sometimes I can't even breathe."

"Yes," I said, pulling him deeper, matching his rhythm. I knew exactly what he meant. "Yes, yes, yes."

"I want to give you everything." He stopped moving for just a moment, his lips hovering over mine. "Everything."

He said nothing else as the need built between us, the compulsion to move harder and faster and deeper—our hearts racing, our skin hot, our breathing ragged and quick. I came first and he followed a minute later, which allowed me to feel every pulse of his release inside me. And I didn't think about anything except that I loved the way it felt to share something so deeply intimate with him, to share myself with him, to share this bed and this night and this experience. It was the most powerful and intense feeling I'd ever had.

No wonder, I thought as we clung to each other in the warm, breathless aftermath. *No wonder this is how a life begins.*

Except it didn't work.

And as I sobbed in the bathroom on a Saturday morning two and a half weeks later, feeling sad and broken and ashamed, I realized how high I'd let my hopes get.

I'd known, even with the Clomid, that it might not work. But the sex had felt so magical. My connection to Enzo so intense. The chemistry between us so fiery.

So I'd thought maybe.

And I'd wished.

I'd prayed.

I'd listened to Enzo tell me how confident he was. And—most humiliating of all—I'd actually *felt* pregnant.

No joke, I'd actually convinced myself that I felt telltale signs for the first time . . . sore breasts, increased appetite, dizziness, a bloated belly. All symptoms of PMS, of course. God, how could I have been so dumb?

I gave in to the need to cry it out, even though I felt guilty about how sad I was, because some women try for *years* to get pregnant without any luck. Then I gave up feeling guilty and cried for them too.

Enzo was at the gym, but we were picking up the keys to the new house today at noon—so I knew he'd be back any minute. I didn't want him to see me like this, so I pulled myself together, took a shower, got dressed, and covered my face with makeup before going downstairs.

When I entered the kitchen, Enzo stood at the island with a cardboard cup of coffee. A second one was on the counter. "Morning, Lucy."

"Morning." I didn't quite meet his eye as I went to the sink and started filling a glass to water the plant in the kitchen window. "How was your workout?"

"Great. I stopped for coffee on the way home. Got you some tea, and don't worry—it's herbal. No caffeine."

"Doesn't matter," I said, choking back tears.

"Huh?"

"Doesn't matter," I said, my tone louder and sharper. I dumped the water into the dirt.

"Hey." He took the empty glass from me and set it aside before taking me by the shoulders and forcing me to look at him. "What's going on?"

I shook my head as the tears spilled over.

He understood without my saying a word, which somehow only made me cry harder. Pulling me to his chest, he wrapped his arms around me and held me while I wept into his sweaty gray shirt. His hands moved up and down my back. "Shh," he said, kissing my head. "It's okay."

"It's not," I blubbered, getting snot and tears and mascara all over him. "I failed. Even on the drug, I failed."

"That's ridiculous. If anything, I failed."

"It's *me*, Enzo. You had the test, and you were fine. *I'm* the problem."

"Hey." He took me by the upper arms again and held me back so he could look at me. "This was one missed chance, that's all. We get more, right?"

I wiped my nose with the back of my hand. "One more."

"Okay, so don't give up. You know what they say, third time's the charm." His lips tipped up on one side. "Right?"

I bit my lip, wishing he wasn't being so supportive and understanding about this. Wishing I didn't have this terrible gut feeling that it didn't matter how many chances we had, it wasn't going to work. Wishing I didn't have these feelings for him that were complicating everything.

"Right?" he urged again.

"Right." I stepped away from him and grabbed a few tissues from the box on the counter. I blew my nose and mopped up my face while he sipped his coffee and looked at me like he felt sorry for me and didn't know what to say.

It was fucking horrible. I didn't want to be the object of his pity.

He cleared his throat. "I forgot to tell you, my nephew James's fourth birthday party is tomorrow afternoon at Pietro's house."

"Sounds like fun," I said without any enthusiasm at all. Moretti family functions were frequent, loud, and went on forever. And it never failed—at least three older female relatives would come over, put a hand on my belly, and ask if I was pregnant yet. When I said no, they'd ask why and caution me not to put it off too long. They'd insinuate that it was because we didn't get married in church. And they all had a story about their cousin or friend or niece who thought she had all the time in the world and put her career first but was sorry later when she struggled to have children.

But Enzo didn't need to hear about that.

"We can pick something up for James in town today," I said, facing him again.

"Good idea. I was thinking of getting him a baseball glove and maybe a batting tee. He starts tee ball next month, and Pietro sucks at baseball, so I figure I better teach him."

I managed a smile. "Of course."

"You gonna be okay?" He moved closer to me and tugged on one earlobe.

"Yes." I gestured toward his chest. "Sorry. I made a mess of your shirt."

"Fuck my shirt. I'm a mess anyway. How about I shower up really quick and we hit the diner for breakfast?"

"Or maybe the bakery," I suggested, thinking how good one of Blair's pastries would taste this morning.

"You got it."

While we were at the bakery, Enzo got a phone call he went outside to take, and Blair came over to the small table where I was sitting and dropped into his chair.

“What’s wrong?” she said, her face concerned. “And don’t say nothing because I can tell there’s something.”

“I got my period today,” I said quietly, picking up my coffee cup.

“Oh.” She nodded sympathetically. “I’m sorry.”

“It’s okay.” I forced a smile. “We can try again next month. I’ll start another round of Clomid Monday.”

“Let me know if you need anything. An ear to rant into, a shoulder to cry on.”

“Thanks.” I took a deep breath and glanced outside at Enzo on the sidewalk. He was so damn handsome. “I cried all over Enzo this morning.”

“Yeah?” She glanced over her shoulder at him. “How are things with you guys?”

“Good. They’re good.” I dropped my eyes to my uneaten scone and shrugged. “We’re picking up the keys to the new house today.”

Her face lit up. “That’s exciting! When will the renovation begin?”

“Right away, I hope.” I broke off a piece of the scone but didn’t eat it. “I could use the distraction. I think we both could.”

“Was Enzo sad about the . . .”

“Yes,” I said. “But he’s been really sweet.”

“Of course he has. He’s not an asshole. And he genuinely cares about you, Bianca. No matter what you think.”

The knots in my stomach pulled tighter. “We’re actually getting along much better than I thought we would.”

“Really?”

“Yes. In fact . . .” I tried to laugh, but it sounded a little desperate. “I’m kind of worried about it.”

“Why?”

“Well, because the longer we live together, the better I get to know him, the more sex we have—the closer I feel to him. He’s not the guy I thought he was.”

"No?"

I shook my head. "No. In fact, he's shown himself to be incredibly kind and understanding through all this fertility stuff. I mean, don't get me wrong, he can still be a cocky bastard, and he loves to get under my skin, but he's actually a really good husband."

Her eyebrows went up. "Any chance you guys might stay together?"

"No," I said quickly. "There's been no talk about that."

"Well, maybe you *should* talk about it. After all, things have changed since you guys drew up that ridiculous contract. Maybe you can give yourselves some more time."

"More time would just make it worse," I said miserably. "If it doesn't work this next month, I have to walk away."

"Without even telling him how you feel?" She gaped at me. "Why?"

"Because the last time I opened myself up to someone like that, it ended with my heart shattered into a million pieces. This arrangement with Enzo was supposed to guard against that. He was supposed to be safe." My tone was sharp.

"But how do you know he isn't? I think you should be honest with him. Men aren't mind readers, you know."

Her choice of words was jarring—it reminded me that I'd promised Enzo I wouldn't make him guess at what I was thinking or feeling. Was she right? Should I just admit the truth to him?

I thought about the night he'd come up to the bedroom dressed like a vampire, and how once the costume was off I'd pleaded to hear something real. Not a day had gone by that I didn't hear his voice in my head.

I never stop thinking about you.

No one has ever made me feel the way you do.

Sometimes I can't even breathe.

I want to give you everything.

But what did that mean? Did he have feelings for me? Did he want me for something more than a temporary wife who'd supply him with offspring? And what if I couldn't even do that? What then?

Enzo came back inside and headed toward me, and I was conscious of the way every single woman in the place watched him. He knew it too, and even though he kept his eyes on me, something deep in my gut told me he'd never trade that kind of attention—let alone his sexual freedom—just to be with me, especially if he wanted kids. And why should he?

If I couldn't even give him a baby, what good was I to him?

"So how's newlywed life?" Pietro's wife Lynne dropped into the patio chair next to me. The sun was out, the temperature was unusually warm for spring in Michigan, and after an early dinner, we'd moved outside for some fresh air.

"Good. Great." I tried not to eyeball her pregnant belly with envy, or worse, bitterness.

"Your wedding dress was so cute. Of course, everything is cute on you. You're so petite." She ran her hands over her belly and laughed. "I'm a whale."

"Not at all. You look fantastic. When are you due again?"

"May twenty-fourth. So I still have four weeks left, if you can believe it." Then she sighed. "But I shouldn't complain."

No, you shouldn't, I thought irritably. What I said was, "It's okay."

"Actually, I love being pregnant," she went on. "I'm not one of those women so concerned about her figure that they worry pregnancy will ruin it."

I lifted my glass of wine to my lips. Whether she was insinuating I would be one of those women or not, the comment just didn't sit well with me.

"I just think it's the greatest gift, you know? Such a miracle.

Good job, honey!" She smiled and waved at James, who was out on the lawn playing with his new bat, ball, and tee. Enzo was coaching him, Pietro was fielding balls, and James's two-year-old sister Lilly was toddling around with a butterfly net. "Enzo has always been *so* sweet to the kids," she went on. "He'd make a great dad."

"Yes, he would." I watched Enzo take the bat from James and demonstrate one more time how to hit the ball off the tee. When it rocketed past Pietro into the makeshift outfield, Enzo scooped up Lilly, set her on his shoulders, and jogged around the bases. When he reached home plate, James begged for a turn, so Enzo set the little girl down and swept his nephew up onto his shoulders, then ran the bases again. As he went by us, he waved, and I smiled and waved back.

"See what I mean?" Lynne asked, as if I'd disagreed with her. "You guys should totally have kids."

"So we've heard," I murmured, a little more sarcastically than intended.

"Let me guess—Mama Moretti is already on you about it. I wasn't married to Pietro for ten minutes before she asked me when I planned on getting pregnant." She laughed and tapped my arm. "Luckily, it happened on my wedding night, can you believe it? We weren't even trying!"

"Wow. That *is* lucky. You have a beautiful family."

"Thank you. You will too someday. But don't wait too long. My sister's best friend Anna—she's an E.R. doctor—was always too busy to date and found herself still single at almost forty. She tried to get pregnant with a sperm donor, but it was too late. Her eggs were bad quality by then." She shook her head sorrowfully. "They never tell you that, do they? That your eggs have a sell-by date."

I tipped up the last of my wine. "I need to use the bathroom real quick. Be right back."

But I never went outside again.

"Hey, you." On the drive home from Pietro's, Enzo took my hand. "What's the matter?"

"I'm fine," I said.

"Except that I know you, and you're not fine. You're wearing your Very Serious Face, the one you make when the sauce isn't quite right and you can't figure out what you need more of, and you're hoping you don't need *less* of something, because there's nothing to be done about that."

I forced a smile. "Ha."

"Come on. Talk to me." He squeezed my hand. "You signed a contract saying you wouldn't make me read your mind, remember?"

"I remember the contract." *Especially the rule about not falling in love with you. And I'm terrified it's happening.*

"Are you still upset about this morning?"

"Yes." It wasn't a lie. It just wasn't the whole truth.

He was silent a moment, and when he spoke again I thought he was going to say something trite or patronizing—in fact, I almost hoped he would, so I'd have reason to be angry with him—something like *every cloud has a silver lining* or *you shouldn't take this to heart* or *it just wasn't supposed to happen yet.*

But he didn't. He took my hand, pressed his lips to my fingers, and held them there. Then he placed our hands in his lap.

My throat closed, and my eyes filled. *Stop it, I wanted to tell him. Stop acting as if you love me, because I'm confused and scared.*

"Lynne said something that made me feel bad," I confessed.

"What did she say?"

"Nothing awful. It was just the wrong day to tell me how much she loves being pregnant, what a miracle it is, what a great dad you'll make, how her sister's friend waited too long to try to have a baby and never could because her eggs got old."

"Why is she saying that shit to you?" He sounded angry.

"It's just how women talk. She didn't mean to make me feel bad," I assured him. Somehow his anger on my behalf took away some of the residual sting from her words. "Half the women in your family—and mine too—love to ask me when we're going to have kids. Sometimes it's a struggle to keep the smile on my face and evade the question."

"They should all fucking mind their own business," scoffed Enzo. "And I'm going to tell them so next time I see them."

I couldn't help smiling. "No, don't. It's okay."

"It isn't. Anyone who messes with you messes with me."

In the dim lights of the dash, I could see him scowling like he was ready to take on the playground bully for me.

And that was the moment I knew—I was madly, deeply, desperately in love with him.

But I couldn't tell him. He could never know.

I swallowed hard, and focused out the windshield again, the streetlights blurring through my tearful eyes. Closing them, I fought back against the sob trying to rise in my chest. This wasn't fair. This *wasn't fucking fair.*

I wasn't supposed to feel this way.

I wasn't supposed to feel anything.

Back at home, I actually dug out the original contract we'd signed and locked myself in the bathroom with it, reading it over and over again, trying to get back to that place—that feeling like I was safe on dry land.

But it was no use. The tide had swept me out to sea, and now I was drowning.

From a distance, I heard myself laughing as I wrote the words: *"Special rule for Bianca: No falling in love with Enzo Moretti, and if you forget for one moment what a cocky, arrogant, egotistical, presumptuous, swaggering ass he is, just come back and look at this list!!!!!"*

I saw his outraged, offended face as he demanded I remove the last part and recalled adding all the exclamation points. I'd promised him I knew exactly who he was and I'd never expect him to be anyone else.

What I hadn't realized was that I could love him exactly as he was, flaws and all. That the very things I used to dislike in him would one day make me smile. And how all the things I'd come to learn about him, how passionate and funny and sweet he could be—and what an incredible father he'd make—would turn my walls to dust.

Tears splashed onto the page, making the ink smear and run.

Enzo knocked on the bathroom door. "Bianca? Are you okay?"

I jumped to my feet, quickly folding up the tearstained paper. "I'm fine," I said, trying to sound as normal as possible. "Be out in a minute."

Then I shoved the folded page in a drawer, right next to the unopened box of Clomid pills I was supposed to start taking tomorrow. I picked up the box and looked at it, anger and resentment and fear and sadness rising in me.

The tears spilled fresh. I couldn't do this again. I just couldn't.

Tucking the box of pills at the very back of the drawer, I closed it, splashed some cold water on my face, and opened the door.

I knew what I had to do to save myself.

Fifteen

Enzo

THE FOLLOWING WEEK, I FELT LIKE I WAS WALKING ON eggshells around Bianca, constantly terrified of saying the wrong thing, so mostly I said nothing at all. I had no idea if she wanted to be left alone or wanted me around, so I tried to strike an even balance, working late some nights and coming home for dinner with her on others. I tried to do things for her I knew she liked—brought her flowers, made her waffles, let her choose the movie.

Nothing made her smile like it used to.

She seemed to retreat inward. Our house was eerily silent without the usual bickering. I wanted to touch her, but it wasn't at all clear whether she wanted to be touched or not, so I didn't risk it. And I certainly didn't ask about sex.

It killed me to see the light go out of her, but I had no idea how to make her feel better. And I was angry—so fucking angry. Why wasn't this pregnancy thing working? I knew I was letting her down. She swore I wasn't, but it was difficult not to feel that way. Her entire reason for entering into this marriage was to get a baby out of it, and I'd been so sure I could deliver. Here I stood ready to inherit the company—after the accident, my mother finally talked my dad into fully retiring—meaning that I'd gotten everything I wanted out of our deal. And she'd gotten nothing.

On Friday evening, I met up with the guys at the pub. When Griffin had first texted about hanging out, I'd hesitated to leave Bianca alone. But when I called and mentioned it to her, she encouraged me to go.

"Are you sure?" I asked.

"Yes. I'm really tired, so I'm just going to heat up some leftovers and go to bed early."

"Okay. Let me know if you change your mind and want company. I could make dinner."

But she never reached out again, so I went to the pub.

Cole, Griffin, Beckett and I caught up over beers and wings and burgers like we always did, but even being at the Bulldog reminded me of Bianca. I kept looking over my shoulder toward the back room where our wedding reception had been. Had it really been less than two months ago? It seemed like we'd been together a lot longer than that. I could hardly remember what it had been like living in my place alone.

I heard my name and looked back at my friends. "Sorry, what?"

"What's with you tonight?" Griffin asked. "You seem kinda out of it."

"Just—just thinking about all the shit I have to get done this weekend." I picked up my beer and took a long drink without tasting it. "Anyone feels like tearing up carpet, removing wallpaper, and ripping out cabinets, come on over to the new house tomorrow."

"I can help," Cole said. "I'm off tomorrow."

"Same," said Beckett. "My sister's in town, so I should be able to get away for a while. She can keep an eye on my dad."

"I'll come too," said Griffin. "Probably around one, after the garage closes."

"Thanks, guys."

Griffin and I stayed the longest, and later, as the two of us were walking to our cars, he asked me if Bianca was okay. "Blair keeps saying this week how worried she is about her."

I frowned. "Yeah, she, uh, didn't get pregnant this month. Again."

"Oh."

"She took it really hard."

"Can't you just keep trying?"

"That's the plan." I tried to keep my voice light. "But I get the feeling she's not all that hopeful anymore. And I feel so fucking bad, you know? I want to be able to give her what she wants. I hate when there's a problem I can't fix."

"Same. But I don't think we can compare this to a blown tire or a kitchen remodel."

"No, we can't," I grumbled. "It just sucks to see her this way. Is it weird that I like it better when she's arguing with me or telling me what an egotistical dickhead I am? She doesn't even seem like the same person."

"Maybe she just needs some time to work through the disappointment."

"We don't really have time. I'm telling you, this fertility stuff is such bullshit. You have to be so precise with the timing, and even then it might not work. What if I can't deliver on the promise I made?"

"Then I guess you guys get a divorce and go your separate ways." He glanced at me. "Wasn't that the plan?"

"It was, but—I feel like I'm abandoning her or something. It's fucked up."

"Do you want to stay married even if she doesn't get pregnant this month?"

My heart thudded hard. "I don't know. If you'd have asked me a week ago, I might have said something different. We were having so much fun—she was happy. I was happy. There was a part of me that thought maybe we should stay together, but then this week is the total opposite. I feel angry and useless and pretty fucking miserable. Not as miserable as she is, but Christ . . ." I shook my head. "I'm remembering all the reasons why I never wanted to get married in the first place. She's not talking to me. I have no idea if she wants me around or not. I'm too anxious to even touch her. We're not fighting, but I even miss the goddamn fights."

"I'm sorry, man. I wish I had some advice. Somehow I figured it out, but . . ." Griffin rubbed the back of his neck. "I feel like Blair must have done a lot of the work."

"But how did you *know*?" I asked. "Seriously, how did you know you could do it, the whole marriage thing, just you and her for the rest of your lives? How did you know you would be good at it?"

"I didn't," he said with a shrug. "But it was either try it or lose her, and I knew I couldn't lose her."

I nodded, feeling even more confused and despondent. "I thought I'd like the certainty of knowing it would end at a certain point. Now it feels like the clock is ticking faster every day."

"So what now?"

"I think we can try again middle of next week. She takes this pill for five days, which she's doing now, and then we wait for five days, then we have sex every other day for like a week. I'm telling you, it's like a fucking math problem trying to get this woman pregnant."

Griffin chuckled. "Sounds like it."

I said goodbye and got behind the wheel. As I drove home, I racked my brain, trying to think of something, anything, that would bring back the moxie of the old Bianca. I remembered our wedding night, how we'd sat up talking and drinking champagne and eating chocolates, how surprised I'd been when she whispered to me in the dark. I wanted that back.

On a whim, I turned around and headed back toward a

drugstore that was still open. The champagne wouldn't be high quality and the chocolates would be mass-produced, but maybe they'd make her smile. Maybe she'd get tipsy and open up a little bit. Maybe she'd invite me to kiss her, touch her, hold her. I didn't need sex—although I wouldn't turn it down—I just wanted to feel close to her again. I wanted to promise her everything would be okay and have her believe me.

And I wanted to keep that promise.

She was already in bed when I got home, but she wasn't asleep. She was sitting up in bed reading, glasses on, makeup off, hair in a messy pile on top of her head. She wore the navy plaid flannel top, but unbuttoned this time, and under it a little white tank. The room smelled like her lavender body lotion—a scent I was now attached to.

"Hey," I said, entering the room carrying a tray holding a bottle of sparkling strawberry wine, two glasses, and a box of chocolates shaped like a heart. "I brought you something."

Her lips curved softly and she set her book aside. "What's this?"

"It's a picnic," I said, "to celebrate our seven-week anniversary. I bet you didn't even realize it was today."

"I didn't," she confessed, watching me set the tray on the mattress.

"Well, lucky for you, I'm a romantic. And nothing says Happy Fake Seven Week Anniversary like some delicious *jampagne* and chocolate that's probably left over from Valentine's Day."

That brought a little laugh. "Who could say no to that?"

I grabbed the wine bottle and popped the cork, which shot up and hit the ceiling, then landed directly in one of the wine glasses.

Bianca looked at it in surprise. "Impressive."

"What did I tell you about my long shot, babe?" I plucked it out and poured her some sparkling pink wine. "I think that means our luck is about to change."

She took the glass I handed her without comment.

I poured myself some wine, sat on the bed, and held up my glass. "To seven weeks of wedded bliss. May the next seven be as fruitful as a glass of sparkling strawberry jampagne." I tapped my glass to hers.

"Cheers," she said, taking a sip. Her face puckered for a second.

I tasted the wine and my mouth did the same. It tasted like a mouthful of fizzy liquid jelly donut. "Mmm."

She nodded. "Mmm."

I pulled the top off the box of chocolates. "Here. Because nothing goes with sugar like more sugar."

"Thank you." She chose one and took a bite.

"Well?"

"Delicious."

I grinned. "And all this time I've been spending money on the good stuff when you're happy with drugstore wine and candy."

She smiled, but it didn't reach her eyes. "How was your night with the guys?"

"Good." I leaned onto my side, propping my head in my hand. "They're going to come over to the house tomorrow and give us a hand."

"Oh, nice."

"I figure we can get the kitchen torn out with the extra muscle."

She nodded. "Sounds good. I'm hoping to get all that wallpaper in the front hall removed over the next few days. I'm afraid to see how many layers there are."

I reached over and rubbed her leg through the blankets. "Don't do anything too strenuous."

"Why not?"

"Because you need to take care of yourself."

"For what?"

I frowned. "What do you mean, for what? For the baby."

She laughed, but it was an empty sound. "There's no baby, Enzo. Remember?"

"Well, not yet. But there will be." I sipped my awful wine. "What's the target shooting schedule like for next week?"

She looked away. "I'm not sure."

"You're not sure?" I was totally taken aback. "How is that possible? Last month, you were like, 'We must bang on Wednesday evening at precisely ten-twenty-two p.m. Eastern Standard Time when the moon is full.'"

She took a drink. "Sorry."

Immediately I regretted trying to be funny. "No, I'm sorry. I shouldn't make jokes. I was just wondering what day would be best."

"Wednesday, I guess. If you still want to try."

"Huh?" I picked my head up off my hand. "Why wouldn't I still want to try?"

"I don't know. I've just been thinking maybe you were getting tired of all this."

"All this what?"

"All this . . . me." She shrugged, and when she lifted her eyes, they were glassy with tears. "I know this isn't what you signed up for."

"What the hell are you talking about? This is exactly what I signed up for, Bianca. You asked me for three months and I said yes, right? Along with some really ridiculous shit?" I set my wine glass on the nightstand. "Where is that contract? Let's look at it."

"Why?"

"For fun. Come on, it will make you laugh. Remember how much fun we had making it up?" I was hoping seeing it would take her back to that moment in time, when she was full of hope and light and firecracker spirit. Even if it only reminded her how much she'd disliked me back then, she'd at least feel something other than sad.

She looked into her wine again. "Things were different back then."

"I know, but it will still be funny. I can't even remember some of the things we put on it." I slid off the bed and stood up. "I know you still have it somewhere."

"It's in the bathroom," she said. "Top drawer on the right. The one you gave me to use."

I raised my eyebrows and headed for the bathroom. "You keep our marriage contract in the can? That says a lot right there."

Switching on the light, I opened the top right drawer and moved some shit around—makeup wipes, cotton balls, Q-tips, toothpaste, dental floss, moisturizer, a box of pills—until I found a small square of folded paper. Unwrapping it, I tried to read what we'd written but could hardly make it out because it had gotten wet. Frowning, I looked at the drawer again. Had there been a fucking plumbing leak somehow?

I felt around and looked at the bottom of the drawer, but saw no evidence of moisture. The cotton balls and Q-tips were dry, and the white Clomid box showed no signs it had gotten wet.

It also showed no signs of having been opened.

What the fuck?

I picked it up and shook it—definitely full. I stared at the box in my hand, wondering if maybe she'd had a different pack. Otherwise, why else wouldn't she have taken them? If I remembered correctly, she should have started them on Monday, which meant she should have taken the last one today. I shook the box again, but it still wasn't empty.

I looked at the contract again, the blue ink diluted and smeared like the watercolor hue of her eyes.

With the page in one hand and the box of pills in the other, I went back into the bedroom. "What's this?" I asked, holding up the Clomid. "You haven't been taking them?"

Color splashed into her cheeks. She sucked in her breath.

"Be honest with me, Bianca. Did you not take the pills because you changed your mind?"

She swallowed and opened her mouth, staring at the pill box. "I . . ." Then she met my eyes again. "Yes. I changed my mind."

My arm dropped. "Why?"

"Because it wasn't going to work anyway, and I figure we might as well just stop pretending."

"And you didn't think to say anything to me about it?" My pulse was hammering in my head.

She set her wine glass on the nightstand. "I was going to. I just needed some time to process everything."

"Bianca, this is . . ." I tried to think of what this was. Plenty of words came to mind—hurtful? Shocking? Wrong?—but none of them were exactly what I wanted to say. She had every right not to take the drug, every right to take time to think, every right to decide whether or not she wanted a child with me.

So why did this feel like a punch in the gut?

She got to her knees on the bed, sitting back on her heels, and looked up at me. Her blue eyes were shining. "Please don't be mad at me, Enzo. Please." She began to cry. "I tried so hard to talk myself into it, but I just couldn't. I don't want the disappointment again. I don't want to feel like I'm letting you down."

"You're not."

"Yes, I am," she insisted, wiping away her tears. "I know you want kids, and you can still have them. You don't need me."

"But—"

"Listen to me, Enzo." She got off the bed, putting even more distance between us. "You tried, and I appreciate that. I couldn't have asked for anything more. And if you need me to stay longer to make sure Moretti & Sons goes to you, I will."

"Otherwise, what?" I asked, stunned to see her grab a pair of jeans from a dresser drawer I'd turned over to her and tug them on. What the fuck was happening?

"Otherwise, I think it's best if I go back to my condo."

"For how long?"

"For good, Enzo." Her tears kept coming as she took off the plaid pajama shirt and pulled on a gray sweatshirt over the white tank. "It's better this way, can't you see?"

"How?"

"Because we can stay friends. I can still help you with the house. We can still talk. We just won't be . . . together."

I was dying to go over and take her in my arms, let her blubber all over my shirt, tell her to stop talking this way and get back in bed.

But I stayed put. How was I supposed to argue with what she was saying? I *did* have what I wanted. She'd fulfilled her end of the deal. And if she'd changed her mind about having a baby with me, there was nothing I could do about it. In fact, I should be glad, shouldn't I? This last week had been so tough—I didn't want to live like that.

So why did it hurt so much to watch her packing up to leave?

I stood there with the pill box still in one hand and the contract in the other while she went into the bathroom. I was still frozen in place when she came out with a small cosmetics bag.

"I'll call you tomorrow, okay?" she said as she brushed by me without meeting my eyes.

"Okay." My voice was wooden. I felt numb.

She went to the nightstand and grabbed her book, then headed for the door.

"Bianca, wait."

She turned slowly, like she was reluctant to look at me. "What?" she whispered.

"This is what you want?" I asked. "You're sure?"

"I'm sure." Her expression was a mixture of fear and sadness, and I didn't have the heart to make it worse.

"Can you—can you let me know when you get there?"

"Yes." Tears filled her eyes again. "I'm really sorry, Enzo. But it's for the best. Please trust me."

Then she was gone.

Half an hour later, I was still sitting on the edge of the bed, drinking shitty wine and trying to tell myself she was right and this was for the best, when my phone vibrated. I looked at the screen. Usually seeing the name I'd entered for her in my contacts made me smile, but not tonight.

Old Ball and Chain: I'm home.

No, you're not, I felt like arguing. But what would be the point?

Me: Thank you.

That was it.

No further words were exchanged between us, despite the fact that we were married, and barely an hour ago we'd been lying here drinking strawberry wine and celebrating our anniversary.

Exhaling, I took the tray downstairs, dumped out the bottle, put the wine glasses in the sink and the heart-shaped chocolate box in the trash.

Back upstairs, I undressed and went into the bathroom, where I saw the diamond earrings I'd given Bianca on our wedding day. They were back in the box, which she'd left open, sitting on the vanity.

Right next to her wedding ring.

The sight made my chest feel like it was caving in. My throat closed.

A few minutes later, I turned off the lights and got in bed. I lay there in the dark, the house strangely silent and lonely as fuck. I could still smell her. Without thinking, I took her pillow and covered my face with it, inhaling deeply.

What the hell had gone wrong? And why was I so upset about it? I hadn't wanted to be married to her in the first place—or to anyone. All I'd wanted was to run Moretti & Sons, and now I did. The papers were signed. My dad was retiring. And even if he was a jerk about Bianca leaving and changed his mind, fuck it—Bianca was right. I could always leave Pietro to run Moretti & Sons and start my own company. I didn't need to prove anything to anyone.

And I could still have kids someday. Hell, men could have kids into their seventies, couldn't they? Maybe it wasn't fair, but that's the way it was.

Angry and sad, I turned onto my side and hugged her pillow the way I'd gotten used to holding her at night. My heart felt like someone was standing on it.

But it was done.

I'd tried my best, like she'd said. I'd tried and I'd failed, and now she wanted out.

Best to let her go.

Sixteen

Bianca

I knocked on the door of my old condo just before ten, but there was no answer. I realized JJ was probably out—it was Friday night, after all—and let myself in with the key I still had on my ring.

Shutting the door behind me, I took a deep breath, glad to discover my place did not smell like a locker room. It actually smelled sort of like my parents' house—like lemon furniture polish and fabric softener.

I peeked into my old bedroom, which *did* smell more like a locker room, wrinkled my nose at the clothes thrown everywhere and the unmade bed, and backed out again.

In my old office, I pulled out the sofa bed and made it up, then brushed my teeth, happy to note that the hallway bathroom was actually clean and freshly laundered hand towels were stacked in the cupboard.

Back in my office, I took a minute to glance at all the photos on my shelf, reminding myself that I still had family and friends. I still had places and memories I loved. In a way, I still had Enzo too—at least, I hoped I did. I couldn't bear the thought of never seeing him again, although I might have to avoid him for a while, at least until my heart didn't feel so exposed and vulnerable. I needed some time to build those walls back up.

I dug through the small overnight bag I'd hastily packed in the guest room at Enzo's and pulled out some pajamas. I put them on and slipped into bed before reaching for my phone. First I texted my brother that I was asleep in my office and I'd explain tomorrow.

Then I took a deep breath and let Enzo know that I'd arrived. His reply was quick and short, and I didn't blame him. I knew I'd blindsided him tonight. I should have told him at the beginning of the week that I'd decided not to take the Clomid again. I had no excuse—I'd simply put off the conversation because I knew it would be hard. I knew I'd have to admit the truth—that I wasn't strong enough to keep going through this rollercoaster of emotions. That I was worried my feelings for him were growing too big to contain. And I knew I'd have to follow it up by leaving.

What I hadn't known was how easily he was going to let me go. No fight. No pleas to stay. No trying to talk me into trying again. Mostly he'd seemed upset that I'd hidden the truth from him about the pills.

It seemed to me like the perfect evidence he was done with me. And why wouldn't he be?

He'd gotten his company. I couldn't get pregnant. There was nothing left, no reason for us to keep up the act.

He didn't love me. He was never going to love me.

I set my phone aside and cried myself to sleep.

Saturday morning, I woke up with my cheek on a damp pillow. I checked the time—it was just after seven.

Swinging my feet to the floor, I stretched and ran a hand through my hair. My head ached, my eyes felt puffy, and my nose was sore from blowing it so many times. There was a pile of soggy tissues on the floor next to the bed.

After dumping them in the trash, I threw on my jeans and sweatshirt, used the bathroom, and shuffled out to the kitchen to make some coffee. Again, I was pleasantly surprised to see that JJ had a fully stocked pantry and refrigerator, complete with fresh fruit and orange juice. Maybe I'd sold my brother short in the maturity department.

When the coffee was made, I poured myself a cup and wandered out to the living room, which is where I discovered JJ asleep on the couch, fully dressed, with a wrinkled, empty bag of potato chips on his stomach, crumbs spilling out onto the floor.

Frowning, I set my cup on the coffee table and went to the front hall closet to grab my hand-held vacuum cleaner. When I turned it on to clean up the mess, JJ jumped. "Bianca, what the hell?"

"You got chips all over the floor," I complained over the noise.

"So you have to clean it up now? It's the middle of the night."

"It is not. It's after seven." I turned off the vacuum. "And why are you sleeping out here?"

"I don't know. I came home and got hungry. I wanted a snack." He sat up and ran a hand through his hair, which was totally matted on one side and spiky on the other. "I must have fallen asleep."

I put the vacuum away and threw the chip bag in the garbage before going back to the living room and opening the blinds.

JJ moaned at the light. "What are you doing here anyway? I thought you got married."

"I did. We're . . . having some issues." I picked up my coffee and sat in the wide-backed chair opposite the couch, tucking my legs beneath me.

"What issues?"

"None of your business."

"Is he annoying or something? The girl I'm dating is *so* fucking annoying."

"No, he's not annoying."

"You're not moving back in, are you?" He looked scared. "I don't have anywhere to go."

"Relax. You can stay for now."

He looked relieved. "Thanks."

I glanced around. "It actually looks like you've kept the place pretty neat."

"Oh that," he said, yawning. "Yeah, Mom comes over once a week and cleans."

My jaw dropped. "Are you fucking kidding me?"

"No. She does laundry and grocery shops too."

I rolled my eyes. "That is ridiculous. You are a grown man, JJ."

"I didn't *ask* her to, Bianca. She insists. I think she's afraid you'll kick me out and I'll have to move back in with her and Dad."

"Well, you need to start looking for a place," I told him. "It's time for you to stop acting like a kid and get your shit together."

"Okay, okay," he said, looking injured. "Jeez. It's too early for this kind of abuse."

"Then go to bed."

"I'm going." He stood up and lumbered toward my old bedroom. "I liked you better when you were married."

I gave him the finger and took another sip of coffee.

Men.

I hid out in my old condo all day, even though I was dying to know how things were going at the Center Avenue house. Part of me wanted to just show up there and get to work, distract myself with good, old-fashioned manual labor and the challenge of a new creative project, but I knew I'd burst into tears the moment I saw Enzo. Ugly crying wasn't something I wanted to do in front of Griffin and Cole. Or in front of Enzo, for that matter. Bad enough he'd seen me fall to pieces last night.

Instead, I holed up in my office, cleaning out my desk, dusting off all the books and photos and knick-knacks on my shelves, then curling up with a book. But every time I thought about Enzo, my eyes filled. I went through an entire box of tissues and kept having to reread the same pages because I couldn't lose myself in the story. A thousand times, I checked my phone to see if he'd called or texted, but was disappointed every time. Then I'd get mad at myself for wanting him to reach out—it wouldn't help. A clean break was best.

But it fucking *hurt.*

By seven o'clock, I'd given up on reading and was balled up under a blanket on the couch watching a Lifetime movie.

My brother came into the living room and blocked the screen. "Hey. Want to order a pizza for dinner or something?"

"Sure. You're not going out?"

"I might go out later." He looked at me closely, probably noticing my bloodshot eyes and puffy face. "What's *wrong* with you?"

"Just stuff."

"Like what?"

"I don't want to talk about it."

"Okay." He turned around and walked away, leaving me staring after him.

Seriously. Only a brother would abandon a conversation like that.

Getting up off the couch, I followed him to the kitchen and took a bottle of wine from the rack on my counter. "Want a glass?"

"Nah." He pulled a beer from the fridge and popped off the cap.

"So tell me about your new girlfriend," I said, pouring a generous amount of pinot noir into a glass. "Do I know her?"

"She's not my girlfriend. We've only been dating for a few weeks."

"What's her name?"

"Reina."

I looked up at him in disbelief. "Reina?"

"Yeah." He leaned back against the counter and pulled out his phone. "What do you want on your pizza?"

"Anything is fine." I re-corked the wine bottle. "Is Reina super young and hot?"

"Yeah, but she's really into herself. It bugs me."

I took a sip of wine. "Well, give her a chance. Maybe she's insecure. Some people come off the wrong way at first because they're shy or nervous."

He shook his head and burped. "I don't think that's her problem."

While JJ ordered the pizza, I started unloading the dishwasher. I wondered if Enzo was still at the new house with his friends and what they were doing for dinner tonight. Would they get takeout and keep working? Call it a night and head for the pub? Would they ask Blair and Chey to join them? Would my friends wonder where I was?

"So are you going to tell me what happened with Enzo or not?" my brother asked, sitting at the island and watching me put away dishes.

I didn't say anything at first, just placed a stack of plates in the cupboard. Two juice glasses. A soup bowl.

"Did you guys have a fight?"

"Not really."

"So why are you here?"

"I'm here because Enzo and I realized that we might have rushed into marriage," I said carefully.

JJ belched again. "I could have told you that."

"We're taking some time and space to figure out the best way to proceed."

"Are you going to get divorced?"

I swallowed hard. "I don't know."

"Do you love him?"

Yes, I wanted to say, just to finally admit it out loud. *I didn't want to, but I do. And that's why I'm here.* But my answer was, "That's a complicated question."

"It is?"

"Yes," I said irritably, yanking out the silverware basket and setting it on the counter. "And even if I said yes, I do love him, it doesn't mean we should stay married. There are other factors."

"Like what?"

Angrily, I tossed forks and spoons and butter knives in the tray lining the drawer. "Like whether or not he feels the same."

"You think he doesn't love you?"

"I know he doesn't love me." I had to stop to take a breath. Brace myself on the edge of the counter.

"Then why'd he marry you?"

"Look, this is why I said it was complicated." I tamped down on the sob trying to work its way from my chest to my throat. "I can't explain why we can't be married anymore, but I just know that we can't. We tried, we failed. That's it, the end."

"Doesn't seem like you tried very hard."

I glared at him over my shoulder, then took my glass of wine and left the kitchen.

"Hey, where are you going?"

"To my office!"

"Why? We're talking."

"I'm done talking!" I went into my office and slammed the door behind me, then took a big long drink of wine. I checked my phone and noticed I'd missed three calls from Blair. She'd texted too.

Blair: WHAT IS GOING ON??? Call me.

I sat down and called her back.

"Hey," she whispered as soon as she picked up. "Hold on."

I listened to her muffled breathing and then what sounded like a door closing.

"Where are you?" she said frantically but quietly.

"I'm at home," I said. "As in my old condo. Why are you whispering?"

"Because Griffin and Enzo are here and I don't want them to hear me."

At the mention of his name, my pulse picked up.

"Why are you at your old condo?" she asked.

"Because Enzo and I are moving ahead with the plan at an accelerated pace. Phase two failed. We're now in phase three—the breakup."

"You're breaking up?"

"Actually, we were never really together."

"You know what I mean. You're moving out? You're getting divorced? You're not trying for a baby anymore?"

"All of the above," I said bitterly, taking another sip of wine.

"I figured something had happened. I went by the Center Avenue house this afternoon with sandwiches and offered to stay and help out. Enzo was acting so weird, and you were nowhere to be found, and he kept saying he wasn't sure where you were or if you were coming."

"What do you mean, acting weird?" I asked.

"He was just not himself at all. Silent and broody. Big scowl on his face. Barking directions at everyone and snapping if anyone asked a question—especially about you."

I put a hand on my forehead and squeezed my eyes shut.

"So you're really leaving?"

"I have to, Blair."

"Because of what you told me?" she asked gently.

"Yes," I said softly, tears leaking from my eyes. "I couldn't stay another month. I couldn't keep sleeping with him. I couldn't bear another heartbreaking disappointment. I couldn't risk falling deeper in love with him. All of it was too much—I felt like I was under water. I couldn't breathe."

"I'm sorry, Bianca. I wish there was something I could do."

I grabbed a tissue from the box on my desk. "I'll be okay. I'm just going to stay away from him for a little while. Try to let my feelings cool off."

"What about all your stuff at the house?"

"I'll have to get it eventually." I paused to blow my nose. "What's he doing at your place?"

"Griffin invited him over for dinner. He said he felt sorry for him."

"How long will he be there?"

"I don't know. We just ordered takeout. Why, do you want to come over?"

"No! I'm wondering if I have time to go get some more stuff from the house. All my clothes are there."

"Do you have to sneak around? Can't you just talk to him?"

"I don't know if I can handle it yet," I said honestly, my voice breaking. "Last night was so hard. I barely held it together. I don't want him to know how I feel—that will only make it worse."

"Why?"

"He'll just pity me. He'll look at me like he did after I got my period. Like he feels sorry for me."

"Well, he does. I do too."

"It's not how I want him to see me, okay?" I was trying not to cry openly—I didn't want my brother to hear me—but I broke down anyway as I paced back and forth. "I want my pride back. I want my strength back. I want him to look at me and see the girl he thought I was. The one with courage and determination, who can handle anything life throws at her. The one with moxie."

"Moxie?"

"Yes. He once said he liked that about me—that I had moxie."

She sighed. "He likes a lot of things about you. He's just being an idiot."

"No, he isn't. He's being exactly who he is." I stopped pacing and took a breath. "Exactly who I knew he was. And it's on me for falling for him when he told me not to."

"I hate this," Blair said. "Tell me what to do to help."

"Can you figure out how long he'll be at your place?"

"Am I supposed to do it without mentioning why I'm asking?"

"If you can." I chewed the tip of my thumb.

Another sigh. "I'll try. And I'll text you."

"Thanks."

Seventeen

Enzo

I was sitting on the couch at Griffin and Blair's apartment, nursing a beer and a bad attitude when Blair came out from the bedroom, her phone in her hand and a strange, plastic-looking smile on her face.

She perched on the edge of a chair adjacent to the couch, her feet side by side and her spine completely straight. She looked like a pageant contestant waiting to be asked about her thoughts on world peace.

"What's going on?" Griffin asked suspiciously from the opposite end of the couch.

"Nothing's going on," she said, false brightness in her voice.

"I know that face. Something is going on. Who called?"

"Called? When?" she asked, as if she hadn't leaped off the chair, dashed into the bedroom, and slammed the door the moment her phone buzzed five minutes ago.

Griffin and I exchanged a look. "Just now," he said.

"Oh. Uh, that was Cheyenne."

"Cheyenne and Cole are at the movies with Mariah tonight," Griffin reminded her.

"Oh, right. Ummm, it was your mom."

"My mom is out of town."

"Oh." Blair looked frantic. "It was a wrong number?"

"A wrong number?" Griffin stared at her. "And you took your phone into the bedroom and talked to this stranger for five minutes?"

"Blair," I said. "Was it Bianca?"

She gave up the act. "Yes, but you're not supposed to know that."

"Why?" Griffin asked as I tipped up my beer and took several swallows.

"Well, she wanted me to find out how long he'd be here, because she wants to grab some clothes from the house without running into him." She met my eyes. "I'm sorry, Enzo."

"Wait a minute. Bianca moved out?" Griffin looked at me.

"Yeah." I finished my beer and stood up. "You guys got any whiskey?"

Blair followed me to the kitchen, and along the way she grabbed a brown bottle off a bar cart. "You want ice?" she asked as she took down a glass and poured.

"Nah."

"I told Bianca I'd let her know," Blair said, handing me the drink. "You think maybe a couple hours?"

I didn't answer until I'd taken several swallows, wincing as the liquor burned its way down my throat. "Why can't she call me herself?"

"I don't know."

"What did she say?"

She shook her head, although her expression was sad. "I can't betray her confidence."

I took another drink. *I* should be the one with Bianca's confidence. I was her husband, for fuck's sake. "I don't understand her. Last night when she left, she said she wanted us to be friends."

"I think she does want that." Blair chose her words carefully. "She just needs a little time to get there. She's . . . she's sad, Enzo."

"About what?"

Blair shrugged. "Everything."

"The whole thing was her idea, did she ever tell you that?" I asked angrily.

"Yes."

Griffin ambled over and opened the fridge, grabbing another beer. After removing the cap and tossing it out, he leaned back against the counter and crossed his arms. "What happened?"

"Fuck if I know." I drank again. "One minute things were fine, the next she was packing a bag."

"I'm sure it was a really hard decision for her to make," said Blair.

I shrugged.

"Did you guys have a fight or something?" Griffin wondered.

I laughed, but it was a cold, angry sound. "No. We haven't fought in a while."

"Trying to get pregnant can be really stressful," Blair said.

"I know that," I snapped. Then I shut my eyes. "Sorry. I'm just—in a bad mood. And tired. I didn't sleep much last night."

"I understand," Blair said gently.

Griffin took a bottle of wine from the fridge. "Want a glass?" he asked her.

"Yes. Thanks, honey."

I watched Griffin pour a glass of wine for his wife and felt a ridiculously sharp pang of envy.

Tonight after dinner, they'd go to bed together. Sleep together. Wake up together. Tomorrow he might do a dozen little things for her—pour her a cup of coffee, kiss her goodbye, put air in her tires, buy her flowers, tell her she was beautiful, compliment the dress she wore or the color of her eyes or the smell of her perfume. And maybe she'd put her arms around him and bury her face in his neck like Bianca sometimes did and inhale deeply, like she wanted to breathe me right into her soul.

"Enzo?"

I looked up and realized they were both staring at me. "What?"

"Would it be okay to tell her she can go to the house?"

I frowned. "It's fine."

"Two hours is safe?"

Nodding, I tipped up my glass again. I fucking hated that she didn't feel *safe* around me. What the hell was that about? What did she think I was going to do? Restrain her? Pick a fight? Beg her to stay? *Fuck that.* I was *glad* she was going. I didn't need this aggravation. She wanted to move out right away? Fine. The sooner, the better. I hoped she took every scrap of clothing, every item she'd used, every trace of herself out of the house tonight. I never wanted to be reminded of her or this stupid idea we had ever again.

As Blair ducked into the bedroom to call Bianca back, I finished my whiskey and went back to the bottle for more.

Fuck it all.

Early the next morning, I heard a noise. I picked up my head, which ached painfully, and opened my eyes. For a second, I was confused—then I remembered. I'd drunk too much to drive home, and I'd slept on Griffin's couch.

Sitting all the way up, I winced at the light coming through the blinds and at the thick, sandpapery texture in my mouth. Closing my eyes, I took a moment to let the dizziness subside. Through the dull, throbbing fog, I heard a soft voice.

"Morning."

I opened my eyes to see Blair set a cup of black coffee on the table in front of me. Then she sat in the chair next to the couch, tucking her legs beneath her, holding her own mug with both hands. She was dressed in sweats, her long hair in a loose braid over one shoulder.

"Morning," I croaked.

She smiled sympathetically and nodded at the coffee. "That's for you."

"Thanks." I picked it up by the handle. "I need it."

"Griffin ran to the bakery for donuts. I have a rare Sunday morning off."

I gulped the coffee, burning my tongue.

"Easy," she said. "It's hot."

I set the cup down and leaned back, closing my eyes to shut out the light again. "I think someone poisoned me."

She laughed. "His name is Jack Daniels."

"Bastard."

"You'll live."

After a moment, I picked up my head and looked at her. Details were coming back to me about the previous night. If I recalled correctly, Blair had taken Griffin's truck and met Bianca at the house. "Did you go help her?"

Blair nodded. "Her brother was there too. We got everything out. She left the key on the kitchen counter."

"Good," I said, although *nothing* about it felt good. She was my wife. She should fucking live with me.

"How do you feel?"

"Hungover."

"I meant about Bianca leaving."

I was silent a moment, then decided to lie. "Fine."

"Really?"

"Yeah." I sat up taller and picked up my coffee cup again. "I feel fine about it. It was always the plan, after all."

"I know, but . . . I don't think *she's* fine about it."

"What do you mean? She's the one who left."

"That doesn't mean she really wanted to."

I shook my head, feeling completely lost and exhausted.

"I'm worn out, Blair. I can't do this. I can't read her mind. Unless she tells me what she's thinking or feeling, all I have to go on is what she says to me and what she does. And what she said Friday night was that she wanted to go. What she did was leave."

Blair nodded, dropping her eyes to her coffee. "She told me you found the Clomid box."

"Yes." I felt validated and sat up taller. "That's a perfect example. She decided on her own not to take them, decided we weren't going to try a third time, knew she was going to leave early, and she said nothing to me about it. I was fucking blindsided."

"She feels bad about that."

"But she still left, Blair. What was I supposed to do, beg her to stay? For what reason?"

"I don't know," she said with a small lift of her shoulders. "Maybe because you guys have feelings for each other?"

"We don't have *feelings* for each other," I scoffed. "We had a *contract*. We had rules. We had a start date and an end date. It was all fake. What do I care if she wants out sooner rather than later?"

"It was all fake at the beginning," she said softly. "But hasn't that changed?"

I rubbed a hand over my jaw. "Part of me thought maybe it *could* change. But that was before she left."

"So your ego is bruised—I get it. But if there's anything to be salvaged," Blair went on, moving to the edge of her seat and putting a hand on my knee, "don't you think it's worth a conversation?"

Their apartment door slammed loudly, and I felt like my skull had been crushed in it. I stood up. "I gotta go."

"No, stay," Blair implored. "You should eat something."

"I'm not hungry," I said, passing Griffin on my way out.

"You're leaving?" he asked, surprised.

"Yeah. I'll call you later. Thanks for letting me crash."

Outside, I inhaled fresh air and walked to my car, which was parked down the street. I couldn't wait to get home and brush my teeth, take a shower, crash. I wanted to sleep for a year, then wake up and not feel this throbbing in my head, this pit in my stomach, this ache inside my chest.

But instead of driving home, I found myself heading for the harbor. Angry about what I was doing, I clenched my jaw as I circled the parking lot at Bianca's complex. Her car was there, and as I passed it, I remembered teasing her about all the shit in it. When I passed her end unit, I slowed down, but her blinds were shut and I couldn't see inside.

Gripping the steering wheel tight, I pulled into a visitor spot and put my SUV in park. Then I sat there scowling at the gray water. Should I go in and talk to her? Demand to know if Blair was right? If there were real feelings between us? If there was something worth salvaging among the wreckage?

I nearly turned off the ignition when I caught myself.

No. Fuck that.

I'd told her from the very beginning that I wasn't going to play games like this. Bianca had never been one to filter her thoughts around me—she always said exactly what she felt like saying. And what she'd said the other night could not have been more clear.

We were done.

I went home, let myself in, and plodded up the stairs, the sharp edges of my anger dissipating, replaced by a dull ache I told myself was the hangover and not missing Bianca. But I couldn't resist going into the guest room and opening up all the dresser drawers—empty. As was the closet.

In the bedroom we'd shared, her nightstand held no stack of books. The drawer I'd given her in my dresser was cleaned out. In the bathroom, the earrings and ring were exactly where she'd left them Friday night. But there were no perfume bottles on the vanity, no shampoo and conditioner specially formulated for redheads in the shower, no girly products or cosmetics to be seen. As I'd hoped last night, she'd removed nearly every physical trace of herself.

Yet somehow, the entire place still smelled like her.

I got undressed and dragged myself into the shower, trying to scrub off the regret, the loneliness, the anger, the memory of her skin on mine.

After drying off, I hung up my towel on the back of the door, where a hook still held her towel. Immediately I grabbed it and held it to my face, inhaling the scent of her shampoo. Then I was disgusted with myself for doing it, and I threw the damn thing into the hamper.

In the bedroom, I pulled on boxer briefs and some sweatpants, shut the blinds, and crashed into bed, pulling the pillow over my head. Belatedly, I remembered that I'd meant to take some ibuprofen, but I was too exhausted to get up and do it.

Feeling like life had beaten me to a pulp, I fell asleep.

I woke up around one, went downstairs and ate some pasta that Bianca had made and left in the fridge, straight from the plastic container without even bothering to heat it up. Standing there at the counter, shirtless and barefoot, I saw the key Bianca had left on the island. With a fresh ache in my heart, I stuck it in the junk drawer and finished eating. Then I went right back to bed and pulled the covers over my head.

I was yanked out of a dream—which was fine by me, because it was the one where my teeth are falling out—by the sound of someone pounding on my front door. The light in my room was gray and shadowy, and when I checked my phone I discovered it was already six o'clock. Sitting up, I rubbed my face with both hands. My scruff was long and scratchy, and my hair was probably a mess. The banging on the door persisted, so I threw on a sweatshirt and Bulldogs cap before going down to answer it.

When I saw who it was, I regretted coming down at all.

"Enzo Moretti, what is the matter with you?" My mother pushed her way inside the house and slapped me upside the back of my head. She was so much shorter than me, she practically had to jump to do it.

"Ow, Ma! I have a headache," I told her, straightening my cap.

"I'll just bet you do." She marched into the kitchen, set her purse on the counter and faced me. Folded her arms over her chest. Narrowed her eyes. "You weren't at church today."

"I slept in."

One brow arched. "Where? Not here, because I know what was going on *here* last night."

Ignoring that, I opened the cupboard where I kept a bottle of ibuprofen. I shook four into my hand.

"Answer me!" my mother snapped.

I turned on the faucet and filled a glass with water. "Sorry. What was the question?"

"Where were you last night?" she demanded loudly.

Wincing at the volume of her voice, I popped the pills in my mouth and washed them down. "I was at Griffin's."

"*Really.*" As if she didn't believe me.

"Really."

"Not another woman's?"

I made a face at her over my shoulder. "What? No!"

"Because I cannot *imagine* why your brand new wife was seen moving out of your house unless you betrayed her in some way."

"Well, I didn't." I wasn't even going to ask her how she'd heard about Bianca moving out—in a town like Bellamy Creek, she'd probably gotten five phone calls from people already, because someone happened to be out walking their dog last night and saw Bianca put a suitcase in her trunk.

"So where is she?" my mother demanded.

"Probably at her condo." Facing my mother, I leaned back against the counter and drank more water.

"Why?"

I shrugged. "She said she'd made a mistake. We rushed into the marriage. She just wants to be friends."

My mother's jaw fell open and snapped shut again. "Bullshit!" Then she pointed a stubby finger at my chest. "You did something to make her mad."

"No, I didn't, Ma. You can even ask her."

"Believe me, I intend to," she huffed. "But in the meantime, you march right over to wherever it is she went and you apologize to her."

"For what? I didn't do anything."

"Then apologize for that!"

I rolled my eyes. "This is ridiculous. *She left,* Mom. Why don't you feel sorry for *me*?"

"I just don't!" Her eyes blazed with anger. "I know you too well."

"What's that mean?"

"It means, you don't take anything seriously. You think life is just one endless good time. A joke. Well, no one's laughing!"

"What the hell are you talking about?" I was getting mad now.

"You never took this marriage seriously. You wouldn't even let the priest bless it."

"Because it was just a piece of paper to us."

She threw her hands up. "See what I mean? Marriage is not just a piece of paper—it's a lifelong commitment. For better or worse, richer or poorer, 'til death do you part. And with your history, Bianca probably suspected all along your heart wasn't really in it. You must have made her feel insecure. If it wasn't another woman, it had to be your job. You're just like your father! You put work first! You didn't make her feel like a priority!"

"You have no idea what you're talking about," I said through clenched teeth.

"Then explain it to me. Why would a woman married less than two months leave the man she's madly in love with?"

"She's not in love with me, Mom!" I yelled.

"Of course she is." My mother rolled her eyes. "Any idiot could see it."

"She's not," I said, lowering my voice. "She's just a good actress."

My mom parked her hands on her hips. "I don't understand."

"We were never in love. We only got married so Dad would leave Moretti & Sons to me when he retired."

Her face drained of color. "No."

"It's the truth. Bianca agreed to marry me because of that stupid family tradition."

"But—but—why would she do that?"

"That's between us," I said, wanting to protect Bianca. "But she's blameless. This was all my doing. I'll come clean to Dad."

"Damn right, you will. I'm not telling him this. It will kill him that he's raised a dishonest man."

The punch landed right in my gut, as intended. I pressed my lips together in a grim line. "Look, I'm not proud of myself. I'll tell him. Just please don't say anything to anyone else. It would be humiliating for Bianca and me both. This is hard enough."

"I don't get it." My mother rested her forehead on her fingertips. "You're in love. I know you are. I saw it. We all saw it."

"You all saw what you wanted to see. What we wanted you to see."

My mother looked up at me. "Then why was she crying so hard?"

“What?”

“Last night when she was moving out, why was she crying the whole time?”

I felt like the wind had been knocked out of me. “How do you know she was?”

“Because people saw her. Edna Dodson lives right across the street and happened to be looking out her window.”

I rolled my eyes. “Of course.”

“Then she went outside to water her flowers, and—”

“At nine o’clock at night, she had to water her flowers?”

“Yes,” my mother snapped, “and thank goodness she did because she called me right away, *very* concerned. I told her she must have been mistaken, but I can see now that I was wrong.”

Rubbing my face with both hands, I exhaled. “What do you want from me, Mom? I told you the truth.”

She came over to me. “I want you to *fix this*,” she said, poking my chest twice for emphasis.

“I told you, I’m going to be honest with Dad. If he wants to leave Pietro the company, fine.”

She waved a hand in the air. “I don’t mean with your father—I mean with Bianca.”

“There’s nothing to fix with Bianca. It’s over.”

“Bullshit!” she said, slapping my shoulder.

“Ow,” I said, rubbing it. “Jeez, I forgot how violent you are when you’re mad.”

“And I forgot how much you remind me of your father when you’re being stubborn and ornery—you look me in the eye and tell me you don’t love that girl, and may God strike you down if you lie!”

I looked her in the eye, fully prepared to say the words.

And I couldn’t. I fucking couldn’t.

“Look, it doesn’t matter how I feel, Mom,” I said. “She’s gone.”

“You know what she needs to hear to come back.”

"No, I don't!" I yelled, my temper flaring again.

"Well, figure it out and say it before you lose her to someone who does!" With that, she turned around, grabbed her purse from the counter and stomped out, slamming the door shut behind her.

I half-expected my dad to come storming into the Moretti & Sons office on Monday morning and demand his company back, but he didn't. He didn't call, either. I had to assume my mother had kept her word to let me confess my wrongdoings myself, and for that I was thankful. I planned on coming clean with him, fully prepared to deal with whatever the consequences were, but I felt like I could use some time to think.

That week, I worked long hours on Moretti & Sons projects, landing a couple good-sized contracts and overseeing the completion—on time—of several home additions. At least my father wouldn't be able to complain about my performance or work ethic.

Each night, I'd head over to the Center Avenue house, where I continued work on the renovation. Sometimes I offered cash to a couple guys who worked for Moretti & Sons for a few extra hours of labor, and by the end of the week, the kitchen was completely torn out, the old bathrooms demolished down to the studs, the carpet ripped out, the wallpaper removed, and tons of old junk had been removed from the basement and hauled away.

I'd hoped that staying busy would keep my mind off Bianca, but I thought about her constantly. Every time someone texted me, I was disappointed it wasn't her. Once I could have sworn I smelled her perfume in a store, and I walked up and down the aisles, sniffing like an idiot, until I was convinced she wasn't really there. Every time I walked into a room at the Center Avenue house, I'd remember her design ideas and feel like shit. The house was supposed to be something we did *together*.

And each night, when I'd go home to my empty house,

it seemed more lonely than it had the night before. It was too quiet. The meals I made were tasteless. The coffee in the morning wasn't as good. The smell of her on the pillow faded, and I was so angry, I threw it across the room.

Nothing was right without her there.

Word got around that she'd moved out, and I felt the curious stares of people who wondered what had gone wrong so quickly. But whenever anyone asked about her, I simply said we were taking some time and space. When my friends checked in with me, I said I was fine, but I wasn't—and lying to them only made me feel worse. I could still hear my mother calling me a dishonest man, and I hated it. When I lay in bed at night, struggling to fall asleep, all I could think about was her body, her lips, the way she'd sigh when I buried myself inside her.

I missed her. I fucking missed her like I'd never missed anyone. Only one week had gone by without seeing her, hearing her, touching her, but I felt like I was losing my mind. And every time I thought about her crying as she moved out, I wanted to put my fist through a wall.

If she didn't want to go, why had she gone?

Saturday, a few Moretti construction guys came over to the new house to help me with plumbing and electrical, and JJ DeRossi was one of them. I waited until he was alone in the kitchen, installing some recessed lights in the old plaster ceiling, before casually asking him how Bianca was.

At least, I tried to sound casual. Inside, I was desperate for any information about her.

"She's good," JJ said. "Hey, can you hand me that oscillating tool?"

Good? That's all I was going to get?

I tried again after handing him the tool. "Has she, uh, mentioned me at all?"

"Nope. Not really." He began to cut a circle into the plaster, and I waited until he was done and the noise stopped.

"What's she been doing?"

"She works a lot, and then she goes out at night."

"She does?" Surprised, I adjusted my cap and crossed my arms over my chest. "Huh. I didn't think she went out much at night, especially work nights. Usually she just likes to read or watch TV."

"Yeah, she's been out pretty much every night."

"With who?"

"Friends, I guess. I haven't really gotten a chance to ask her because she gets home so late."

I frowned. "How late?"

"I dunno. Two or three maybe."

My arms came undone. "In the *morning*?"

"Yeah. Like after the bars close."

Furious with myself for asking, and with Bianca for apparently handling our breakup much better than I was—and with any guy out there who'd see her out and about and assume he could flirt with *my fucking wife*—I left the kitchen and walked around the house, looking for a project that would require the use of a sledgehammer.

The whole rest of the day, I couldn't stop thinking about what JJ had said. Was she really as happy as he made it sound? Was she seriously going out every night until two in the morning, closing down bars? It did not sound like the Bianca I knew *at all.* Nor did it sound like the Bianca that Blair had described, the one who was "not okay."

I stayed late at the house, working by myself, growing more agitated every hour. By the time I got home and took a shower, I was nearly unhinged.

I had to see her.

After hanging up my towel, I turned back to the mirror and studied my reflection. Once upon a time, the Moretti smolder had been a force to be reckoned with. Did I still have it? After all, I *was* getting older. A couple grays were creeping into my dark hair. Lines had begun to etch themselves faintly into my forehead, and all the frowning I'd been doing lately wasn't helping. I tried to relax the muscles in my face, glad when the lines mostly disappeared.

Turning sideways, I double-checked that I wasn't developing a big gut, then I faced the glass again and attempted my signature expression, the one I'd been using for almost twenty years to charm my way into or out of any situation. I lowered my lids a little—not too much, because the eyes were the most important factor in the smolder—and arranged my mouth into that slightly crooked half-smile, half-smirk women could not seem to resist. I tilted my head. I tousled my hair. I cocked one eyebrow just enough to suggest an invitation.

Oh yeah. I still had it.

Now I just needed an excuse to see her so I could use it.

I couldn't just show up on her doorstep like a sad, lonely puppy—I needed a reason to go there. An excuse. I didn't want her to know how badly I missed her, how much I cared, how hurt I was that she'd gone, how lost I felt without her.

While I thought about it, I hunted for a pair of tweezers. I opened the drawer on the top right, which was where I'd stuck the unopened package of Clomid, along with the diamond earrings and the ring I'd put on her finger, back in its velvet-cushioned box.

Ignoring the ring, I took out the pills and the earrings.

I had an idea.

Eighteen

Bianca

OVER THE NEXT WEEK, I FORCED MYSELF TO PICK MY head up and carry on. After all, I had deadlines to meet. Clients that needed me. A company to keep afloat. I'd lived through a broken heart before, hadn't I? I'd get through this one too.

I tried hard.

I meditated every morning. I canceled my appointment at the fertility clinic and scheduled an appointment with my therapist. I got my nails done with Ellie. I colored my own hair a slightly deeper shade of red. Thursday, I took a day off work and spent the entire afternoon making zeppole, then boxed up little batches of them and delivered them to family and friends.

But I still missed being with Enzo. I still mourned the loss of what we'd had. And I continued to cry myself to sleep at night, terrified I'd never find that kind of magic with anyone else.

On Friday after work, I met up with Blair and Cheyenne for drinks at a wine and cheese bar called The Avignon.

"So how are you?" Cheyenne asked, her eyes wide with concern across our high-top table.

"I'm okay," I said, taking a deep breath. "I'm doing okay."

Blair smiled tentatively. "Did you get your hair done? It looks great."

"Actually, I did it myself," I told her, laughing a little. "I wanted a change, and I was too impatient to wait for an opening with my stylist. I hope she doesn't kill me."

"I'm sure she'll understand," Cheyenne said. "We've all been there."

We ordered glasses of wine, some cheese and charcuterie, and chatted about our work weeks, our weekend plans, and the warmer weather. May in Michigan was always unpredictable—you could have snow or eighty-degree days full of sunshine. Luckily, this spring had been mild, and the temperatures were warming up nicely. People were starting to put their boats in the water, and Bellamy Creek was busy with tourists again. But we couldn't avoid the ghost at the table forever.

Blair broke down first. "So no word from Enzo, huh?"

I shook my head. "Nope."

"I haven't seen him either," she said. "Even Griffin said he's been strangely MIA."

"Same." Cheyenne picked up her pinot noir. "I asked Cole before I left if he'd heard from Enzo at all this week, and he said no. Evidently, he's not even responding to texts."

I shrugged, trying to ignore the worry they were putting in my head—I hoped he was okay. "He could be busy at work, now that he's in charge, or putting in a lot of time at the Center Avenue house. But he certainly hasn't been with me."

"I don't get it!" Blair said angrily. "He was so miserable the day after you left, I thought for sure he'd beg you to come back by now."

"I think he was just mad about the way I did it," I said, "without consulting him first. Or that I'd been dishonest about the Clomid."

"I think there was some of that," Blair said. "He admitted

he'd felt blindsided, and his ego definitely took a hit. But he was hurt too, Bianca. I could tell. He didn't want you to go."

"Then why didn't he try to stop me?"

Cheyenne and Blair exchanged a look.

"What?" I said.

"It's just . . . These guys don't always know exactly how to express what they're feeling," said Cheyenne. "They're either too stubborn or they seriously just can't think of the right words or they're plain old scared to be that vulnerable."

"The only thing Enzo is scared of is someone falling in love with him," I said, "but then, of course, he goes and does everything he possibly can to *make* you fall in love with him."

"Not before you," Cheyenne said firmly, shaking her head. "I've known Enzo Moretti *forever,* and I've never seen him act this way about anyone."

I stared at the fourth finger of my left hand, where he'd put that ridiculous ring that had always been a joke. "But it wasn't real," I reminded them—and myself. "It wasn't real."

By eight o'clock on Saturday night, I was in my usual spot on the couch, wearing sweatpants and a ratty old hoodie, damp hair hanging loose around my face. I'd just wrapped a blanket around me and was reaching for the remote when my brother came into the living room dressed to go out.

"I'm leaving," he said, patting his pockets like he was looking for his wallet or phone. "You seen my keys anywhere?"

"On the kitchen counter."

"Thanks." He started to walk away and turned back. "Hey, I forgot to tell you. I did you a favor today."

"What favor?"

"Enzo was asking about you, and I—"

I sat upright. "What? Where? At work?"

"Yeah. He's paying a few guys cash under the table for side

jobs at this new house he bought to flip. Anyway, he asked about you, and I said you were doing great."

"Oh." I lay down again. That didn't mean anything. That was just being polite.

"Then he asked if you ever mentioned him, and I said no."

"Good."

"Yeah, he looked kinda mad about that, so I kept going with it."

I eyeballed my brother from above the edge of the blanket. "What do you mean?"

"I mean I told him you seemed totally fine and you were going out every night until two or three in the morning." JJ looked pleased with himself.

I bolted upright again. "*What?*"

"Well, what was I supposed to tell him, that the minute you get home from work you put your pajamas on, eat ice cream for dinner, and cry the rest of the night?"

"No, but—"

"Or that you spend so much time on the couch, the cushions are now shaped like your butt?"

I glared at him. "It's *my* couch!"

"Or that you told me you loved him but you left because he doesn't love you?"

"No!"

"All right then." He shrugged. "You're welcome."

I frowned at him a moment longer before deciding I didn't have the energy to argue. What did it matter anyway? Why shouldn't Enzo think I was happier without him, going out to bars at night, talking or dancing with other guys? It's not like he cared.

JJ left and I turned on the TV. I was trying to decide which sappy romantic comedy would cheer me up most when someone knocked on the door. Figuring my brother forgot to grab his keys, I got off the couch and opened it.

But it wasn't JJ. It was Enzo.

Immediately my heart began to gallop. He looked *so good.* Hair combed, scruff trimmed, wearing a gray cashmere sweater that made me want to press my body to his and rest my cheek on his chest.

"Hey," I said, trying to keep my expression neutral. I touched my damp hair self-consciously, tucking it behind one ear.

"Hey," he said. "Can I come in?"

"I guess." I backed up, giving him plenty of room to enter without coming close to me. Shutting the door behind him, I carefully side-stepped around him into the kitchen. "Can I get you anything?"

"No, thanks," he said, following me. "I just came to bring you some things you left at the house." He set a brown paper bag on the island.

I frowned at it and pushed my glasses up my nose. "I didn't think I left anything."

"It's not much."

Curious, I peeked into the bag. First I pulled out a big gray T-shirt that said *Ciao* on it. "This isn't mine."

"It isn't?"

"No." I checked the tag. "Enzo, it's a men's extra large."

"Oh." He cleared his throat, tucking his hands into the pockets of faded jeans. "I must have made a mistake then."

I set it aside and pulled out a pasta and ravioli cutter. "These aren't mine either."

"I know, but you really seemed to like them whenever we made homemade pasta," he said enthusiastically. "I thought you should have the set."

"Oh." I did like them—they were professional tools, beautifully made of brass with wooden handles—but mostly what I'd liked about making those meals with Enzo was how much fun we'd had cooking together. "Thanks."

I put the tools next to the shirt on the island and reached into the bag again, pulling out the unopened box of Clomid.

"I wasn't sure if you wanted those or not," Enzo said. "I was just going to throw them out, but then I thought maybe you could use them in the future."

I swallowed hard and set the pills down. "Thanks."

"There's only one more thing in there."

I put my hand in the bag again and as my fingers closed around the small velvet box, I realized what it was. Even though I wasn't going to accept the gift, I pulled it out. "These aren't mine, Enzo."

"Yes, they are. I gave them to you."

My eyes filled, and I frantically tried to blink away tears. "I can't keep them."

"Why not?"

"Because they belong in your family."

He was silent for a moment. "But I want you to have them."

Finally, I looked up at him. "What is this? What are you doing?"

"I'm—I'm giving back what's yours."

I looked down at the random assortment of things in front of me. "The only thing I want back from you is something you don't even know you took."

"Huh?"

"Never mind." Shaking my head, I tossed the Clomid in the garbage, put the shirt, the pasta cutters, and the earrings back in the bag, and shoved it across the island toward him. "Here. I don't want this stuff."

He looked angry for a second, like I'd offended him, then seemed to notice my appearance. "You're not going out tonight?"

I remembered what my brother had told him. "Later," I lied.

"With who?" He tried not to sound jealous, but I knew him too well. Knew that angry squint of his eyes and tight clench of his jaw.

"No one you know."

"Where?"

"Just some places in town."

"Your brother said you've been going out a lot."

I shrugged, neither confirming nor denying it.

"Any chance you'd rather stay in and hang out with me?" His mouth eased into an inviting, familiar smile. "I miss those Manhattans you make."

"I don't think so."

"Why not?" He moved around the island, and I backed up against the counter.

"Because I have plans."

He came closer. Caged me in against the counter with a hand on either side of my hips. "Cancel them."

"No," I said defiantly, crossing my arms over my chest.

"Come on." He tilted his head, looking at me with half-closed eyes, one eyebrow arched. "You know you miss me."

I stared at him in disbelief. Was he trying to seduce me right now? "Seriously, Enzo?"

"What?" He moved even closer, his sensual mouth hooking up on one side.

"That isn't going to work."

"What isn't?"

"The smolder." But I turned my face away so I wouldn't have to see it.

"Come on, it always works." He brushed his lips against my jaw, barely touching my skin, and inhaled deeply. "God, you smell good."

"Enzo," I whimpered as his mouth moved down my throat. He smelled good too, and my body was reacting to his nearness in ways that made me want to start taking off his clothes. But I had to be strong. "You need to stop. You're only here because of what my brother told you. You don't like the idea of me going out."

"That's true," he said, his voice low and soft, his breath tickling the base of my throat. "I don't."

I frowned—he'd basically just confirmed what I suspected. He was only here because he didn't want anyone else to play with his toys.

"But I also miss you, Bianca," he breathed. "I miss your smell and your taste and your body. Come back."

"To your bed?"

"Sure, we can start there."

"And end up where?"

"The kitchen table? The shower? The back of my car? You name it."

Gathering all my strength, I shook my head and pushed him away. "No. That's not what I *meant*."

He exhaled and backed off. "So tell me what you *meant*, because every time I try to guess, I guess wrong."

"Just forget it. You should go." I prayed he'd do what I said, because I was one breath away from falling apart.

Either that or fucking his brains out on the kitchen floor.

"What happened to us, Bianca?" Enzo shook his head, like he was truly baffled. "I thought we were having a good time."

"We were, but . . . I got confused, okay?"

"Confused about what?"

"When we first made the deal, I knew exactly what I was getting into and why. You wanted a wife, and I wanted a baby, but the two lines weren't supposed to cross. We were each going to get what we wanted without making a mess of the other person's life. But it didn't go down that way."

"Are you saying I made a mess of your life?"

"I'm saying it happened." Trying to hold myself together, I inhaled and exhaled. "I'll take all the blame. It's my fault. But jumping back into bed tonight would only make it worse."

"How?"

I broke down and started to weep. "Because I'm not like

you, Enzo! I can't separate sex and feelings as easily as you can. Yes, I miss you. Yes, I lie awake at night wishing you were next to me. Yes, I am aware that I will probably never have orgasms as good as the ones I had with you. But those orgasms are not a good enough reason to toss my heart on a cutting board and hand you a knife!"

"I never asked you to do that!" he said angrily.

"No, of course not. In fact, you told me flat out not to fall for you. You're into bodies, not hearts. I haven't forgotten."

"And this is why!" he yelled, gesturing back and forth between us. "This is what happens when people let their feelings fuck them up!"

"What feelings?" I cried. "You don't have any feelings for me. You came here looking for sex!"

"I came here looking for *you*," he said, pointing a finger at me. "But believe me, I regret it."

"I can't do this, Enzo." I spoke softly, tears running down my face.

"Fuck, forget I said that." He rubbed his face with both hands. "I didn't mean it."

"Let's just end this here and now, okay?" I pleaded. "Before we both say things just to hurt each other, things that we don't really mean? We've known from the start that we were never meant to be. It was just a piece of paper, remember? Just a business deal."

He hung his head. "Yeah."

"I'm—I'm sorry I lied to you about the pills."

"I don't care about that."

"And I'm sorry I left so suddenly. I didn't do it to hurt you—I did it to save myself."

"From what?" he asked, looking up again. "I don't get why all of a sudden you're afraid of me."

I took a deep breath, looked him in the eye, and spoke the truth. I had the feeling it was the only weapon I had left in my arsenal, the one thing that would send him running. "From falling deeper in love with you than I already am. From getting so attached to you that I'd never be able to walk away. From the crushing heartbreak of having to endure *you* leaving *me*."

He looked stunned and stricken, almost like I'd punched him.

"Because you would have left, Enzo. Sooner or later, you would have left." I made a fist and pressed it to my stomach. "I can't give you what you want."

His eyes closed briefly, his shoulders drooping.

Moving past him, I went to the door and pulled it open. "And before I lose all self-respect and do something stupid like sleep with you anyway because I even miss the damn smolder, I need you to go."

He didn't move for a moment, just stood there in the kitchen with his back to me, still and silent. For a moment, I wondered if there was still hope for us.

Say it, I begged silently. *Tell me you love me too. Tell me I'm enough.*

But he turned around and headed straight out the door without stopping—without a word, without a nod, without so much as a backward glance.

I closed the door and rested my forehead against it, crying softly and wondering why love had to hurt so much.

Nineteen

Enzo

I DIDN'T SLEEP AT ALL ON SATURDAY NIGHT.

I lay on my back, hands behind my head, staring into the darkness and wondering if I'd just made the biggest mistake of my life by walking out on Bianca, or if she was right and we were never meant to be.

I'd never felt more messed up. She said she *loved me.*

But then she threw me out, like in her very next breath!

Talk about whiplash. I'd been so stunned, I hadn't been able to think straight.

Had she meant what she said? Did she really love me? Did I love her too? Did that explain the incessant ache in my chest since she'd gone? Or the way I sometimes couldn't catch my breath around her? The way I hated the thought of those blue eyes looking at someone else the way they'd looked at me? The way my heart felt as if it was tucked inside her fist, like she *owned* it? I'd never felt anything like it before she came barreling into my life and plunked herself down at my table and offered to marry me.

I scowled at the ceiling. This was all her fault! The whole

thing had been *her idea*! She said we could just *pretend* to be in love, and then not only had she gone and fallen in love with me—when she'd sworn she wouldn't—but she'd made me fall in love with her too!

Witchcraft.

I'd said it right from the start.

But now that I was under her spell, what the hell was I going to do about it?

On Sunday morning, I got out of bed early and went to Mass. My family was in a pew up front, but I sat alone in the back. I didn't really feel like looking my dad in the eye or suffering my mother's scorn or answering anyone's questions.

In all honesty, I was hoping to get some kind of message from beyond about what to do next. Let her go? Try again? Be a gentleman and respect her wishes? Go full-on caveman and demand another chance? Play it safe and cut my losses? Take the risk that she'd reject me *yet again*?

I listened carefully to every prayer, every reading, every hymn, every word of Father Mike's homily, hoping to discover some hidden meaning that would make the answer clear.

But I didn't.

Maybe it was because I was distracted by this family of six that came in late—the dad carrying a crying baby in his arms, the mom clutching a toddler to her hip with a massive bag slung over one shoulder, each of them holding the hand of another small child. The parents looked harried and exhausted—the guy's shirt was wrinkled, the woman's hair looked like it had been in the same ponytail for a few days—as they herded their brood into a pew across the aisle from me a couple rows up. They took turns holding and soothing the fussy infant, and at one point the dad fed her a bottle—at least, I was guessing it was a her by the giant pink bow on her bald head. The mom handed out snacks—Goldfish crackers by the looks of what was dropped onto the floor and sometimes thrown at a sibling. Both parents also dug through the bag countless times, hunting for the object that would quiet and distract their kids while Father Mike droned on . . . books and toys and sippy cups and pacifiers.

I felt a tug of sympathy for the poor parents, trying to keep four kids silent and still for a solid hour, but also for the kids—I remembered very well being in their position, knocking around in a pew with my siblings trying to avoid my father's *be quiet or else* stare or my mother's pinch.

But I was envious too. Of the unspoken language between the husband and wife. Of their closeness. Their connection. They clearly knew each other so well they were able to communicate with just a look, a smile, a nod, a headshake and silent, rueful laugh that said, *What is this life? Whose idea were all the kids? Remember when it was just the two of us?*

But they were happy too, you could just tell. I watched the husband put his hand on his wife's lower back and rub gently as she swayed with the toddler in her arms. I saw the wife brush her husband's hair off his forehead as he fed the baby. They were in something together, something they had built, something they would continue to grow. It hit me that even though I'd always wanted to be a dad, I'd really never considered what it would be like to *share* that experience with someone else. Watching that couple in church, I saw myself and Bianca as we could be. I looked down at my wedding band, which I'd never removed, and then at the family again.

It wasn't a perfect life, it wasn't glamorous or easy—there would be spilled juice and Goldfish crumbs and fights to break up and endless crying and sleepless nights and exhausted days. But it would be *our* life, and somehow I knew there would be more than enough laughter and joy and pride and happiness to balance out the difficult times. And at the end of every day, there would be a little space and time carved out for just the two of us, where we'd hold each other and act like it was just the two of us again—at least until our rambunctious little rug rats got old enough to come busting into our room demanding to sleep in our bed.

At one point, the couple's oldest kid—a little boy about four years old with dark hair, big brown eyes, and a clip-on tie—wandered away from his parents and came down the aisle. He saw me watching him and hesitated, then he slipped into my pew and stood next to me.

Smiling, I moved over to give him more room. His dad noticed his absence right away and frantically looked around. When he spotted the kid next to me, he gestured for him to return, and his face said he meant business. But the kid refused, shaking his head no and crossing his arms over his chest. It totally reminded me of something I'd have done at his age. I gave the man a smile and an all-good gesture, and he telegraphed his thanks.

The kid stood next to me solemnly for a few minutes, and when Father Mike asked his congregation to share peace with one another, he turned to me and offered his hand. I shook it, and right afterward, he scooted back toward his family. I watched him go, and then noticed for the first time that Bianca was standing on the far side of the church, at the back, in the same row I was.

Our eyes met for ten full seconds, and I couldn't breathe. She looked toward the altar again, wiping her eyes. My chest felt like an eighteen-wheeler had parked on it.

A moment later, we lined up for Holy Communion, and when I got back to my row, I fully planned on going to sit next to her. Taking her hand. Whispering in her ear and asking for another chance.

But when I looked for her, she was gone.

Dejected, I snuck out of church, went home, changed my

clothes, and spent the rest of the day at the Center Avenue house.

Thinking of her every second. Missing her fiercely. Wishing she was there to argue with me, tell me I was removing the wallpaper wrong or bought the wrong color paint or chose the wrong light fixture or bathroom tile. I trusted my taste, but hers was better, and I hated that we weren't doing this together anymore. I hated the thought of another night without her. I hated the thought of my *life* without her. I wanted what I'd seen in church today—a messy, beautiful life with her by my side.

At five o'clock I called it a day and drove over to Griffin and Blair's apartment. I felt like I needed some advice.

Blair answered the door, looking surprised to see me and not all that pleased about it. I figured she'd probably heard about my showing up at Bianca's place last night.

"Hey," I said. "Griffin here?"

"No. He's at the store." She studied my face and seemed to soften a little. "But he should be back any minute."

"Can I come in? I really need to talk to you guys."

She hesitated, but then gave in. "Okay."

I entered the stairwell and started up the steps. "I take it you've talked to Bianca today."

"Yes," she said, following behind me.

At the top of the stairs, I turned to face her. "Do you think I'm an idiot?"

She reached the landing and looked me dead in the eye. "Yes."

Frowning, I ran a hand over my jaw. "I need advice, Blair. I'm fucking miserable."

"I can tell. You look like you haven't eaten or slept in days."

"I'm not sure I have."

She parked her hands on her hips. "Stay for dinner. Want a beer?"

"Yes, please. Thank you."

She went over to the fridge and pulled out a beer, popping off the cap. Just as she handed it to me, we heard the door slam downstairs, and Griffin appeared at the top of the steps with a grocery bag a moment later.

"Hey," he said. "What's up?"

Blair took the bag from her husband. "He came for advice, but I need to feed him too. He looks awful."

Griffin looked at me. "What's going on?"

I took a drink. "I fucked up with Bianca."

"Again?" He headed over to the fridge and pulled out a beer for himself. "I thought she broke things off last weekend."

"She did. But I went over there last night to give her some things she'd left at my house, and maybe try to talk to her, and it didn't go well."

"That's because you tried to do more than talk," put in Blair, chopping garlic with her back to us.

Griffin looked at me. "Is that true?"

"Uh, yeah. My approach *might* have been a problem."

Blair sent me a look over one shoulder. "You think?"

"Well, I couldn't help myself," I said defensively. "I miss her, and I was all worked up because her brother had told me some bullshit about her going out every night, and I was picturing her talking to guys and getting jealous." I stopped and shook my head, thumping my chest. "Me! Getting jealous of other guys!"

Griffin laughed. "*What* is the world coming to?"

"Fuck off. I'm not used to this, okay? I don't like missing her. I don't like this *feeling*."

"What's the feeling?" he asked, leaning back against the counter.

"I don't even know what to call it, but it's *horrible*. It feels like the worst flu I've ever had. My chest hurts, my stomach is churning all the time, and my head is all foggy and fucked up."

Griffin nodded. "You're in love with her."

"For sure," added Blair, pouring some olive oil in a sauté pan.

I hung my head, closing my eyes. "I saw her in church this morning, and I couldn't even breathe. What am I going to do?"

"Get her back," said Griffin.

"She doesn't want me, Griff. She kicked me out last night."

"Because you did it *wrong*," Blair said, tossing the garlic into the pan. Within seconds it was sizzling and fragrant. "You strutted in there like a peacock and expected her to just fall into bed with you. You didn't tell her how you felt."

"Yes, I did," I argued.

Griffin looked at me with suspicion.

"Okay, I *sort* of did," I said, rubbing the back of my neck.

At the stove, Blair was shaking her head.

"What did you say?" Griffin asked.

"I told her I missed her—I said *lots* of nice things about missing her—but then she started in with all these questions, and I panicked."

Griffin sipped his beer. "What kind of questions?"

"Like about the future," I said, growing unnerved all over again. "She asked where we'd end up, and I didn't *know*. I felt like she was expecting me to predict exactly what will happen. It's impossible, isn't it? How can you promise someone something like forever—until fucking *death do you part*—and not feel like you're just gambling on it? To me, it seems like building a house without a blueprint. Hmm, let's just start laying bricks and see what happens." I shook my head. "It's madness. And yet . . . I can't see forever without her. I don't want to."

"You're not *wrong*, Enzo," Blair said, dumping a can of diced tomatoes into the pan. "It *is* a kind of madness. And it *is* a gamble. You have to be willing to take a risk."

I exhaled. "Even if I am willing, how do I convince her to give me another chance? She keeps pushing me away. Even *after* she said she loved me, she pushed me away."

"Okay, but think about that," Blair said, stirring her sauce.

"Let's say she's being honest about her feelings—because I think she is. She does love you. She didn't want to, but she does. So why do you think she would push you away?"

I crossed my arms over my chest. "I have no fucking idea."

"I bet you do."

I glared at her back. "You sound just like my mother. If I had all these answers, I wouldn't be so miserable trying to read her mind—or yours!"

Blair adjusted the gas under the pan and turned around to face me. "Look, I'm trying to navigate this without betraying my friend. I'm sorry it's frustrating for you. But I really think you can piece together why Bianca believes breaking it off with you now will save her a lot of heartache later."

I thought back to her exact words last night. "She did say this one thing."

"What was it?" Griffin asked.

"She said that she had to leave me before I left her."

Griffin tilted his head. "Why does she think you'd leave her?"

"I got the feeling it was because of the baby thing," I said, my chest aching again. "She doesn't think she can get pregnant, and maybe she's afraid I'd leave her because of it."

"Bingo." Blair pointed at me. "And Enzo, as much as I want you two to end up together, I think you have to ask yourself that question. If you want your own biological kids and Bianca can't get pregnant, that's an issue."

I walked away from them and over to the living room windows, which looked out over Main Street. It wasn't as busy as it would be in a month, once school was out and tourism really picked up, but there were a decent amount of people wandering up and down the block, parents pushing strollers or holding the hands of toddlers, kids racing around with ice cream cones.

Blair came up beside me and looked out too.

"I do want kids," I said, watching a father lift a little girl onto his shoulders. "But I want them with her, no matter what. Nothing feels right without her."

"I think she needs to hear that," she said gently.

"But what if she rejects me *again*?"

She laughed. "Do it right this time, and she won't."

I frowned.

"The good thing is, you're already married to her." She elbowed me.

"No, I'm not," I scoffed. "That wedding was bullshit. Everything was bullshit."

"I was there."

"Then you know." I tipped up my beer again. "It's not what she deserved. None of it was."

"Then do it all again, and give her what she deserves this time," Blair urged. "Change all the things you messed up. Say all the things you should have said. Make it real this time."

I looked down at her. "That's actually a really great idea."

She smiled and curtsied. "Thank you." Then suddenly her face turned menacing—or as menacing as a Tennessee debutante's face can get. "But if you hurt her again, Enzo Moretti, I will *hunt you down and destroy you.*"

"I'm not going to hurt her," I promised, my mind already clicking. "I'm just going to get her back. But I might need help. Yours and Cheyenne's."

"Whatever you need, we're there." Sweet as apple pie again, she stuck her arm through mine and tipped her head onto my shoulder. "But mostly, we just want to tell her we were right."

The next morning, I went to my parents' house to see my father.

My mother answered the door. One of her brows peaked and she crossed her arms over her chest. "Well? Did you do what I said?"

"Not yet."

She harrumphed.

"I need to talk to Dad, okay? I can't do anything until I clear my conscience about lying to him."

She harrumphed again, but she let me in. "He's in his office. I don't know why he calls it retirement since he still gets up early, takes his coffee into his office, and stays at his desk for hours."

I had a pretty good idea why he liked being alone in his office every morning, but I didn't say anything to my mom. "Thanks."

I knocked twice on my dad's office door, then opened it up. "It's me. Can I come in?"

Seated behind his desk with his laptop open in front of him, he picked up a mug that said MY NONNO CAN BEAT UP YOUR NONNO. "Sure."

I shut the door behind me and sat in one of the two leather chairs across from him. "How are you feeling?"

"Good." He sipped his coffee and eyeballed me over the rim of the cup.

Nervous, I ran a hand over my hair. "So I need to tell you something."

"Okay."

"I fucked up."

Another slow sip. A slight squint of the eyes.

"I did something I'm not proud of, and I need to come clean about it to you before I can fix things with Bianca—this involves her too."

"I'm listening."

"I only married her so you wouldn't give the company to Pietro." I closed my eyes a moment. "I know it was wrong, and I'm sorry."

He said nothing.

I opened my eyes again and met his gaze squarely. "It was dishonest and shady, and that's not the kind of man I am. It's not the kind of man you raised."

"No, it isn't."

"If you want to turn Moretti & Sons over to Pietro, I'll understand. And I'll help him run it."

He took one more sip and set his coffee down. "I was never going to give the company to Pietro."

"Huh?"

"Your brother is good at a lot of things. Being CEO would not be one of them."

"So . . . so I didn't need to get married and start a family in order to prove that I was responsible enough to run the company?" I sputtered.

"No. You needed to get married and start a family because that's what you want out of life. And you were never going to do it if you didn't sense some kind of pressure to get it done." He shrugged. "That's the way it always is with Moretti men. We like our independence too much. We're selfish and stubborn. We need a shove in the right direction."

I shook my head. "So I did all this for nothing?"

My father frowned. "Are you listening to me? You did it because deep down, you wanted to. You were tired of being alone. You were ready for a family. But like all Moretti men, you needed a push, so I gave it to you—just like my father gave it to me."

I stared at my hands in my lap, at the gold band on my finger. Was he right? I had to admit that if I hadn't felt pressured into faking the relationship with Bianca, I never would have realized how much I wanted to be with her. Or what it was like to love someone. How it felt to put someone else first. "Maybe you're right," I said slowly.

"Of course I'm right." Then he tapped his temple. "You think I didn't see what you were doing? I raised you. I taught you everything you know. And I wasn't born yesterday."

"You knew I wasn't in love with Bianca when I married her?"

He rolled his eyes.

"Why didn't you say anything?"

"Because I had a feeling."

"What feeling?" A shiver moved up my spine.

"That she was the one for you. I saw it that night at the table when you announced your engagement. I wasn't sure what kind of game you two were playing, but I saw pretty clearly how it would end as long as nobody interfered."

I stared at him in disbelief. "She *is* the one. I see it now."

"Better late than never, I guess. Now go make sure she knows it."

Rising to my feet, I nodded. I was almost out the door before he spoke again.

"You have to say the words, son. And you have to mean what you say. Bianca's the kind of girl who will see right through your bullshit—that's why she's perfect for you."

His words made me grin. "I know."

"Good. Now get the fuck out of here, and don't come back until you've made things right with your wife—and get used to doing it, by the way. That's married life."

I laughed. "Thanks, Pop. For everything."

Right in front of my parents' house, I called DiFiore's and left a message, requesting a reservation for Friday night. Then I went directly to the nursing home to speak to Grandma Vinnie. From there I went over to the jewelry store and talked with Paulie. Later that afternoon, I went over to the rectory to speak with Father Mike. When the hostess at DiFiore's called me back to confirm my reservation, I asked if they'd please hold a particular booth for me. Then I texted Blair and Cheyenne, begging them to make sure Bianca showed up at the restaurant for dinner Friday at seven.

It was torture staying away from Bianca for four more days, especially knowing that she was as miserable as I was, but I forced myself to be patient so I could surprise her.

On Friday morning, I woke up at the crack of dawn and jumped out of bed. Each hour seemed to pass more slowly than the last, but eventually it was time to get ready.

I took twice as long as I usually did. I dressed in my best suit. I made sure my hair was doing the *thing*. I shined my shoes, put on her favorite cologne, and re-knotted my tie five times. Everything had to be perfect.

Because there comes a day in a man's life when he enters a room with hope in his heart and a ring in his pocket, fully prepared to get down on one knee. To pledge his eternal devotion. To take his soul mate's hand in his and pop the question, promising to love, honor and cherish her forever and ever until death do them part, amen.

This was that day.

I'd never loved anyone the way I loved Bianca, and I was going to tell her that. I was going to put a new ring on her finger, one I'd had made just for her. And I was going to ask her to be my wife—for real, and for always.

No pretense, no expiration date, no conditions.

I had a feeling she'd say yes, but just in case, I practiced my smolder in the mirror before I left.

Oh yeah. I still had it.

Twenty

Bianca

On Friday night, Blair picked me up at quarter to seven for a girls' night out to celebrate Cheyenne's thirty-first birthday and the fact that she and Cole had set a wedding date—they'd get married in late June in the backyard of their new house.

Plenty of people thought she was slightly crazy for setting a wedding date that was only six weeks away, but she said she'd waited long enough to become Mrs. Cole Mitchell, and I didn't blame her one bit. For a lot of brides, maybe it was about the custom gown and the engraved invitations and the guest list with three hundred people on it, but Cheyenne felt—and I agreed—all that stuff was nice, but it was just window dressing. What mattered, what was real, was the way they felt about each other. The life they had planned. The family they were becoming.

I was thrilled for them both. So in spite of the fact that my own heart was still in a million unhappy little pieces, I put on a new dress, swapped my glasses for contacts, strapped on some heels, and painted my lips a cheerful shade of poppy red.

What I *wasn't* thrilled about was that Cheyenne had chosen

DiFiore's as the restaurant for tonight's celebration. I'd been there several times with Enzo since our engagement dinner, and it felt like *our place.* I was trying so hard to move on instead of look back, and I worried that being there would be a painful reminder of what I'd lost, of the terrible mistake I'd made. But tonight wasn't about me, so I would go and smile and celebrate Cheyenne like a good friend should. She deserved that.

Tomorrow, I could cry if I needed to, maybe take out those diamond earrings he'd left at my place and put them on, along with his big gray CIAO T-shirt, curl up in a ball and bemoan the fact that I hadn't had the nerve to start divorce proceedings yet, but knew it was something I had to do. He wasn't coming back.

"You look great," Blair chirped after I got in her car. "Is that a new dress?"

I glanced down at the floral minidress with flowy sleeves and low-cut neckline. "Yeah. I felt like I needed to get out of my all-black rut."

Blair sighed. "It was a long winter, wasn't it? But this summer will be great. We have lots to look forward to."

I nodded but said nothing.

Blair pulled up in front of the restaurant and looked around. "Shoot. I don't see any parking spaces."

"There's one over there," I said, pointing up the street.

"But you're wearing heels, and that's a long walk. Why don't you jump out and grab our table?"

"Blair, don't be silly. They're not that high." I glanced down at the nude, block-heeled sandals I had on. "I'll walk with you."

"No!" she said vehemently. Then she looked alarmed. "I mean, no." Her tone was softer. "You go in. We're a little late already, and I bet Cheyenne is in there waiting for us."

I shrugged. "Okay. I'll see you inside."

She smiled like she was relieved. "Yes, good. See you inside."

Slinging my bag over my shoulder, I shut the passenger door of Blair's little green MGB and head into the restaurant.

Inside, it was dark and warm and smelled delicious—like garlic bread right from the oven and fresh herbs like rosemary and oregano. Taking a deep breath, I approached the hostess stand, fighting tears as I recalled Enzo's hand on my lower back the night we walked into our engagement dinner. Then I remembered the way he called me his little meatball, and it nearly made me laugh.

The hostess, a young, dark-haired girl named Victoria, recognized me. "Hi, Mrs. Moretti. Your table is all set."

I sniffed and blinked, trying to compose myself. "Uh, thanks. Is my friend here?"

"Yes," she said, smiling widely. "Right this way."

I followed her through the restaurant, doing my best not to glance at the back room where the DeRossis and Morettis had gathered just a few months ago to celebrate the joining of our families. I'd hoped that Cheyenne would be waiting for us at one of the tables near the front windows or maybe one of the high-tops over in the bar, but to my dismay, Victoria was leading me toward the booths along the back wall—which was where I'd sat across from Enzo and offered to marry him. In fact, she seemed to be leading me toward the exact booth where I'd stupidly, blindly put everything in motion.

As soon as we reached it, I stopped and gasped. Someone was sitting there, but it wasn't Cheyenne.

Enzo slid out and stood up, looking so gorgeous in his suit and tie, my heart stopped. His sensual mouth curved into a smile. "Hi."

"What is this?" I glanced at the table, which was set for two. Candlelight flickered and glowed. A bottle of Barolo was open, two glasses poured.

Instead of answering my question, he looked at the hostess. "Thanks, Victoria."

"You're welcome, Mr. Moretti." She gave him a longing, wistful smile.

When she'd left us, Enzo gestured across the table from where he'd been sitting. "Will you sit down?"

I glanced at the booth and saw myself so blithely sliding in—uninvited—across from him last February. "I don't know. What's going on? Where is Cheyenne?"

Enzo looked a little guilty. "They're not here."

"They're not?"

"No, I just needed their help getting you here. I didn't think you'd come if I asked you myself, and I wanted to surprise you."

"Well, it worked. I'm surprised." I shook my head, feeling unsteady on my feet. "But I'm also upset. I feel tricked."

Enzo put a hand on my shoulder. "Don't—it's not like that, I promise. Just please sit. Give me five minutes, and if you still want to leave, I won't fight you." He gestured again at the booth.

I glanced over my shoulder and back at the table. I didn't have to stay. I could walk out now, before I broke down again. Before I gave him another opportunity to hurt me. "I don't owe you anything," I said, desperately wishing I could make my feet obey my head and not my heart.

"No, you don't." He took a step closer and cradled my face in his hands. "But I owe *you* something. Please give me another chance to give it to you."

When he looked at me that way—no teasing smile, no pretense, no smolder—I couldn't say no. Maybe it would turn out to be the second biggest mistake I'd ever made, but I slid into the booth.

"Thank you," he said, sounding relieved as he sat across from me. He indicated the wine glass closest to me. "That's for you."

"I'm fine," I said, even though I was dying for a sip. "What is it that you think you owe me?"

He picked up his wine glass and took a slow swallow. After setting the glass down, he slid out of the booth again, came to my side, and got down on one knee. Then he reached into his inside coat pocket and took out a small box. Before I could even suck in my breath, he opened it up, and nestled in the black velvet cushion was a stunning emerald-cut diamond in an art deco setting on a platinum band.

My jaw fell open. Chills swept across my back and down my arms. "What is that?"

"That is a very close—as close as I could get inside a week—approximation of the ring your great-grandfather the bootlegger gave to your great-grandmother . . . with a slightly bigger diamond, of course." He gave me a mischievous little grin.

"Oh my God. Enzo." I covered my cheeks with my trembling hands.

"What I owe you is the truth, Bianca," he said, his eyes dark and serious. "All my life, I didn't think it would matter who I married. I wanted kids for the sake of carrying on tradition and the experience of fatherhood, but it wasn't until I fell in love with you that I understood what that really means. I don't just want to have children so I can be a dad—I want to have children *with you.* I want to raise a family *with you.* And when it's just us again in that big old Center Avenue house, I want to sit on the porch in a rocking chair and argue *with you.*" He smiled as he took the ring from the box and showed me the inscription: *Per cent'anni . . . Enzo.*

I swallowed hard, but the lump in my throat only grew bigger.

"I love you," he said, taking my left hand and slipping the ring on my finger. "More than I've ever loved anything or anyone. I'm sorry I made you wait to hear it. I want to spend the rest of my life with you."

"But Enzo." I made myself say the words. "I might not be able to have—"

He silenced me with two fingers over my lips. "We're a family no matter what."

I smiled through my tears, and he lowered his hand. "Do you mean it?"

"Yes." He took both my hands in his. "You're the most beautiful, the most caring, and the most exasperating woman I've ever known. You can infuriate me like no one else—but you make me happier than anyone else ever could. And the love I feel for you is the truest, *realest* thing I've ever known."

A sob escaped me, and a tear slid down my cheek. "I love you too."

"I want a love story like your great-grandparents—one that will outlast our time on earth, one that our great-grandkids will still be talking about a hundred years from now."

I nodded as more tears slipped from my eyes. "I want that too."

"Will you marry me?"

Laughing, I wiped my cheeks. "I'm already married to you."

"But you deserved a better proposal. So what do you say? Still want to be my wife?"

"Yes," I said, laughing again as I took his face in my hands and kissed his lips. "Yes."

He kissed me briefly before rising to his feet and turning to the crowded dining room. "She said yes!"

The entire place erupted in shouts and applause, and I felt heat in my cheeks as he slipped into the booth across from me.

"Whew," he said, loosening the knot in his tie. "I'm sweating."

"Why? Did you think I was going to say no?" I stared at the gorgeous ring on my finger, my heart thumping happily.

"Honestly?" He hesitated. "No. I figured you'd say yes. But I'd have deserved it if you said no."

I rolled my eyes and picked up my wine glass. "Oh, good. You're still you."

"I'm still me." His smile made my breath catch—I hoped it always would.

Suddenly Blair and Cheyenne appeared at the side of our table, clutching hands and barely able to contain their excitement. "We heard cheering! Did it happen?"

"It happened," I said, holding up my hand to show off the ring.

They squealed and grabbed my hand to examine it more closely. "Oh my God, it's beautiful!" Blair looked at Enzo. "This is the replica?"

"It's close," Enzo said. "My cousin Paulie did the best he could on short notice." His eyes met mine. "I wasn't willing to wait."

"I love everything about it," Cheyenne gushed, tears in her eyes as she put a hand over her heart. She leaned over to hug me, and then gave Enzo a kiss on the cheek. Blair did the same, pausing to whisper something in his ear before straightening up.

"We'll leave you to your dinner, but we're all at the bar if you guys want to join us afterward," she said.

"Who's we?" I asked.

"Just Griffin, Cole, and Beckett." Blair poked Enzo's shoulder. "We weren't allowed to tell anyone else."

I laughed. "Okay, we'll head in there after we eat."

"Perfect." She linked arms with Cheyenne and the two of them looked at each other and then at me like smug, satisfied cats. "Also—and we mean this in the nicest way—"

"Told you so," said Cheyenne, before they both dissolved into laughter and headed for the bar.

I shook my head. "Those two are ridiculous. They were convinced all along that this would happen."

"They're good friends," Enzo said, reaching for my hand. "And they love you. You don't even want to know about the threats they issued if I fucked this up."

"I can just about imagine," I said. "What did Blair say to you just now?"

"She said she was glad she didn't have to kill me."

I burst out laughing. "We're lucky to have such great friends."

"We're lucky, period." He locked his fingers with mine. "And I'll never take this for granted."

I met his eyes and smiled. My heart was whole again.

While we ate, we talked a mile a minute about the Center Avenue house and what would need to be done before we could move in. He told me about the work that had been completed in the last two weeks, and I was so anxious to see it, I made him promise to at least drive me by it tonight after dinner.

"But it'll be dark by then," he said.

"I won't care," I insisted. "I want to see it tonight."

After we finished our meals, we went into the bar area, where our friends were waiting. Blair and Cheyenne hugged us all over again, and Beckett, Cole, and Griffin each kissed my cheek and told me they'd known pretty much from the start that Enzo had met his match in me. We ordered a round of drinks and held up our glasses for a toast.

"To old friends," said Griffin.

"And new ones!" exclaimed Blair.

"To second chances," offered Cole, taking Cheyenne's hand.

"And second basemen," added Beckett with a laugh as Enzo took a small bow.

"*Per cent'anni,*" I said, looking around at our friends, my throat growing tight. I took Enzo's hand and hoped with all my heart for one hundred more years of this.

Enzo raised his glass even higher. "To the best friends a guy could ask for . . . and fuck the Mavs."

All the guys made caveman noises and drank, while Blair, Cheyenne and I exchanged a look. "Old man baseball," Cheyenne said with a sigh. "Better get used to it."

We left our friends at the bar after just one drink, Enzo tugging my arm. "Come on. We have to be somewhere."

"We do?" I asked as he opened the door for me. "Where?"

"You'll see."

I could not imagine where he was taking me, but I didn't have to wonder long—less than ten minutes after leaving the restaurant, he pulled up in front of St. Paul's Catholic Church. I looked over at him. "What's this?"

Instead of answering, he turned off the car, came around to the passenger side, and helped me out. Taking my hand, he led me up the church steps.

"Enzo, what is this?" I whispered as he pushed the heavy wooden door open, and we stepped into the vestibule. It was dark and silent and smelled like incense.

"Come on." Speaking quietly, he kept my hand in his and we walked up the nave toward the altar, our footsteps echoing in the empty space.

Shivers swept up my spine. The sanctuary was dimly lit, and I saw no one else until we reached the crossing, and he gently pulled me to the left, into the north transept. There, in front of some beautiful stained-glass windows lit by the moon from behind and flickering votive candles on a table below, stood Father Mike.

He smiled at us. "Welcome."

"Thank you for this, Father," Enzo said.

"Of course. Are you ready?"

"Give me one second." Enzo turned to me, taking both my hands. "I know we're technically already married. But we did that for a piece of paper. For an audience. And definitely for the wrong reasons. I wanted to do something more meaningful." He glanced up at the stained glass. "My great-grandparents donated these windows when the church was being built a hundred years ago. I've looked at them a thousand times and never thought twice about them. But now when I see them, they remind me of the importance of family, of putting down roots, and of having faith in something bigger than ourselves. And that's because of you."

I wanted to say something, but my throat was too tight.

"I asked Father Mike here tonight to give our marriage a blessing," he went on. "I didn't want to do it before—neither of us did—because it would have felt wrong. And it would have been because our parents pressured us into it. This is just between us."

"And God," Father Mike reminded.

"Oh, right," said Enzo. "Him too."

I smiled through tears. "I love it. And I love you."

"I love you too." Leaning toward me, he pressed his lips to my forehead and rested them there for a moment. Then he straightened up and turned to Father Mike. "Okay, we're ready."

After we left the church, Enzo drove me by the Center Avenue house, as promised. Hand in hand, using the flashlights on our phones since many of the lights had been disconnected, we walked through the house. I was impressed with the progress that had been made in the last two weeks, but sad that I'd missed out on seeing it happen.

"Don't worry," Enzo said, squeezing my hand. "There's a lot more work to do to get this place livable."

In the middle of what would be—I hoped—a child's bedroom, I turned to face him. "We're really going to live here?"

"Of course we are." His arms came around me.

"And have a family?"

"Of course we are. If biology isn't on our side, we'll adopt. I don't care how we get our family, I just want to have one with you."

Slipping my arms around his waist, I rested my head on his chest and closed my eyes.

"We're going to be happy here, Mrs. Moretti," he said, rocking me side to side. "We're going to fill this house with a bunch of noisy, messy kids who are going to drive us crazy, but we're going to be happy. I can feel it."

I held him tight, breathing deeply. "I feel it too."

Walking into his house again—his hand on my lower back—felt like coming home. Falling into his bed again, feeling his skin on mine, watching him move above me, was like a dream. Taking him deep inside me, hearing his quickened breath and his low, thick growl, set my body on fire the way only he could. And when we came together, our bodies in perfect, blissful harmony, it was like recompense for everything I'd been through.

"God, I missed you," he whispered in the dark, raining kisses over my face and neck and chest. "Don't ever leave me again."

"I won't." Laughing, I rubbed his back and wrapped my legs around him. "You're stuck with me now. God says. *And* the state of Michigan."

"Good."

"Plus my ring says a hundred years. So I figure I should at least honor that promise."

He picked up his head and looked down at me. "You better. I don't want to be without you. I don't even feel like me without you anymore."

I smiled. "You couldn't even smolder?"

"I couldn't even fucking smolder."

Laughing, I grabbed his face and kissed his lips. "That is a clear sign that we'd better stick together."

"Damn right. After all, I need to pass that on to future generations of Morettis. Even if I don't pass it through DNA, it can still be taught."

"I have no doubt our boys will inherit the smolder."

"And our girls will inherit the moxie. It's what made me fall in love with you."

A few minutes later, we were snuggled up just like we used to, my head on his chest, his arms wrapped around me.

"Did you mean what you said?" I asked softly, brushing my fingertips across his chest. "About adoption?"

"Of course I did."

I tried to cuddle even closer. "I haven't made up my mind yet about trying again with Clomid. I'm taking a little break."

"Good," he said. "You deserve some time to breathe. And whatever you decide—Clomid, turkey baster, adoption, kidnapping—I'm with you. We're a family, no matter what, remember?"

"I remember."

He kissed the top of my head. "Night, Lucy."

I smiled. "Night, Ricky."

SIX MONTHS LATER

Enzo

"I'm sorry, what did you say?" I stared at the ultrasound tech, certain I'd misheard her.

She smiled, keeping her eyes on the screen. "There are two heartbeats here."

"Oh my God," whispered Bianca, squeezing my hand.

"What do you mean, two heartbeats? Why would the baby have two heartbeats?"

The tech laughed gently, glancing at me. "There are *two babies.*"

"But we only ordered one," I said, my voice cracking.

"It happens," said the tech. "See?" She gestured to the screen, where I saw what looked like two black balloons nestled in a sea of gray. Inside each balloon was a kidney-bean-shaped blob flickering in the center.

"Those flickering things," I said, my throat tight and scratchy. "Those are hearts?"

"They sure are, Dad."

My jaw dropped and I looked over at Bianca. Behind the lenses of her glasses, her blue eyes were wide and unblinking. "Two," I croaked.

"Two," she said, looking as shocked as I felt.

For a moment, I felt slightly dizzy. *Two?*

But then a wave of pride crashed over me—TWO!

I stood up taller, puffing out my chest. "Well, damn," I said. "Talk about overachieving."

Bianca laughed. "Pretty sure it was the Clomid."

"Even with Clomid, the chances of twins aren't *that* high when conceived naturally," the tech said. "I think it's something like five to ten percent."

"See?" I bent over and kissed her forehead. She'd been through so much over the last six months. In fact, we'd agreed that this cycle would be the last one trying to conceive without additional intervention. "You're a rock star."

She smiled up at me, making my heart pound even harder. *I love you,* she mouthed. To the tech, she said, "Does everything look okay?"

"Everything looks great," she said.

Bianca's eyes closed, and she breathed deeply, in and out. Tears leaked from both eyes. "Thank you," she whispered.

My eyes were blurry too.

Later on that night, we lay in our big bed in our new bedroom at the Center Avenue house. Rolling onto my side, I put a hand on her smooth, soft belly. "I still can't believe it. How on earth are two humans going to grow in there? It doesn't seem like there's enough room."

She laughed. "Um, I'm going to get really big."

"Like how big?" I propped my head on my hand.

"Massive. Like I could be wider than I am tall."

I gasped in mock horror. "No."

"Yes. Will you still love me?"

"Even more." I flipped around and rested my head on her stomach.

She smiled at me, playing with my hair. "What are you doing?"

"I'm listening to them. It's never too early to start eavesdropping on our kids."

She laughed. "Hear anything good?"

"Shh." I pretended to concentrate.

"Girls or boys?" she prodded.

"One of each."

"Really?"

"Yes."

"And what are their names?"

"Ricky and Lucy, of course."

"Of course." She grinned. "What are they up to?"

"They're arguing. Ricky is taking up too much space. Lucy drew a line and told him not to cross it, but Ricky likes to provoke her."

"Sounds about right."

"Are you happy?" I asked her, my heart about to burst.

She nodded with shining eyes. "Are you?"

"More than I ever thought possible. And I know it's just going to keep getting better."

"I'm scared too."

Immediately I sat up. "Why?"

She shrugged. "All of this . . . You, the house, the babies. It's everything I've ever wanted. I'm scared of losing it."

"Hey. Come here." I lay down again and gathered her in close. "Nothing can take away what we've got."

"But what if—"

"You talk too much. Have I ever told you that?"

"Probably."

"And you're always leaving your books in piles around the house, you constantly rearrange shit in the kitchen so I can't find anything, you're a big know-it-all, and you turn the thermostat up so high it's like a sauna in here."

She giggled. "Sorry."

"Don't be." I kissed her head. "Because you're also my favorite person in the world. You brought light into the egotistical and immature darkness that was my soul."

"That's right, I did," she said, laughing again.

"Plus you're the best wife ever. And you're going to be an amazing mom."

"You think so?"

"I know it." I paused. "And I'm always right. In addition to being so good-looking and awesome at baseball, that's your favorite thing about me."

"It's really not."

"What?" I pretended disgust. "Come on. What could you love more than those things?"

"Hmmm. I love how generous you are. How hard you work. How you treat everyone you meet with kindness. I love the way you can make me laugh so easily. I love that you have the same three best friends now that you had when you were twelve—that says you're loyal and trustworthy. I love the way you smell. I love how protective you are. I love walking into a room with you and seeing everyone stare because you're so gorgeous, and feeling your hand on my back that tells me you're mine."

"Always," I said, rubbing her spine.

"And," she added reluctantly, like it pained her to say it, "I suppose I have grown to love the smolder."

I laughed. "It was only a matter of time, babe."

She tilted her head back and looked up at me with those blue eyes that melted all my defenses. "For once, I don't even want to argue with you."

"Good." I kissed her softly and held her close, marveling that there were three heartbeats in my arms. My own heart thrummed hard inside my chest.

With love, with gratitude, with protectiveness . . . with the certainty of knowing that we'd taken a crazy leap of faith and landed exactly where we were supposed to be.

For real, and for always.

THE END

Want a peek into Enzo and Bianca's happily ever after?
Subscribe to my mailing list and you'll get instant access to an exclusive CALL ME CRAZY bonus scene!

Pappardelle and Sausage with Kale and Spicy Tomato Sauce

Ingredients

2 Tbsp. extra virgin olive oil
5 cloves garlic, minced
1 small yellow onion, chopped
1 lb. ground hot Italian sausage
1 bunch or 6 oz chopped kale
28 oz can whole plum tomatoes
1/4 tsp. red pepper flakes
2 Tbsp. chopped fresh basil
1/2 cup Parmesan
1/4 cup heavy cream
Salt and pepper

1 lb Pappardelle

1) Heat oil in large, deep saucepan. Add onion, garlic and Italian sausage. Cook for 5-8 minutes on medium-high until sausage is cooked through and onions are softened and just starting to turn golden.

2) Add chopped kale and cook down, around 3-4 minutes. Add can of tomatoes and break the tomatoes down with a wooden spoon. Add basil, red pepper and salt and pepper to taste. Simmer for an additional 3 minutes.

3) Add 1/4 cup Parmesan and heavy cream, stir to thoroughly combine. Turn heat to low while you cook the pasta.

4) Bring 6 quarts of salted water to boil. Add pappardelle and cook for 5-7 minutes or until al dente. Drain and add to sauce, along with remaining 1/4 cup Parmesan. Stir to combine and serve immediately.

Meatball Subs

Ingredients

Meatballs:
1 lb ground beef
3 cloves garlic, minced
1 egg
1/8 cup plain breadcrumbs
1/4 cup grated Parmesan
1/8 cup chopped fresh parsley
1 tsp. salt
1 tsp. freshly cracked black pepper

Sauce:
1 lb. 12 oz can plum tomatoes
2 Tbsp. extra virgin olive oil
3 garlic cloves, chopped
1/2 tsp. kosher salt
4 large basil leaves, torn in half
6 slices Provolone
3 sub rolls
1/4 cup chopped fresh parsley
Parmesan for sprinkling

1) Preheat oven 400 degrees.

2) In large, deep saucepan, sauté garlic in olive oil on medium-high until golden. Add can of plum tomatoes and break up with a wooden spoon. Add basil leaves. Season with salt and pepper. Simmer for 8-10 minutes on medium low. Keep on low heat while you prepare the meatballs.

3) Meanwhile, mix all meatball ingredients together in large bowl and form into 6 balls about the size of a lime. Place meatballs on a tinfoil or parchment-lined sheet pan. Drizzle with olive oil and bake at 400 degrees for 15 minutes.

4) Remove meatballs from oven and nestle them into the saucepan with the tomato sauce. Simmer on medium-low for 10 minutes, then flip the meatballs over and simmer for another 10 minutes.

5) Prepare the subs:
If the bread isn't pre-sliced, slice the bread making sure not to cut all the way through. Open up the roll, and place a slice of provolone on each side of the bread. Place the rolls, cheese side up, under a broiler for 5 minutes or until melted and bubbly. Place 3 meatballs in the roll, and top with a spoonful of sauce. Sprinkle with Parmesan and chopped parsley.

Pizzelles

Ingredients

3 1/2 cups all-purpose flour
1 1/2 cups sugar
1 cup (two sticks) butter, melted
2 Tbsp. grated orange peel
2 tsp. vanilla extract
1 tsp. anise
1 Tbsp. orange juice
4 tsp. Baking powder
1 tsp. ground cardamom
1/4 tsp. salt
6 large eggs
Powdered sugar for dusting

1) Preheat electric pizzelle iron

2) Measure all ingredients into a large bowl. Mix at low speed until well blended, scraping sides of bowl with rubber spatula.

3) Follow the instructions of pizzelle iron manufacturer (you might need to use cooking spray). When iron is ready, spoon a small amount of batter into the center of each form. Close the iron and cook until light golden-brown, about 1-1 1/2 minutes (check instructions on your iron). Gently transfer cookies to cooling rack—they will crisp up as they cool.

4) Dust with powdered sugar before serving.

Italian Wedding Soup

Ingredients

Meatballs:
1 lb. ground beef
3 cloves garlic, minced
1 egg
1/8 cup breadcrumbs
1/4 cup Parmesan
1/8 cup fresh parsley, finely chopped
1 tsp. salt
Olive oil

Soup:
4 cups chicken broth
1 bunch escarole, roughly chopped
1 lb. raw chicken breast, bone in

1) Preheat oven to 350 degrees.

2) Mix meatball ingredients together in medium bowl until well combined. Form meatballs into marble-sized balls. You will get around 60 meatballs, but can freeze about half of them for future use, depending on your preference.

3) Place meatballs on silicone or tin foil lined sheet pan. Drizzle with olive oil. Bake for 6 minutes.

4) Meanwhile, place chicken in large pot and cover with water. Boil for 20 minutes. Remove chicken from water and let cool. Once cooled, remove meat from bones and shred. Discard the bones and water, and set shredded meat aside.

5) Heat broth in large pot on medium-high heat. Add escarole and cook on medium until the escarole is cooled down, around 10 minutes. Add shredded chicken and meatballs. Simmer on medium-low heat for 5-8 minutes to let the flavor from the meatballs infuse the broth. Season with salt and pepper to taste.

6) Serve the soup topped with grated Parmesan.

Toasted Sourdough and Tomato Bruschetta

Ingredients

1 lb. tomatoes, diced
1/2 red onion, diced
2 cloves garlic, minced
2 Tbsp. fresh basil, about 5 large leaves, chopped
1/8 cup grated Parmesan
1/4 cup extra virgin olive oil
1/4 tsp. salt
1/2 tsp. black pepper

12 slices sourdough bread
1/4 cup extra virgin olive oil

1) Add tomatoes, onion, garlic, basil, Parmesan, salt and pepper to medium bowl. Stir until combined. Add 1/4 cup olive oil and combine.

2) Brush tops of sourdough slices with olive oil. Place under broiler for about 3 minutes or until golden brown. Serve with bruschetta.

Zeppole

Ingredients

Dough:
4 oz unsalted butter
1 cup whole milk
1 Tbsp. sugar
1 tsp. orange zest
Pinch of salt
1 cup flour
4 eggs room temperature

Filling:
1 lb. ricotta, drained
1/2 cup heavy cream
1/2 cup powdered sugar
1 tsp. vanilla extract
1/2 cup mini chocolate chips

Vegetable oil
Powdered sugar
Cherries in syrup

Filling:
1) Place ricotta, powdered sugar and vanilla in food processor and and blend until smooth. Slowly add the heavy cream while the mixer is on high and blend until the ricotta is smooth and thick, about 20-30 seconds. Add chocolate chips and pulse about 10-15 times to combine.

Dough:

1) In a medium pot, bring butter, milk, sugar, orange zest and salt to a boil. Immediately add the flour and stir vigorously with wooden spoon until the dough comes together to form a ball. Remove from heat and continue to stir dough to cool down slightly, 2-3 minutes.

2) Add eggs one at a time and mix until well incorporated between each addition. Once all eggs are added, you will have a smooth, thick paste. Add the dough to a piping bag fitted with a large star tip.

For Fried Zeppole:

1) Cut 12-14 four-inch square parchment pieces.

2) Fill a deep saucepan with 1-2 inches of vegetable oil or shortening. Heat oil to around 350-375 degrees.

3) Pipe 2.5-3 inch rings onto the parchment squares. Drop the rings, dough side down into the hot oil. The parchment will peel away once heated. Fry until golden brown, then flip. Flip several times to cook evenly until deep golden brown and puffed up.

4) Remove from oil and place on paper towel to remove excess oil. Let cool. Once cooled, slice in half and fill with ricotta cream. Dust with powdered sugar and top with a cherry.

For Baked Zeppole:

1) Heat oven 400 degrees.

2) Pipe 3 inch rings on a parchment lined or silicone lined sheet

pan. Bake for 25 minutes. Turn off oven, and let puffs sit in oven for another 10 minutes or until deep golden brown.

3) Remove from oven and let cool. Slice in half and fill with ricotta filling. Dust with powdered sugar and too with a cherry.

Acknowledgments

Once again, I need to thank Dina Cimarusti for all the delicious recipes in this book. I hope you enjoy making them as much as I do!

As always, my appreciation and gratitude go to the following people for their talent, support, wisdom, friendship, and encouragement . . .

Melissa Gaston, Brandi Zelenka, Jenn Watson, Hang Le, Devyn Jensen, Kayti McGee, Laurelin Paige, Corinne Michaels, the entire Social Butterfly team, Anthony Colletti, Rebecca Friedman, Flavia Viotti & Meire Dias at Bookcase Literary, Nancy Smay at Evident Ink, Julia Griffis at The Romance Bibliophile, proofreaders Michele Ficht, Shannon Mummey, and Alison Evans Maxwell, Stacey Blake at Champagne Book Design, Katie Robinson at Lyric Audiobooks, narrators Teddy Hamilton and Samantha Brentmoor, the Shop Talkers, the Sisterhood, the Harlots and the Harlot ARC Team, bloggers and event organizers, my Queens, my betas, my proofers, my readers all over the world . . .

And once again, to my family, with all my love.

About the Author

Melanie Harlow likes her heels high, her martini dry, and her history with the naughty bits left in. In addition to the Bellamy Creek Series, she's the author of the Cloverleigh Farms Series, the One & Only series, the After We Fall Series, the Happy Crazy Love Series, and the Frenched Series.

She writes from her home outside of Detroit, where she lives with her husband and two daughters. When she's not writing, she's probably got a cocktail in hand. And sometimes when she is.

Find her at www.melanieharlow.com.

Also by Melanie Harlow

The Frenched Series

Frenched

Yanked

Forked

Floored

The Happy Crazy Love Series

Some Sort of Happy

Some Sort of Crazy

Some Sort of Love

The After We Fall Series

Man Candy

After We Fall

If You Were Mine

From This Moment

The One and Only Series

Only You

Only Him

Only Love

The Cloverleigh Farms Series

Irresistible

Undeniable

Insatiable

Unbreakable

Unforgettable

The Bellamy Creek Series

Drive Me Wild

Make Me Yours

Call Me Crazy

Co-Written Books

Hold You Close (Co-written with Corinne Michaels)

Imperfect Match (Co-written with Corinne Michaels)

Strong Enough (M/M romance co-written with David Romanov)

The Speak Easy Duet

The Tango Lesson (A Standalone Novella)

Made in the USA
Las Vegas, NV
13 October 2024